STRANGE FAMILIAR

BY
JEFFE KENNEDY

Thank you for reading!

<u>Credits</u>
Cover: Ravven (www.ravven.com)

Librarian Cillian Harahel and Wizard Alise Phel have fled Convocation Academy in the dark of night and grip of winter, taking with them the hidden archives they liberated from hiding. The effort of magically holding onto the massive archives—everything to do with House Phel and the conspiracy against it—is draining Cillian nearly to death. Alise wants only to get him to the house of his birth, and hopefully save his life.

But the young lovers are soon separated by their warring families. While Cillian remains at House Harahel to begin the painstaking work of restoring the archives, Alise goes home to the only home she has left: House Phel. There, she finds her sister, Nic, giving birth. But the joyful event is soon shattered by the arrival of their father, Lord Elal.

Forced to make a choice between her niece's wellbeing and her own, a broken-hearted Alise returns to House Elal with her father, agreeing to be molded into his creature.

Cut off from each other, Cillian and Alise struggle to find the answers they desperately need—and, perhaps, find one another again.

DEDICATION

To Sean,

who will understand the ERS episode.

ACKNOWLEDGMENTS

Many thanks to Minerva Spencer for doing so much heavy lifting on this book when I was out of strength to lift. I owe you big time! Also for long, boozy, talky afternoons at Jinja.

Much love and gratitude to the usual suspects: Grace Draven, Darynda Jones, Jennifer Estep, Megan, Mulry, Kelly Robson, and Jim Sorenson, who keep me afloat every day.

As always, immense gratitude to Carien Ubink and Sullivan McPig, for catching the details I forget and for All The Assisting.

And love to David, ever and always, for being there for me.

STRANGE FAMILIAR

~ I ~

ALISE WAS WORRIED about Cillian, which was a major role-reversal and one she didn't care for. She'd been helplessly fretting over him for several hours as the elemental-powered carriage glided through the cold winter night, and as the magical burden ate away at him. Now she was starting to get angry. From the beginning of their quasi-friendship that had progressed to this undefined romance—despite her best efforts to define it—Cillian had been the one to fret over her, with his nourishing affection and baked goods.

To herself, she could admit how much she'd liked that. Being taken care of felt special and lovely. It was certainly unprecedented in her life as the daughter of a high house. Her father, the very Lord Elal considered by many to be the most-powerful—or at least most terrifying—wizard in the Convocation, hadn't been much of a nurturer. Quite the opposite, in fact. Piers Elal didn't believe in coddling his children, instead raising them to be forces of power and influence in Convocation society. Not that this was unusual for the scions of high houses. Wizards in the Convocation, and by extension the houses they ran with iron fists and oppressive magic, continually maneuvered for position, all aiming for total supremacy, even if they paid lip service otherwise.

Well, not all high houses, Alise mentally amended, eyeing Cillian who pretended to sleep on the plush seat of the carriage opposite her. The librarian wizard hailed from House Harahel, one of the few high houses dedicated to the service of their calling, rather than the rapacious acquisition of wealth and power. The wizards of House Harahel focused entirely on books, archives, and maintaining the records of the Convocation to be as factual and as free of political bias as possible. They remained in the background of the often fierce and usually lethal conflicts of Convocation society. As a result, and as Cillian had cynically noted, Harahel possessed little wealth or influence.

Alise, a true child of House Elal whether she liked it or not, had a difficult time understanding that life. One part of her—the side newly awakened by Cillian's quiet enjoyment of simple joys—rather envied the sheer peacefulness of being a nonentity. It must be nice to grow up with a grandmother who gardened and baked and to live in a house full of people who cared only about books. And it must be rewarding to be a wizard talented enough to score a position as a librarian in the Convocation Archives, but not possess the sort of power useful only for spying, controlling, and destroying people's lives.

But the other side of her, the part that made her exactly the kind of wizard born and bred to ruthlessly run a high house and serve the interests of Elal above all else, privately held House Harahel in a bit of contempt. She'd never confess it to Cillian, but she found it hard to understand their house policy of observing from the sidelines, of endlessly recording events and never stepping in to influence them. Wasn't it a form of cowardice, in the end? A kind of hiding away from the world and avoiding the sharp edges of the conflicts it brought.

Just as Cillian was doing at that very moment. He wasn't truly asleep. She'd know that even without her finely tuned wizard senses reading the alertness of his spirit. As an Elal, Alise possessed unusual proficiency with spirit magic, and the spirits inhabiting human bodies were subject to her abilities as much as any disembodied entity or lowly elemental. Maybe "subject to" was putting it too strongly. The simpler an entity, the easier they were to contain and manipulate. Spirits sufficiently complex to inhabit human bodies—not to mention human brains—presented immense challenges. Which was fortunate as those powerful and unprincipled types like Alise's father would skip the intermediaries and go straight to controlling people with wizardry. Not unlike the methods employed by the psychic wizards at House Hanneil, in particular Gordon Hanneil, the saboteur who'd telepathically wrested Cillian's will from him for a short time.

That little battle outside of Convocation Archives—small only in the sense of numbers and not at all the epic levels of wizardry slung about—had traumatized them both. Alise's nerves were still strained from the terror and tension, her heart jumping unevenly at the least sound or movement. Shouldn't they be commiserating, cuddling, comforting each other? Not ensconced on separate benches with him so obviously pretending to sleep that even a mundane human with zero magic would detect the deception.

She'd only shared a bed with Cillian a few times, but she

already knew the pattern of his breathing in easy sleep, the slow and even susurrus of his breath, the relaxed line of his high cheekbones and the way his lush black lashes fanned over them in rest. He had striking eyes when awake, but only in sleep could she truly study—and, all right, revel in—the sheer beauty of those gloriously long lashes. Well, and his gorgeous face in general. Cillian only wore his spectacles for reading, but he was pretty much *always* reading, so the rare moments of repose when he removed them felt like a special window. He didn't look better without them, necessarily, but the spectacles tended to age him a bit, to disguise the pretty-boy face he'd been blessed with.

Her pretty boy, no matter how her fellow students at Convocation Academy had sighed over him and tried to get his attention. Cillian had wanted her before she truly registered his existence, and she'd liked that. No, to be fully honest, she'd come to love his ardent attention, even the way he badgered her to eat and sleep. That's what really annoyed her. How dare he seduce her with his kind, sweet ways, making her accustomed to, even dependent upon, his frank adoration? *Look at him,* cocooned in the furry blankets, snuggled in them up to his pointed chin, pretending to sleep.

Was she supposed to likewise pretend that she believed this sleeping fakery? Cillian was her first affair, pretty much first everything, and she had no idea what the rules of the game should be. Maybe he thought *she* was sleeping and was being his usual considerate self, staying still and quiet so as not to disturb her. That would be in character for him and sadly also consistent with *her* character to be annoyed with him when he was only being kind.

Testing the theory, she shifted abruptly, scrabbling with her own furry blankets and rearranging them with unnecessary roughness. Nothing from Cillian. Eyes on his purposefully blank face—she was sure of it now—she coughed, loudly. Nothing. Tempted to kick him, to see how he'd fake his way through *that*, instead she heaved a sigh of exasperation and said, "I know you're not asleep."

He stirred, making sleepy noises—she had to roll her eyes for that bit of playacting—and cracked one lid open, blinking in an approximation of fuzziness that would convince no one ever. Good thing he hadn't gone into the theater, really.

"Did you say something?" he asked, his words slow and vague. She should have led with kicking him.

Instead, she measured her patience, finding that she didn't have much, but knowing any she did possess should go toward being pleasant to this man she maybe probably almost certainly loved, who definitely deserved only compassion from her after all he'd given with unstinting generosity. "I *said*," she answered patiently, "that I know you're not asleep, which means that you continuing to try to deceive me on the matter is more than a little insulting."

Ah, some objective part of her noted. *It bothers you most that he would try to deceive you.*

No, it bothers me that he's avoiding dealing with this problem, a situation we share. Never mind that she sounded defensive to her own mind.

You're being *defensive*, that objective self pointed out.

I just thought that.

I know, I'm just reinforcing. It's important to be honest with yourself, at least in your own mind, even if you're not honest with anyone else.

I'm honest!

Are you though? It's not really an Elal forte.

Cillian sighed and sat up, interrupting her circular internal argument, and good thing, too.

"I was *attempting* to sleep," he said, emphasizing the word with a sharpness she'd never before heard from him. "You should be, too." The concern in his words came as a pale echo of what he'd shown her before, more of a reflex, she thought, a habit. Another pretense.

"Do you want to talk about what happened?" she prodded. This is what he would do for her, what he *had* done for her, nagging and poking until she confessed the dark fears haunting her. "It wasn't your fault that Gordon Hanneil—" She broke off when he held up a hand to stop the words.

"I really do not want to talk about it," he said the edge in his voice not entirely disguised by his attempt to gentle it, the weak smile he offered in the muted glow of the fire elemental-fueled lanterns. "Let's just sleep," he added, almost pleadingly, pulling the blankets tighter around himself as if they could protect him. From her?

She really hated the thought that he didn't feel he could turn to her with his problems. Worse, she feared he—perhaps rightfully—blamed her for those problems, that he might resent her. This was why he should be the one comforting her, telling her that everything would work out fine. This was his strength, not hers.

What is exactly is your strength? Her inner voice inquired silkily.

Brooding, acting impulsively, and causing destruction, she answered with biting chagrin.

Exactly.

Fine then. If she was such a terrible person—and Cillian loved her anyway, or thought he did, or did before this—then she might as well continue as she'd begun. "I can't sleep," she informed him. "I'm too upset and it's frankly inconsiderate of you to lie there, *pretending* to sleep, when I'm this upset."

Cillian emerged enough from his protective cocoon to rake a hand through his dark curls, sending them into greater disarray. He looked adorably tousled and she wanted only to climb inside that furry shell and allow him to kiss and reassure her. They'd started out the carriage ride that way, cozied together under the blankets. Until he'd moved away from her, taking the other bench on the pretext of sleeping.

For a painfully hopeful moment, she thought he might be about to open his arms to her, invite her in, but he only rearranged his furry armor, wrapping it more indelibly around his slim body, firmly shutting her out. For the first time, Alise understood what Cillian's frustration must have been like all those times she'd refused to talk to him, to unbend even a little. She supposed she deserved this turnabout, but she didn't have to like it.

~ 2 ~

"FIRST OF ALL," Cillian told Alise, the pulse of overwhelming and unfamiliar anger edging into his vision, "I wasn't *pretending* to sleep."

"Ha to that," she fired back, her wizard-black eyes catching the soft light and turning it into a glare. Those eyes dominated her piquant face, giving her the aspect of a fairy with her delicate bones and lush mouth. She shimmered with magic, the intensity of it intertwined with her fierce personality and ferocious intelligence. He loved all of that about her and at the same time could only acknowledge how woefully he paled in comparison. He'd always known he wasn't good enough for Alise, but he'd never thought he'd be an actual burden on her. But after Gordon Hanneil so easily stripped him of his will, turning him into a mindless puppet, Cillian had to face the fact that he was and always would be a liability to Alise.

His heart turned over a little. He wanted her, needed her, but the rest of everything was crushing him and he couldn't seem to reach past any of it. All he could do was put her off.

"By using the phrase 'pretending to sleep,' you're implying deception on my part," he continued calmly, reasonably, taking refuge in his own strength: relentless academic debating. "I argue that I was attempting to sleep by creating all of the outward appearances of sleep in the hope that the power of suggestion would lull me into the true depths of somnolence I crave."

There, that sounded good, and wasn't entirely untrue. Never mind that he'd be leaving out the critical piece of information that nothing could possibly lull him to the level of relaxation needed for sleep with his mind and heart in such turmoil, let alone the soul-crushing, magic-draining weight of the archives he'd stolen.

Alise gazed back at him in something more than mild astonishment, her full, bow-shaped lips actually parting in surprise. "Did you just lie to me using a whole bunch of jargon to cover it up?"

No. Well, yes, sort of. He pulled the blankets tighter around him; he couldn't seem to get warm, a damp chill lurking in his bones. Though the Refoel healer, Jonathan, had poured magic into bringing him back from the damage that vile Gordon Hanneil had done to him, weakness still ate away at the core of him. *It's the magic drain,* he realized. Never had he used his library magic to accomplish such a massive feat.

First, the immense effort in the archives to locate the artfully hidden folders that had tucked away all reference materials related to the history of House Phel, where they'd been stowed in spaces outside of physical reality. But he'd found them, when no one else could, and he'd unlocked them, too. It had taken every bit of cleverness and drained him of his admittedly median levels of internal magic pulling off that trick, along with all the magic Alise had given him so generously.

Then this: carrying those Phel archives, centuries worth, folded up inside himself, continued to pull from him, eating away at the wizardry that had always been available, though he'd always used it for minor work like indexing manuscripts and keeping track of where he'd put everything. At this rate, even with Healer Jonathan's heroic efforts to shore up his strength, Cillian would be a hollow shell of a wizard by the time they reached House Harahel with the stolen archives. *Stolen.* What would his grandmother say? After the entire business of Szarina when he, dazzled by her and stupidly in love, helped her cheat, his grandmother had agreed with the Convocation Academy Provost to give him a second chance. But no third.

"Cillian." Alise sounded terse, torn between aggravation and worry. How perverse of him that he loved her equally for both. "I asked you a question and you're just staring blankly. I can't decide whether to kick you or call for help."

"What help would you call for?" he asked, more curious than anything. Distantly, he observed that he wasn't making an enormous amount of sense.

"Oh, now there's a completely unhelpful response," she muttered. "I'm turning this carriage around. We're going to House Phel instead of Harahel. At least there Wizard Asa might be able to help you and Nic and Gabriel will know what to do."

"You can't," he said, wishing he could put more force in his voice. This was a very bad idea though he couldn't fully recall why.

"Oh, I can," she replied, brows lowering in threat. "I can

program this air elemental to take us off the edge of the known world if I so choose and if you don't start making sense very soon."

"I love you, too," he said, flush with the warmth of knowing she cared. Then he belatedly remembered she'd yet to say she loved him. He thought she probably did, although that wouldn't factor into the future of their relationship. Life wasn't like the fairytales: it took a lot more than love to conquer most obstacles.

"It's like you're drunk." She knotted her fingers together, worrying the slender bird bones with such force he feared she'd break them. One thing about Alise, though—people might mistake her slim, youthful appearance for weakness, but she was made of unbreakable determination, possessing a core of strength beyond what most people could muster. At the moment, he could wish she had a bit less determination. Any other person would be sleeping off their ordeal, not badgering him. "Or it's exhaustion," she continued, narrowing her sharp black gaze and prodding him with her wizard senses. "How do you feel?"

Like utter shit. "I just need to sleep," he practically begged.

"Except you *weren't* sleeping," she retorted with remorseless logic. "I sat here for hours, watching you 'create all of the outward appearances of sleep'"—she put air quotes around the words—"which I don't believe for a minute was in the 'hope that the power of suggestion would lull you into the true depths of somnolence you crave.' You were trying to fool me into leaving you alone, and I did, for quite a while, but that's over now. You need help, whether you'll admit it or not.

We're going to House Phel."

"No," he managed to say.

"Yes, Cillian. I'm not going to sit here and watch you die, which is what I'm afraid is happening."

Was it? He didn't think so, but what did dying feel like? Maybe this sense of fatal weakness, of emptying out inside meant death. Still, it seemed like he should be more upset about it if that were the case. He forced himself to focus, dimly aware of Alise using her formidable wizardry on the—for her—simple task of redirecting the air elemental. They couldn't go to House Phel, he knew that, but why?

"House Harahel is closer," he whispered.

She barely flicked him a glance. "By a slim margin. More important, I have no guarantee of our reception there. At least at House Phel I know they'll listen to me."

Ah, he should have realized she'd worry about her reception at House Harahel. Her concerns weren't unfounded. The House Elal heir-apparent arriving unannounced wouldn't be a welcome event. But she wasn't alone in this.

"They will listen," he said, though he wasn't sure if she heard him. She didn't appear to, her focus on the air elemental driving and directing the carriage, which slowed as it changed course. "You'll be with me."

"That won't do me any good if I arrive with you dying or dead," she replied. "Call me selfish, but I'd prefer not to engage in combat with another high house, even if they are a bunch of supposedly peaceful librarians. I've learned from you that you all might seem quiet and mild-mannered, but you possess hidden skills that can be scary."

He wanted to explain that they couldn't take the stolen House Phel archives to the actual House Phel. "Alise, listen to me. This is important. Come here."

She heaved a sigh, but responded when he wormed a hand from the blankets and offered it to her. Her composed expression crumpled and he realized she'd been waiting for the gesture of welcome. So easy to forget with all of Alise's formidable competence and regal mien just how uncertain she was, how insecure of her place in his heart, despite all evidence to the contrary. She'd spent far too much of her life feeling unloved, so much so that he doubted he could undo that damage. Still, she came to him with alacrity that did his heart good, burrowing inside the blankets with him, her warmth like a hot coal against him.

"You're so cold," she said, rubbing her hands over him. "Maybe we should go to House Refoel or back to Convocation Academy. I could—"

"Alise," he interrupted, lacking the force, but she stopped talking. "No. Harahel."

"Just because that's home..."

"Harahel," he repeated. "Promise."

"Please don't do this."

"Promise."

She made a deeply unhappy noise, but the carriage changed direction, accelerating. "I promise," she answered on a whisper. "But you have to promise me you won't die. I mean it, Cillian. Promise me!"

"Promise..." he breathed and, at last, blessed sleep dragged him under.

~ 3 ~

WHEN ALISE HAD agreed to journey to House Harahel with Cillian the first time, she'd envisioned a formal approach and negotiated visit with all the appropriate etiquette observed.

That would have been infinitely preferable to arriving without invitation in the pre-dawn hours with Cillian's cold, limp, and unconscious body. Better than his corpse, but barely. She didn't kid herself that anyone at Harahel would be pleased to see an Elal on their doorstep. House Harahel wasn't exactly an enemy of House Elal, but neither were they allies.

In truth, given the way her father ran business, Elal enjoyed very few allies—and the ones they'd had seemed to be meeting with reversals of late. Fortunately, a couple of those had converted to allies of House Phel, where she owed her loyalty, but unfortunately, the bulk of the Convocation didn't know that. To most everyone she was heir to House Elal, her father's daughter, and with every indication of being as powerfully gifted with magic and as unprincipled with it as the head of the house of her birth. She didn't blame any of them for being wary of her.

At the moment, she was pouring every drop of that powerful magic into pushing the air elemental to maximum speed. She'd enlarged and empowered the simple creature, giving it as much fuel as she could from her dwindling reservoir, while using the lion's share of it to keep Cillian's spirit in his body. She had no experience with doing such things, but his essential self kept attempting to tug away, to rid itself of the drained flesh it seemed done with occupying. Alise refused to allow that to happen, no matter the cost to herself.

If she had a familiar available to replenish her magic, she'd promise them anything in exchange. But she didn't and the nearly deserted landscape en route to House Harahel offered no possibilities to find a familiar, even if one had been willing to help. All she could do was hold onto Cillian, physically and magically, hoping to warm him with her body and keep her mental hooks in him with her wizardry.

She bitterly regretted promising to take him to Harahel and repeatedly reconsidered the wisdom of capitulating to Cillian's wishes. Him and his cursed integrity. She knew full well that's why he insisted on House Harahel, because of the archives he carried, the archives currently killing him. Obdurate, high-minded Cillian, so determined to prove his integrity and honesty after that awful Szarina Sammael used him so brutally and tainted his reputation.

Well, regardless of how Lady Harahel received Alise, hopefully they'd take care of Cillian and someone there would be able to relieve him of the burden of carrying those archives. She privately had her doubts. Cillian himself had said that he didn't know of any wizards, library-magic-gifted or not, who'd managed to perform the monumentally difficult feat that he had. At this point, she didn't even care if the archives survived the procedure; she only wanted Cillian to live.

Alise counted the minutes until their arrival at House Harahel, which didn't help much as she had no idea how much longer it would take to get there. Feeling as if she held herself together with mental fingernails, she periodically diverted a sliver of attention to the air elemental, prodding it to determine if she could get it to go even a little faster. Full of fierce glee at the unprecedented freedom and power she'd bestowed on it, the creature had gone almost feral. That was partially her fault. In order to strip away the enchantments constraining the elemental's size and power, she'd gone for the quick and dirty method of unbinding the entity entirely—which meant removing the spellwork cast by whatever Elal factory wizard had manufactured it—and rebinding it to her own specifications.

Because she'd been working fast, she'd performed the bare minimum required to keep the elemental leashed to her will instead of haring off on its own. The lax binding had also served to allow her to inflate the elemental's size and propulsive force, so that the carriage hurtled along on its skids, practically flying over the snow-covered road. Left to the elemental's instinctive desires, and if not for the constraints of gravity, they might have become airborne. As it was, they were fortunate the recent winter storm had left everything deeply buried. Otherwise the barely controlled elemental would have crashed them. The instructions she'd embedded kept them on course and following the markers buried within the road by the builders, but without those, nothing would have stopped the elemental from dragging them through any obstacle in its programmed path, living or not.

Checking on the creature, she noted the fraying strands of her control, barely keeping it tamed to her will. Given time and opportunity—and more magic than she currently possessed—she'd rebind the elemental and do it correctly this time. She could just imagine the horrified expression on the face of her Professor of Manipulation and Control of Noncorporeal Entities upon discovering her slapdash methodology. But reworking the binding would take time and energy she couldn't afford. Also, with the air elemental so swollen on her magic and glutted on unaccustomed freedom, Alise had to consider she might not be able to bind it again. It might wrest free of her and then she'd have to gather up a new elemental. They were ubiquitous and she could do that, but—again time and energy. Therefore, she left it as it was and hoped.

Hoped the elemental wouldn't break free.

Hoped they made it to House Harahel in time to save Cillian.

Hoped she hadn't destroyed everything that mattered to her before she'd even had a moment to savor it.

Hope. Hope. Hope.

So it was that, sometime later, they flew at blazing speeds onto the grounds of House Harahel. Alise had expected to be stopped at the Harahel border, or at the very least at the boundary of the grounds of the house itself, but apparently Harahel didn't employ shields or guards. The Elal in her blanched in horror, deeply uncomfortable with such lax security. No one could cross the borders of the extensive lands belonging to Elal, not without being admitted by a border guardian. Even Houses El-Adrel and Sammael, who flaunted their supreme confidence—and general lack of interest in the safety of their populations—by leaving their borders open, closely guarded the approach to the houses themselves.

Alise didn't realize they'd reached House Harahel itself until the air elemental slammed to a stop, throwing her hard against the thankfully padded backrest. At first, she feared they *had* collided with something. Pulling aside the heavy, insulating curtains, she gazed out the carriage window in considerable surprise.

The house loomed directly overhead, a few warm lights in its many windows. They'd pulled up in a circular drive directly in front of a wide wooden porch, not unlike the design at House Phel, which also seemed far too inviting and lacking security to her. Alise should have been able to predict that House Harahel, like Cillian with his relaxed and friendly ways, would be open and approachable.

In the pre-dawn half-light, the edifice seemed to be mostly gray and black, but she suspected it would be colorful in the light, with its fanciful gables, ginger-breaded eaves, and slender towers ringed with wide windows and peaked roofs. Spindly silhouettes of whirling things topped several of those conical peaks, glinting with a metallic shine as the sun tipped its rays over the hilly horizon.

No one had emerged from the house, for which Alise judged them with edged anger. Noses in their books, no doubt, while one of their own—no matter how lowly Cillian's rank might be within House Harahel—lay dying on their doorstep.

Well, she would get their attention.

The spurt of righteous rage leant her a bit of magic from her nearly empty well, and she summoned a spirit to pound on the big doors of the manse and send up a banshee wail while at it. She stayed inside the carriage, unwilling to unwrap Cillian and expose him to more of the chill, but she did kick open the carriage door so they'd see her within.

It took far too long for anyone to emerge and, when the doors finally creaked open, it wasn't a guard or servant who peered out, but an ancient fellow in a robe and slippers, a striped stocking cap dangling crookedly from his head, a lantern in his hand containing an actual candle and not a fire elemental. Alise was hard-pressed not to roll her eyes, instead keeping them fixed in demand on the old man who peered blearily past the circle cast by the feeble lantern light.

"Eh, someone out there?" he asked. A book fell from where he'd clearly tucked it under his arm to open the door and he bent to pick it up, wedging the door open with his body. A cat ran out, bounding into the snow. Dark arts protect them all.

"Get help right now," Alise called out in a firm voice, abandoning any pretense at correct etiquette. "I bring Wizard Cillian Harahel, in dire need of immediate assistance from the house of his birth."

"Cillian, ah?" The man, book retrieved, shuffled onto the porch, slippers sliding on the sheen of ice from overnight, and peered sharply at her. "Young Wizard Cillian is to be at Convocation Academy, not screaming through the night in a carriage run by an altered air elemental in the company of an

Elal Wizard. Piers Elal's daughter and heir, too."

Alise bit back her impatient frustration at the delay, cautioning herself against further assumptions. How this frowsy-looking man discerned so much about her with barely a glance, she didn't know, but she'd best tread carefully. It wasn't easy to see in the growing light, but it seemed he sported the black eyes of a full wizard. "All true," she conceded, "and I'm happy to explain, but—please—summon help for Cillian. There's no time to waste."

"A statement that elicits many thoughts and is highly debatable, beginning with the definition of 'waste,'" he observed, coming down a couple of steps without holding onto the railing. "Once we've agreed on what is a waste, which would likely take doing, as I imagine you and I have very different priorities, then we could move on to a discussion on the mutable nature of time itself."

Why hadn't she gone to House Phel? Alise dragged in a breath with the last crumb of her patience, barely restraining a scream of frustration. "I beg of you, Sir Wizard, summon help for Cillian and I'll submit to all the debates you like."

"Now there's a good bargain." He cackled in glee. "Not many sharp-minded youngsters want to sit and debate the nature of time with the likes of me these days."

Alise set her teeth, scraping up the last vestiges of her magic to find another spirit to summon someone besides this venerable obstacle of an old wizard. But she didn't have enough to even fetch an elemental. "With all due respect," she grated out, "please fetch someone to help Cillian!"

"Not as patient as you'd like to appear, eh?" He perched on

the middle step, swaying a bit. "I think you'll find that's a character flaw you'll want to remedy young Alise. Impetuosity leads only to trouble." He cackled again, well pleased with himself.

She was opening her mouth, maybe to release that scream of sheer frustration and to alert the household that way, like a mundane human with no magic, when the doors burst wide, expelling a horde of people with blankets and a stretcher.

Before she could blink, she and Cillian had been extracted from the carriage with gentle, but urgent hands, separated, and Cillian carried off into the house. Alise teetered there uncertainly, with one blanket still wrapped around her, having been divested of the others, the old wizard still on his step watching her with chiding amusement, a vibrant older woman at his side holding his arm and regarding her with interested, wizard-black eyes.

"Alise Elal on my doorstep at a winter's dawn, bearing my grandson on the verge of death by magic drain," she observed. "Seems like a bad omen. I'll have to consult the oracles."

"You worry too much, Órlaith," the old wizard said, patting her hand on his arm. "They're just children up to youthful shenanigans."

"And you shouldn't be on these icy steps in these slippers," she returned, gripping him tighter, never taking her probing gaze from Alise. "Well, you're here and I'm not sending you back in your state only to have Piers Elal on my doorstep next demanding recompense for the loss of yet another heir. He's been quite careless on that front and you'd think he'd know better by now. You'd best come inside and get warm. Come along."

"I'd like to go with Cillian," Alise began, "and there is something you need to know." But Órlaith had already turned her back, leading the old wizard back up the steps, and so Alise tagged along after them. As the tart woman had indicated, Alise really had no other option at this juncture. And, as Alise had accurately predicted, she noted to herself with sour vindication, she wasn't at all welcome at House Harahel.

She really should have taken Cillian to House Phel. At least she more or less belonged there. Curse Cillian and his stubborn insistence. They'd better be able to help him—which meant she needed to explain what had happened to him and what they needed to do to relieve him of the burden he carried. She was plain exhausted, which was why she was being so thick-headed. Feeling like the child they named her, she chased after the pair, skidding a bit on the icy steps and earning a caution-ary glance from Órlaith. "Don't be breaking your neck on the House Harahel steps either, Alise Elal."

"I prefer Phel," Alise said, catching up to them. "As in House Phel," she explained further, when neither said anything. "My sister, Nic, is wife and familiar to Lord Gabriel Phel, and they consider me part of their house now."

Órlaith gave her a shrewd look. "Names don't change your blood. You're an Elal. It's written all through you and that won't change your content, no matter how you try to alter the title and cover."

She *really* should have gone to House Phel. "Nevertheless, I'd like to see Cillian now. And I need to speak to Lady Harahel. There are things she needs to know, in order to help him."

"I doubt that," Órlaith responded. "Harahels pride themselves on knowing everything that is knowable."

"And a great deal that isn't," the old wizard added with another of his gleeful cackles.

"True enough, Uncle," she agreed with a laugh.

They stepped into the carpeted warmth of the front hall, the space long and narrow, with high ceilings and sparsely lit, gothic-looking chandeliers suspended in the heights. Closed doors lined the hallway, interspersed with tall mirrors in elaborate frames, a table beneath each. Some held antique tomes bookended by sculptures of various creatures, others bowls of things or small chests of drawers, still others various knick-knacks and objets d'art. The place smelled of old wood, dust, and candlewax. It whispered of age, treasured histories, and a lack of coin to keep any of it in good repair. Not at all unlike House Phel in that way.

"We have to keep the doors closed," Órlaith said, gesturing vaguely at the hall, "as we avoid heating rooms in the wintertime that we don't need to use. Expensive, you know. But the library is warm and we can talk there. I assume that's where you were reading, Uncle?" she asked the old man, guiding him down the hallway before opening a door that allowed heat and light to spill through.

"I wake so early," he said to Alise over his shoulder. "Even on these dark mornings. More quiet time to read."

"Indeed." Órlaith settled him into a worn armchair by the fire, feeling the teapot on the table beside it. "I'll send for more tea and there should be fresh pastries. You can sit anywhere you like, Alise Elal, but I suggest this settee nearer to the fire. You look cold and pale enough to see through. And painfully young. How old are you?"

"Eighteen." Alise supposed Cillian came by his fussing and nurturing honestly. *Still.* "I don't mean to be rude," she said, not taking a seat, but standing tall, spine straight as her maman would have expected, "but it's urgent that I speak with Lady Harahel. And I'd like to see Cillian."

"Yes, so you mentioned," Órlaith replied mildly. "Cillian is being cared for and you'll see him in due time. As for Lady Harahel..." She raised her eyes to the skies as if seeking the woman. "Well, it's quite early in the day for her to make an appearance. Besides, she's always getting in the way when I want to know something. I'm Cillian's grandmother, Órlaith. You'll go through me first. Tell me this important thing."

Alise opened her mouth to protest, taken aback at the casual dismissal of the head of House Harahel. Not something that would occur in House Elal, where her father had spirit spies everywhere and knew all that was spoken about him. At the woman's stern look, however, Alise closed her mouth again. Cillian had spoken fondly of his grandmother.

"I greet you, Wizard Órlaith Harahel," Alise said, remembering her manners. "I realize that it's very early and our arrival strange and alarming, but I really must insist on explaining—"

Alise broke off as a servant entered the room and the older woman turned away. Alise shook her head to herself. Manual messages, a real fire in the fireplace. These people lived as if magical conveniences didn't exist.

"What?" Órlaith turned back from giving instructions to the servant. "You think you need to explain that my grandson nearly killed himself to carry a massive folded archive to us that he stole from Convocation Center?"

~ 4 ~

WELL, YES, ALISE rather *had* thought she'd need to mention that—and the fact that Cillian's grandmother had leapt to the wrong conclusion only proved it. At least she didn't have to explain about the non-physical burden he carried. "He didn't steal the archive."

"Shall we debate the definition of 'theft'?" the old wizard asked absently from his chair, the big tome he'd carried now spread open on his lap.

"In so far as it is the sacred duty of all Harahels to ensure that the Convocation Archives remain intact and inside the Convocation Archive walls, and considering that my grandson, with an employment contract to Convocation Academy, has indeed removed a sizable chunk from those archives, then I believe I'll stick with how I described the situation." She gave Alise an owlish look over her spectacles. "And I'm very interested in your explanation for why these are House Phel archives, given your earlier speech about affiliation with that house, which—if I'm not mistaken—is still on probationary status."

"You're not mistaken, Órlaith," the elderly wizard inserted. "In fact, the progress of House Phel toward regaining their high house status has hit so many setbacks that one must regard their movement as going backward."

How could these reclusive sorts in the backwoods know so much? Most wizards actively involved in the Convocation didn't know that much about the challenges facing House Phel. Alise wrestled with how to respond. This had been Cillian's idea, to request aid from House Harahel on comparing the records on House Phel in the Convocation Archives with those maintained at House Harahel. It had become abundantly clear that House Hanneil—possibly conspiring with other high houses—had arranged for those records to be hidden away. The possibility remained that they'd also altered key information, probably to disguise the reasons and methodology in bringing about the fall of the high house generations ago. Alise knew that Cillian also worried about the potential involvement of a Harahel wizard in the conspiracy. Only sophisticated library magic could have hidden the archive to begin with.

All of this meant that Alise was out of her depth and really needed Cillian to handle this. But they needed to save him first. "Please tell the wizards helping Cillian that the folded archive is pass-coded to him. They won't be able to unlock it without that."

"They've already relieved him of the burden. He can unlock it later."

Oh. Abruptly deflated, mostly relieved, Alise considered what to say next.

Órlaith threw up her hands then pointed at a settee with a low table before it. "Oh, for dark arts' sake, sit already. I'm not pleased to have an Elal on my doorstep, but I'm not going to eat you."

Almost reflexively, Alise obeyed, the tone of command making the realization click in her tired brain at last. Something she should have realized much sooner. "*You* are Lady Harahel," she said in a tone of wonder.

Órlaith snorted and the elderly wizard by the fire—possibly the retired Lord Harahel?—cackled. "Not as stupid as she looks, eh, Órlaith?"

"Gee thanks," Alise said sourly, not sure if she was more bothered that she'd been dense or by the implication that she looked that way. "I am not at my best."

Órlaith dropped onto the couch beside Alise with a sigh. "Well, my little attempt at subterfuge wasn't going to last long. I apologize for the deception. I wanted to have a conversation with you as Cillian's grandmother, not as Lady Harahel."

That penetrated Alise's fuzzy brain, too. "Cillian… is a scion of House Harahel—in line to be your heir?" she squeaked.

Órlaith waved that off. "Technically, but the boy isn't at all interested in heading a high house. No more than I am, truth be told, nor would I be Lady Harahel if *some* people hadn't decided they'd rather spend their days reading." She glared at the elderly wizard's back and he hummed a jaunty tune, turning a page and otherwise ignoring her.

Alise was still coping with the news that Cillian had failed to reveal. In all their conversations about her feelings on being her father's heir or not, and their few, minimalistic relationship discussions, Cillian had never seen fit to mention that his beloved grandmother was the head of his house. She should have kicked him when she had the opportunity. In fact, once he was recovered—and he'd better recover—she *would* kick him. "Wait, a moment," she said, sitting up straighter. "Cillian said that you garden. And bake. And quilt. And send him dried herbs."

"Does he use those then?" She looked pleased, then narrowed her wizard-black eyes, her formidable power mantling. Alise had underestimated this woman, not accustomed to sussing out the subtler, academic magics. But Órlaith was no fool and she was definitely wizard enough to pose a threat. "What *is* your relationship with my boy, by the way?"

Oops. Definitely not a conversation she wanted to have without Cillian present. She had no idea if he'd want his family, his house—the head of his house!—to know about their affair. It was so new, too tender for public scrutiny. Besides, clearly Órlaith already didn't approve of Alise. "I'm a student at the academy," she answered evenly, "and Cillian assisted me on an independent study project, assigned by Provost Uriel," she added, thinking that bit of authority would lend credence to the perception that her relationship with Cillian was entirely professional.

Órlaith wasn't fooled, however. She regarded Alise cannily. "Tandiya Uriel is involved in this?" She considered, pursing her lips.

"Uriel hates Hanneil," commented the wizard by the fire. Alise wondered why he even pretended to be reading when he clearly listened to every word of their conversation. It was no accident that these two had her cornered in this library, conducting what could only be called an interrogation.

Just then, the doors opened and two young servants wheeled in a cart. They bustled about, replacing the retired Lord Harahel's teapot with a freshly steaming one, and setting a full tray on the table before Alise and Órlaith. Once they left, closing the door behind them, Alise teetered on the edge of etiquette anxiety. As a guest, she could not reach for anything before her hostess did. Certainly she couldn't serve herself before Lady Harahel did. But the servants had all left and the head of a high house wouldn't—

Órlaith Harahel reached for the teapot and poured for them both, bringing Alise's thoughts to a stuttering halt for what felt like the fiftieth time in the last half an hour since they'd arrived. She knew exactly how long it had been, as they at least had an El-Adrel clock on the mantel, one she kept eyeing, wondering how long it would be until someone brought news of Cillian.

She accepted the cup on its pretty saucer, both antiques, but not matching each other or anything else. Órlaith put a steaming cinnamon roll on a plate and set it before Alise. "Eat. Drink," she instructed crisply. "It's no fun to interrogate a waifish wizardling who looks about to pass out on my settee."

Alise smiled at the cinnamon roll, which looked exactly like the sort Cillian baked for her, and unexpectedly had to choke back tears. Órlaith patted her on the shoulder. "There, there, dear. Cillian will be fine. Your compassionate interest in the health of your independent study advisor is quite moving. Convocation Academy must have changed since my day, cultivating such close relationships between staff and students."

The wily old bitch. Alise took a hearty sip of the steaming tea, willing the burn to clear her head and wake her up. Eyes dry, she looked over to Órlaith, who watched her knowingly. "It's rather impolite to read my thoughts without permission," she noted candidly.

Órlaith smiled thinly. "House Harahel may not be one of the movers and shakers of the Convocation, not like—let's say, House Elal—but neither are we doddering backwoods fools. I use the weapons available to me. Also, your mental shielding is appallingly bad."

Alise knew for a fact that wasn't true. She'd recently learned to barricade her mind following Gordon Hanneil's attempt to mentally control her. Professor Seraphiel had declared her more than adequate. Nevertheless, Alise took a moment to strengthen that shielding, which she'd admittedly let sag a bit, thinking herself amongst harmless librarians, not politically savvy mind-readers.

"Better," Órlaith said with a nod, sipping her own tea. "I'm unusual in Harahel, to answer your unspoken question, in that my late mother was a Hanneil. Everyone seriously questioned my esteemed father's choice in taking her as his familiar."

For once, the elderly wizard did not comment.

"The skill comes in handy," Órlaith mused, seemingly unbothered by the silent implication that the old wizard was one of those who'd questioned the choice. "Also, there's no reason I can't enjoy hobbies like baking, gardening, and quilting and still run a high house. It's remarkable how little time it really takes to do so when one isn't constantly jockeying to add to already immense wealth or scheming to take over the Convocation."

Alise lifted her cup in silent toast to the obvious jab at House Elal. She could hardly retort, even if she felt any inclination, as her father arguably did spend all of his time on those activities. Taking up her cinnamon roll, she briefly pondered how to eat it, recalling Cillian's detailed observations on how each person's method revealed essential character. From the way Órlaith continued to study her, Alise was willing to bet Cillian had learned that personality litmus test at his grandmother's knee, as he clearly had so much else. Deciding to throw off the predator currently cornering her, Alise deliberately ate differently, defiantly plucking out the soft center and eating that first.

Órlaith threw back her head and laughed. "Well played, wizardling. You are more intimate with my grandson than you'd like us to know. He's baked for you. Fascinating. The question is, will you be another Szarina?"

"No," Alise answered firmly, perfectly willing to both firmly close off that avenue of speculation and reveal that she knew about that tawdry incident. "Though I must say that I'm surprised that you, Lady Harahel, allowed a Sammael scion to so badly use one of yours. You won't convince me you didn't know."

Órlaith lifted her cup in the same silent toast as Alise had given. "Foolish young people don't grow into older and wiser ones if they're protected from everything that might give them pain," she observed. "Especially regarding one's scions, as you like to remind me, a parent and head of a high house prefers them to be toughened by the non-lethal lessons life offers."

"Non-lethal life lessons?" Alise echoed incredulously, abandoning her manners in her indignation. "Szarina badly hurt Cillian, wounded him as only a sensitive, caring person like him can be."

"And are you aiming to pick up the pieces of his broken heart, young Elal?" Lady Harahel returned sharply. "As I might point out that you share a great deal more with Szarina Sammael than you don't. You and I both know you'll be wanting to acquire a familiar to fuel your wizardry at the level of power you'll need and—let's be frank—will crave, just like your father. There is no place in your future for a sweet and sensitive lover like Cillian."

Alise was aware of this assumption about her—and not only because Cillian had said almost the exact same thing to her. She was growing exceedingly tired of literally everyone else telling her what she wanted from her life. However, she had no intention of confirming or denying Órlaith's probing insinuations. She and Cillian should have discussed how to represent their relationship, but they hadn't and that was water under the bridge; she was on her own.

"Szarina manipulated Cillian into helping her cheat," she said pointedly, "smearing his reputation at Convocation Academy and causing him to question his own integrity."

"As well he should," Órlaith fired back, all stern high house lady as she hadn't fully demonstrated before that moment. "Manipulated him, indeed." She snorted in contempt. "My boy got his head turned, thinking with his little one, bamboozled by a pretty face and a sob story. Cillian has always seen himself as the savior of damsels in distress. It's an unfortunate character flaw."

Alise gaped at her. "Cillian's caring nature is hardly a character flaw."

"Isn't it?" Órlaith's expression was as hard as glass. "There's no place among Convocation wizards for tender hearts, squirreled away in the archives or not. The Convocation high houses are constantly at war, overtly or covertly, which you know Daughter of Elal. You judged me and found me wanting, assuming I have no security and no sense. Just a granny puttering in her garden, but I am the head of House Harahel, one of the first houses in the Convocation, and we have not survived by accident."

To steady herself, Alise sipped her tea, then set it down, cursing herself for simply eating and drinking with blind trust.

"No, I didn't poison or drug your food," Órlaith said in exasperation. "I just finished telling you I'm not a fool. I don't want Piers Elal bringing down the fury of the entire spirit world upon my house. Nor do I have any wish to incite the vengeance of Lord Gabriel Phel, especially fueled by your powerful sister. Of course I know about that rogue upstart with his unusual—and obviously unconstrained—powers, and I can assess the likely fate of House Phel. Harahel survived where Phel did not, which I'd think would give you pause before casting your judgements."

"I apologize," Alise said, wishing viciously that she'd minded her thoughts—and checking her mental shielding again.

"No, I didn't read your mind that time, child. Your thoughts were all too apparent in your actions. You are, however, competent at controlling your facial expressions. You're quite like your father, you know."

Alise was glad she'd set down her tea, as she would have choked on it, or bobbled her cup. "I am not like my father." The words came out too harsh, too emotional, and Lady Harahel knew it, smiling thinly.

"I knew Piers Elal, at Convocation Academy," she said in a conversational tone that didn't fool Alise. Not anymore, anyway. "Same class, in fact. I had my children early; he had you all later. I wanted my child-bearing done with while my body was young and my powers still new. After all, a woman can continue to increase and enhance her wizardry all her life, but the ravages of pregnancy… best left to the vigor of youth. Something for you to keep in mind, perhaps." Her gaze slid down Alise's slim body in speculation and she resisted putting a hand on the belly she knew was flat.

Alise hadn't had a Refoel healer unlock her fertility—for very good reasons—and in fact didn't know if she ever would. She returned Lady Harahel's inquiring gaze evenly, saying nothing, betraying nothing of her thoughts. Finally.

"Piers was very like you at this age," Órlaith continued as if the silent battle hadn't occurred. "He was never a big man, short and slight, like you are. You know how short men can be, always overcompensating, and Piers was no exception. Worse, he craved power, determined to be the best at everything, to control everything."

Alise couldn't argue with this assessment of her father—it was all too true—but she took exception to the rest of Órlaith's implications. "That's not who I am."

"So you claim and so it remains to be seen. Forgive me if I'm not feeling generous enough to simply take you at your word, Alise Elal." She smiled broadly, her wizard-black eyes ice cold. "I'm not actually interested in what your relationship has been with my grandson."

"I've already tried to explain," Alise replied stiffly, more than aggravated to be continually called out on this, like she was some kind of predatory female like... Well, like Szarina Sammael, looking to use and twist up Cillian. After all, Cillian had pursued her. Relentlessly, in his adorably velvet-clad hammer fashion. She'd been minding her own business, focused on her project, when Cillian had *inserted* himself into her life. And her body. Her first lover and he'd always be special for that reason. She cut off that thought before she blushed and gave herself away.

"Then by all means," Lady Harahel said, smiling into her tea, "please do explain."

"Cillian is my mentor. We sought the Phel archives and he found them, because he is a brilliant, clever wizard of library magic. They'd been deliberately concealed and we have very good reason to believe House Hanneil culpable. Cillian removed the Phel archives, lest they be lost again, or even destroyed. He believes there is critically important information in there, and that they were tampered with. He was deter-mined to bring those archives here, to the house of his birth, to you, in order to run a side-by-side comparison with the House Harahel mirrored archives for House Phel. Provost Uriel is aware of this mission and endorses it."

Alise left out the part where Provost Uriel had also fired

Cillian. That should be his news to share, if at all. Besides, the way the provost had saved them at the last moment and destroyed Gordon Hanneil made Alise think she might relent. Cillian loved working in the Convocation archives; he belonged there. Surely Provost Uriel would know that.

"I see," Lady Harahel said, nodding thoughtfully. "Thank you for that explanation." She set down her teacup and saucer with a crisp clink. "I'll see that supplies are packed for you. We removed the air elemental that you… modified from the carriage and substituted a standard, Elal-brand entity."

"You can't take my elemental."

"Can and did, young Alise. I must say, I'm surprised you were so ambitious—and careless in your arrogance—as to create a monster like you did with the elemental you arrived with. It had to be contained."

"I was in a hurry," Alise said through gritted teeth, defensive and confused, a bad combination. How had the librarian wizards handled sophisticated spirit magic like that? "All I cared about was getting Cillian here before the burden of those archives killed him."

"I'm not unappreciative of your motivation," Órlaith said, graciously, not unkindly, but with steel beneath. "Still, I urge you to bear firmly in mind what I told you about your father and his ambitious nature, which you clearly share. The greatest danger is when we are willing to discard ethics and rationality in the name of expedience. All villains believe they're making choices for the right reasons, even with good intentions, but if they've abandoned their integrity, breaking the rules to achieve a goal… Well, that's when you go bad."

Alise, even more deeply offended, struggled to keep up. She'd never been in control of this conversation and now she found herself firmly on the losing end of it. It didn't help that Lady Harahel had put her finger exactly on Alise's greatest fear: that she was inherently a monster and would become like her father.

"My sympathies on the passing of your dear maman, by the way," Órlaith said with what looked like a genuine smile. "I always liked her and was sorry when she succumbed to the Fascination and bonded as Piers's familiar. She was far too young to die."

Pierced through the heart, Alise froze, unable to summon a reply. She had set her grief and guilt aside, knowing she'd caused Maman's death, no matter that no one else blamed her for it. She had been arrogant, thinking herself so clever to discover and execute a method to sever the wizard-familiar bond. She'd thought to free her mother from her father's tyranny and neglect, to save Maman's life, but her mother had wasted away, passing without ever regaining consciousness. At least only a handful of people knew what had really happened.

Except… did Lady Harahel somehow know this, too? Órlaith gazed at her steadily, her dark curls, so like Cillian's except threaded here and there with silver, giving her a softer appearance than those hard, black eyes evinced.

"Thank you for your sympathies," Alise replied through numb lips, the habitual reply seeing her through the roar in her mind.

"Of course." Órlaith patted her on the hand and stood. "Now, I'll see to supplies for you so you can be on your way."

"On my way?"

"Yes." Lady Harahel gave her a sunny smile. "I want you gone. As soon as feasible."

~ 5 ~

CILLIAN AWOKE WITH a sense of refreshed wellbeing, aware first and foremost that he'd been relieved of the terrible, voracious burden of the stolen archive. Thank all the dark arts for that. Coming home had been the correct solution.

For home he was, lying in his bed in his old room at House Harahel. Though he came home less often these days, often preferring to spend academy breaks pursuing his own projects in the Convocation Archives to traveling, his room hadn't changed much. Outside his mullion-paned windows, made of warped, human-made glass and lined with lead solder, not the perfectly clear glass made by Byssan wizards, a thick snow fell. Inside, it smelled of woodsmoke, old wood, and the distinctive scent of books. All sang quietly of his cozy childhood and the comforts of home, down to the warm quilt covering him, made by his grandmother.

He couldn't wait to show Alise around and—he wasn't embarrassed to admit to himself—show her off to his family. His mother and father would love her as he did. They'd admire her incisive intelligence and delicate beauty. Most of all, they'd see through her cool reserve that protected her huge heart. Alise had never had a loving family, the comforting tokens of a cherished and protected childhood as those that now surrounded him. He wanted to give her that. There weren't that many things he could offer Alise that were his alone to give, but this was one.

Stirring, he sat up, finding the expected teapot under a cozy on his bedside table, his favorite tea within, and poured himself a cup. He told himself he wasn't disappointed Alise wasn't there, waiting for him to awaken. She wasn't the sort to sit by the bedsides of invalids. Hopefully she slept, recovering from her own ordeal. The El-Adrel clock on his bedside table showed it was a little after six, but he couldn't tell from the dim wintry light if it was morning or evening. He could have slept the clock around, as worn out as he'd been.

Drinking the tea down and pouring another cup, he willed his mind to clear. He didn't remember much about the journey to House Harahel. Wanting to sleep and being unable to. His head aching as if boulders had been stuffed inside, cracking open his skull. Alise's worry.

But it was all fine now. They'd made it to House Harahel safe and sound, with the precious House Phel archive intact. All was well.

Eager to find Alise—he was quite sure the light was growing, not dying—he flung off the enfolding quilts and hurried to the bathing chamber. A long time ago, when he'd only daydreamed about having Alise, never truly believing she'd return his feelings, even temporarily, he'd fantasized about showing her his home. They could go ice-skating, one of his few—all right, only—athletic skills. She would be so surprised by his prowess. Though he'd be rusty. His life at Convocation

Academy left him little time for frivolities like ice-skating.

If Alise slept still, he'd go down to the pond and warm-up a bit. He should make sure it was swept free of snow anyway. Perhaps he could put a few surprises in place, like some hot chocolate and cookies. Happily anticipating Alise's delight, he quickly bathed. No grooming imps or water elementals in House Harahel. The Harahels were prickly in their insularity, deeply distrustful of the rest of the Convocation, and abjured magical conveniences made by other houses, with very few exceptions.

With a sigh, he acknowledged to himself that they had good reason. Especially now, with the high houses taking sides in what seemed to be shaping up into an all-out war. But those were thoughts for another day. He wanted to enjoy being at home, to share all of his favorite parts with his beloved. They'd earned a moment or two of peace, a little time to simply enjoy each other.

Entering the breakfast room, he found his grandmother with her ubiquitous pot of tea, an empty breakfast plate pushed to the side to make room for several open books before her. He'd hoped to find her there, though he'd expected more of his family to be there also. As he entered, she glanced up and smiled, springing from her chair to embrace him.

"My boy," she cried, holding him close. "It's so good to have you home." She pulled back scrutinizing him. "How do you feel?"

"Excellent," he answered, meaning it. The vigor of extensive Refoel healing coursed through him, making him feel fresher and brighter than in ages. He mentally corrected himself that House Harahel didn't eschew *all* wizardry from other houses. They did keep an in-house Refoel wizard—though it was always someone with a good portion of Harahel blood, and loyalty, along with it. "Where is everyone?"

"It's early yet and, besides, I wanted to talk to you alone, so I sent the few early risers along when I sensed you awake. Sit. Have some breakfast. Tea?"

Cillian let her pour, happy enough to have her fuss over him. When he'd been a kid, he'd thought everyone's grandmother knew exactly what they were up to. Only after he grew up some, and after hearing warnings from his siblings and cousins, did he discover his beloved gran was not only an accomplished mind-reader, but she also had no regard for privacy when it came to looking after her family and house. Oh, she didn't pry deeply—so far as he knew—but she kept a mental finger on the pulse of surface thoughts at House Harahel. She considered it part of her sacred duty.

"Now," his grandmother said, twinkling at him, clearly pleased to see him fill his plate, "tell me everything."

He nodded, his mouth full of freshly baked and frosted cinnamon roll. No matter how he tried, he could never make his own taste like the ones at home. One of the pastry chefs at the academy had suggested that it could be the water at House Harahel that made the difference. Cillian had been tempted to carry some back with him, to test the theory, but had never gotten around to it. Maybe this was his opportunity. Alise could help him perform the taste-test.

Oh. Except he wasn't going back to Convocation Archives. Tandiya Uriel had fired him. Had Alise told his grandmother that? Surreptitiously, he studied his gran. No, he didn't think so. Alise would have respected his privacy. Still, it was worth finding out. "What has Alise told you so far?"

His grandmother waved that off. "As if I'd trust anything from the forked tongue of an Elal snake. I want to hear from you."

Cillian paused at that. "Alise claims House Phel as her affiliation now, and they claim her."

She snorted. "Yes, so the chit mentioned. I don't believe it for a moment and neither should you."

"Grandmother," Cillian said slowly. "I know full well you'd have checked her thoughts to see if she was telling you the truth."

"Oh, I tried, of course, and I managed to glean some thoughts, which were not at all flattering to you or House Harahel by the way. But I couldn't get past her shielding. A tightly guarded mind on that one, which is suspicious right there. What young wizardling has shields against telepathy like that?"

One who'd been terrorized by a Hanneil wizard who'd imposed a mental block on her and further traumatized her with threats of sexual assault, that's who. And Alise had nearly destroyed herself fighting that all alone, all to protect him. Cillian sighed to himself. As a result—at Cillian's own insistence—Alise had only a few days before learned advanced shielding to extract herself from Gordon Hanneil's vile extortion and to protect herself in the future. It didn't seem likely that House Hanneil would stop targeting her, even if their reasons weren't fully understood.

It was a bitter irony that Alise's newfound skills would backfire in this way, undermining his grandmother's trust in his beloved. Still, the situation was easily corrected.

"Alise has very good shielding for a reason," he explained. "I can't tell you all the details, as its very personal to her, but Alise was mentally attacked by an unprincipled psychic wizard. She received a crash course in protecting herself."

"You don't say." His grandmother didn't sound convinced. Quite the opposite, though Cillian didn't understand why she'd be so suspicious.

"It's all tied in with the archives I brought. When we go through them, I suspect we'll find—"

His grandmother cut that off with a wave of her hand. "We can discuss that later. I have considerable reservations about the safety of those archives. You'll have to establish a protocol that assures me this house will be protected if anything untoward is secreted in those spelled stacks."

Ah. He hadn't expected that, but he shouldn't be surprised, given his grandmother's suspicions regarding outside magic, so he nodded in acquiescence. "Anyway, the point is that I trust Alise implicitly and so can you."

"Like you trusted Szarina Sammael?" his grandmother asked, raising her brows as she sipped from her cup.

Oof. That was a low and unexpected blow. The subject of Szarina was clearly still a tender spot—and possibly always would be—and the jab shocked his breath to a stop for a moment, temporarily stopping his thoughts.

His grandmother stepped into the fraught silence with a crisp nod. "As I thought. You have a weakness, Cillian, for beautiful, young, and highly ranked wizard girls. Especially ones that frame themselves as in need of rescue and—"

"Alise didn't 'frame herself' as in need of rescue," he interrupted, perhaps unwisely and certainly uncharacteristically. "She faced a terrible danger all alone, even doing her best to keep me out of it, hurting herself in order to protect *me*. You are being incredibly unfair to her."

"Am I?" She set her cup down and steepled her fingers under her chin. "Take a moment to consider this from my perspective. She is an Elal, a house notorious for their political scheming, and one deeply embroiled in the current cold war instigated by Gabriel Phel's reckless attempt to reinstate a house best left forgotten in the annals of history. Do you think it's a coincidence that Lady Veronica Elal became his bonded familiar, that the betrothal trials oh-so-conveniently decided the case there, so that none of us could dispute the alliance? History teaches us that there are no coincidences."

It sounded so plausible, put that way, even though Cillian knew the truth. "Nic—Lady Phel—ran away from the bonding. She tried to escape it. That doesn't sound like political scheming to me."

"Or was that the perfect distraction, to allay our potential concerns? Regardless, she is only a familiar, a tool to be used by her father and her husband."

"Clearly you've never met Nic," he muttered.

His grandmother ignored that. "She might not have known. *Or*, she did know, and attempted to avoid her fate with that unlawful escape attempt."

Nic and Gabriel loved each other, Cillian knew that beyond a shadow of a doubt. One only needed to spend a few minutes in their presence to know that, to sense their intense regard for one another—along with the considerable erotic charge between them. When they'd visited House Phel, he and Alise had been only friends and barely that, though he'd obviously wanted her far longer than that. It had been torture to be near her and know she barely gave him a thought, all while Nic and Gabriel demonstrated what he most wanted, and could never have.

Even now, he knew full well that he could never have that with Alise, even if she somehow returned the love he felt for her. They were both wizards, so they could never experience that deep intimacy between bonded wizard and familiar. And that didn't begin to address their very different stations in life. His grandmother wasn't wrong there. But she *was* wrong about everything else.

"I can understand how you'd form these opinions based on the surface appearance of events," he said, keeping his words slow and measured, "but the information you don't have, that can't be put in books and reports, is the heart and integrity of the people involved. Gabriel—Lord Phel, that is—had no idea that, by simply wanting to reestablish the legacy of his house, he'd be kicking over an anthill of ancient conspiracies."

"How do you know that's the case? I understand that you met and liked the wizard. I'm sure he appeals to you in that same way Szarina and Alise do, seeming to be non-traditionalists, exciting and not adhering to Convocation expectations, but those sorts don't survive what Convocation society and law require of us."

Cillian sat back in his chair. The cold winter light showed his grandmother's face in a different way than he'd seen before. Just like the breakfast room, with its lead-paned glass sunroom filled with flowering plants and chirping birds in cages mitigated but didn't erase the frozen landscape outside, her serene, seemingly practical assessment didn't change what he knew to be true. "I know because I've met these people. I know *them*."

"You know what they want you to know," she corrected implacably. "You've never been an accurate judge of true character, my boy, which the entire Szarina debacle proved. Do you think these people don't know that about you? That incident is hardly a secret. You have to at least consider that you were carefully selected as a target for this operation."

As much as he bristled at his grandmother's assessment of his character, Cillian had little foundation to argue against it. He *had* completely misjudged Szarina, wanting to believe that the dazzlingly gorgeous and popular Sammael scion truly loved him. She'd been skillful enough in her manipulation that she'd never introduced the topic of him helping her cheat. *He* had come up with the plan, so anxious to comfort her fears of her father's reprisals, to dry her tears and make her smile again in that radiant way of hers. He'd been gobsmacked to discover she'd picked him out, seduced and cozened him entirely according to the strategy she'd devised. Never would he forget Szarina spitting hateful words at him during that horrible meeting in the provost's office, how she'd laughed in his face that he'd ever believed a woman like her would want a meek librarian with no future.

The memory pained him still, so much that it worked like acid on his confidence that Alise was different. But his relationship with Alise wasn't the same at all. For starters, he had pursued her. "Alise didn't seek me out," he informed his grandmother. "She ignored me for the longest time."

His grandmother nodded, passing him a plate of scones. "How did you meet her?"

"She came into the archives. I saw her then." Night after night, Alise would arrive late, illuminating the quiet, shadowed space like a slim candle, her magic and fey beauty shining to eclipse all else.

"During *your* shift," his grandmother noted.

"It was an independent study," he explained, doing his best not to sound defensive. "She had to work on it late at night."

"And then she, inevitably, needed your help."

"I do work in the archives at the reference desk. It's literally in my job description to provide exactly that kind of assistance."

His grandmother held up her hands in a mockery of surrender, her expression set and wizard-black eyes hard. Belatedly, Cillian realized he was speaking with Lady Harahel, not his loving and beloved gran. He should have realized when she made that statement about the questionable safety of opening the folded archive. For the first time in his life, his grandmother was speaking to him as the head of a high house, questioning one of her wizard minions, one she wasn't happy with.

"Believe it or not, Cillian," she said, seeming to note the change in his internal weather, "I am on your side here. I do not mean to make you defensive, only to point out that there is a recognizable pattern in your behavior. Not to mention that you did what no one else could do. *You* were the one to locate the hidden Phel archives and extract them. *You* carried them here to House Harahel, drawing us into a conflict not of our making. Who else could have accomplished what you did?"

"We didn't know I could. *I* didn't know it, until I tried."

"You have always been far more talented and full of potential than you give yourself credit for," she observed, and he wished he felt less miserable and could take pleasure in the compliment. "Your MP scores are exceptional—and are a matter of public record."

"No one cares about exceptional MP scores in library magic," he retorted. It was like being champion moss-grower.

"Until they do," she retorted remorselessly. "In this case, I posit that they cared deeply. Alise Elal escorted you here personally, to ensure the mission was completed."

How to refute that except to explain that Alise had come with him because she loved him and cared about him? It sounded like more of the Szarina thing on the surface, sure, but he shared something different with Alise. Something intimate and heartfelt, a meeting of like minds and spirits. In contrast, he could look back on the time with Szarina and see that it had all been a lie from the beginning, a shiny fairy tale he'd wanted desperately to believe in. It had all been surface without substance, like Szarina herself. Whereas Alise was substance, through and through, feeling more deeply than anyone he'd ever known. She simply wasn't capable of that level of deception.

"All I can say is that you're wrong about Alise. You'll understand when you get to know her. I wanted to wait until we were together to tell you all about us, but I'll share with you now: Alise and I are in love. We know there are challenges to our relationship and that it might be for only right now. Still, I want that right now, whatever I can have of her. And I'm telling you so you'll understand that Alise brought me here because I asked her to help me. She was afraid for me and worried. There's no collusion, no hidden agenda to her. Alise is my girlfriend and my lover. I wanted her here to meet my family, see my childhood home. To meet *you*." He finished his impassioned speech feeling as if he'd lost steam along the way, fading in the face of his grandmother's stony reception. Worse, she almost seemed to be regarding him with… sympathy?

"My dear boy," she said, shaking her head. She took a deep breath, glanced out the window where the snowfall thickened. "It grieves me to see you go through all of this yet again, but if what you say is true, why did she leave?"

Leave? Cillian's heart, already chilled, dropped like a rock through his stomach. Alise wouldn't leave him. She especially wouldn't leave without making sure he'd recovered, without saying goodbye. But his grandmother—no, Lady Harahel—regarded him remorselessly, waiting out his shock.

"Alise wouldn't leave," he said, but he sounded tentative.

"She would and did. She left yesterday morning, shortly after she divested herself of you. Alise is gone."

~ 6 ~

A LISE RODE IN the elemental-powered carriage through the heavy snowfall, glad of the runners that let it function as a sleigh, through El-Adrel cleverness. Though she'd buried herself in the furry blankets, she couldn't seem to get warm. A cold, numb core of herself refused to thaw.

She couldn't bear to contemplate Cillian's hurt when he discovered she'd left. But what could she have done? Cillian's grandmother hadn't even allowed her to leave a note. She could hardly stay at House Harahel without Lady Harahel's permission, in the face of her express instruction to leave. Though Alise might not care if House Elal got called upon to make reparations for an intrusion by one of their own, she would care if House Phel got in trouble because of her. Nic and Gabriel had already gone out on a limb by taking her into their house, paying for her education at Convocation Acade-my—which she'd screwed up, yet again—and being so forgiving about Maman's death. She couldn't possibly jeopardize everything they'd struggled to build and protect by adding to House Phel's already too-long list of enemies.

Leaving had been the only thing she could reasonably do. The current problem was, she didn't know where to go.

She couldn't return to Convocation Academy, not yet. Maybe not ever. She certainly wasn't going to House Elal. She could live her entire life without returning to those spirit-infested halls. There was only one place she could feasibly go, the place she'd wanted to go in the first place and probably should have, even if she might not be wholly welcome.

So, she programmed the air elemental—one perfectly tamed and bonded, exactly to House Elal factory specs, as Lady Harahel had indicated—to take her to the only real home she had anymore: House Phel.

Then she tried to sleep, though she didn't think she'd be able to, with her mind racing and her heart breaking. Exhaustion must have caught up with her, however, sending her into sleep at some point, because she jarred awake, steaming hot and sweating, at the jolting of sleigh runners on rocks. Hastily, she halted the air elemental's single-minded—if you could call it a mind—forward progress and stepped out of the carriage, shedding blankets like the fur of some stinking mammal after hibernation. She felt greasy and filthy, unable to recall when she'd last bathed.

Worse, her shoes, adequate for the heated halls of Convocation Academy, sunk ankle-deep in muck when she stepped out of the carriage. "Welcome to the swamps of Meresin," she announced to herself, spreading her arms and smiling maybe just a little. She didn't have much humor in her, but the moment made her think of Nic and her sister's unrelenting needling of Gabriel over Meresin being one big swamp. It wasn't, of course, but much of the place did sit at or below sea level, with wildly prevalent wetlands of all varieties.

It was also warmer in Meresin, in these more southern and western climes, though not actually *warm*. In truth, the pervasive moisture generated a chill that penetrated to her bones in a way the frozen weather hadn't. Of course, it didn't help that she stood outside in her shirtsleeves, sweat cloying on her skin after being buried in the furry blankets.

Alise supposed she was fortunate the snow had given way to this waterlogged excuse for a road, rather than dry ground. As it was, the sleigh runners looked a little chewed up. In the exigency of their midnight escape from Convocation Academy, Alise had "borrowed" the plush House Elal carriage from the storage facility. Maybe she was having a hard time breaking the childhood habit of worrying about what her father would say or do, but she was relieved that she hadn't actually broken the cursed thing. Finding the button to trigger the El-Adrel mechanism, she watched as the clockwork devices extended wheels and withdrew the sled runners. Not ideal for the swampy ground of Meresin, but Nic's joking suggestion of carriages that could convert to boats had yet to be taken seriously, let alone implemented.

With the carriage on wide rimmed wheels that only sunk partway into the muck, Alise sat in the open door of the passenger compartment and pried off her mud-soaked slippers, then knocked off as much of the gunk as she could before setting them in a far corner inside. Pulling on a more judicious blanket or two, she set the elemental into motion again, sorry to find that the earlier speed over snow had slowed to a boggy crawl. The carriage lurched and heaved as it hit a rock one moment and a water-filled hole the next.

It pleased Alise to see that her sentries remained in place, notifying Lord and Lady Phel of her incipient arrival. Or so she was extrapolating from her tests of the entities' responsiveness. To be certain, she'd have to check the messaging system she'd set up at House Phel for timeliness and accuracy. And, while there, she'd also inspect and refuel the other imps and elementals she'd set up for Nic, though her sister, while a familiar and not a wizard, still had a knack for coaxing the creatures along. Nic possessed considerable Elal magic, though she couldn't wield it directly.

Midday was a propitious time for arrival at House Phel, the early spring sunlight warm on the gracious manse with its long wings, large windows—only Byssan glass used in the restoration, so all gleamed flawlessly clear in their white-painted, wooden frames—and the wide porches and balconies. The more temperate climate allowed the vast lawn to remain evergreen, studded with tufts of colorful spring flowers. The rolling lawn surrounded the perfectly still lake that mirrored the graceful lines of the manse. With the soft blue sky above, barely touched with a few fluffy white clouds, the whole scene was an idyllic portrait of gentle, rural splendor.

Alise released a long sigh of relief and sorrow, twined indelibly together. House Phel felt like home in a way Elal never had—and apparently as Harahel never would. She couldn't get over the sinking sensation that she'd let Cillian down by leaving. She knew he'd wanted her to see the house of his birth, to meet his family. It was just like him to blithely assume that his family would embrace her, not to mention "forgetting" to mention that the grandmother he'd portrayed as a sweet old lady spending her days baking and quilting was in fact an intimidatingly sharp dragon of a wizard and actually Lady Harahel. Seriously, Cillian couldn't have warned her?

Knowing him, he probably thought it wasn't important. And, knowing him, he wouldn't understand why she'd been compelled to leave. He'd be hurt, upset, possibly angry. And knowing that simply exhausted her. She'd been clear from the beginning that she couldn't give Cillian what he wanted and needed. He possessed the heart of a true romantic. With his particular aspirations for a good and quiet life, he could afford that kind of softness and vulnerability where she couldn't. Plus he possessed that dragon of a grandmother to protect him, which Alise could heartily agree he needed. Lady Harahel was wrong about Alise, but her logic was impeccable. Were the situations reversed, Alise wouldn't let herself near Cillian either.

Which served to prove, right there, that their relationship shouldn't be. She'd been deluding herself about that, seduced by cinnamon rolls and sweetness, and it was time to stop.

During her morose musings, the carriage had circled the lake and slowed to a halt before the manse, the echo of her arrival at House Harahel a bit unsettling. But, where that moment had been dark, cold, and desperate, the house there like something out of a gothic romance, this arrival was the exact opposite. The sunshine, flowers, birdsong, the lovely white manse with its sparkling windows—and an incredibly pregnant Nic coming slowly down the wide steps, a huge smile on her face. Her black curls bounced around her high-cheekboned face, emerald eyes brilliant.

"I wasn't sure if you'd get the message in time," her sister exclaimed, hugging her, the embrace made exceedingly awkward by Nic's enormous and enormously hard belly protruding between them. Then it rippled. Nic gasped, and Alise leapt back. Nic's forest-green Ophiel gown clung lovingly to the rounded surface, magically adapting to even the large mound of her pregnancy like a second skin. Skin that rippled like a wave.

"You're in labor?" Alise demanded.

"Yes." Nic laughed, an hysterical edge to it. "Finally! Isn't that why you're here? And what in the dark arts happened to you? Barefoot, mud-spattered, and you smell like you haven't bathed in days."

"I love you too," Alise responded sourly, figuring that answered that.

"This pregnancy," Nic explained. "I can smell anything rotten or unpleasant from a league away."

"Even better. Should you be standing out here on the steps if you're in labor?"

"No," Gabriel Phel said, emerging from the house, his magic billowing around him like a cloak in a high wind. His startlingly white hair contrasted with his tawny skin, the lone black streak at his temple matching his snapping wizard-black eyes. "Hello, Alise. Good to see you and I'm glad you made it in time." He gave her a hug that was quick, perfunctory, and felt so much like what a brother—a real brother, not her actual turd of a one—would give that she nearly teared up. "Now," he continued, turning to glower at Nic, "do me a favor and make your obstinate sibling go lie down."

"Wizard Qaya, the midwife House Gaia sent me," Nic explained to Alise, "says that it could be hours and hours and that walking is good for me."

"Nic," Gabriel grated, sounding like a wizard on the edge. Silver sparkled in the air, the humidity condensing into tiny silver specks, transformed by Gabriel's water and moon magic, Alise realized. He'd clearly been working on blending the two kinds of magic, but not with perfect control.

"Mind your magic, my only love. Go terrorize the minions or something," Nic told him impudently, patting him on the cheek and giving him a kiss. She looped her arm through Alise's. "My sister will walk with me."

"Don't upset her," Gabriel instructed Alise.

"She can upset me all she likes," Nic retorted. "I'm bored of being treated like I'm breakable. *You* stay here and practice being calm. This is all your fault anyway."

Gabriel actually made a growling sound under his breath, the palpable surge of his magic causing the once-fluffy clouds to gather into heavy-bottomed threats of rain.

Alise eyed the gathering storm with unease. "I don't think your cautions are working," she said *sotto voce* to Nic.

Her sister shrugged that off. "We could use the rain. And it would help him to blow off a little steam, as it were." She cast a coquettish glance at Gabriel over her shoulder, fluttering her lashes. "One day my wizard will learn I only like it when he bosses me around during sex."

Startled, Alise blushed. Nic rolled her eyes. "Oh come now, you're an adult now and—dark arts!" she suddenly exclaimed, startling Alise. "I forgot your natal day. I'm a horrible sister."

Alise laughed. "You are not." In truth, with all that had been going on, she'd practically forgotten it herself.

"I don't suppose our father acknowledged it."

"Does he ever?"

"No." Nic let out a sigh. "And now I'm no better."

"It's all right, Nic. It really is."

"All right then. Then tell me this, what's with this whole 'Cillian Harahel is looking after me' thing?" Nic squeezed her arm. "You had to know that your missive would only pique my interest. You and the shy librarian wizard a romantic item now. Tell me everything."

Alise really regretted having put that in her letter to Nic.

"He's not shy, really. He's—" Alise broke off when Nic's grip vised on her arm as she bent over, propping her other hand on her knee, blowing out her breath rhythmically. "Nic! We should go back to the manse."

"No, no, no," Nic panted, straightening and waving a hand in the air. "They'll just all hover, which you know I can't bear, as it really will be hours and hours of this, and besides Wizard Qaya *did* say that walking is good for me. I need a distraction. Tell me more about adorable Cillian. Did you have sex with him yet?"

"Nic!" Cheeks scalding, Alise tried not to choke.

"Oh, you *have*," Nic crooned. "Tell me every little detail."

"No."

"It's your job to distract me. I'm in pain," Nic wheedled.

Alise sighed. "You're just nosy is all."

"Exactly so," Nic replied jauntily. "Tremendously curious. Insatiably so. Only a dense recitation of every intimate detail will satisfy me. So: spill." She'd turned them on a pretty path leading around one of the wings of the manse, far away from any eavesdroppers.

"There's really nothing to tell," Alise said, deciding this was a ripe opportunity to set the record straight regarding Cillian and her, and to cement what she knew their future must be. It was over between them, no matter how the thought pained her. Denying reality any longer would serve nothing. Not only couldn't she and Cillian ever be; they shouldn't have ever *been*. She might as well make it official.

"I apologize that my wording made our relationship sound like more than it was. I only meant that Wizard Harahel had been assigned as my independent study mentor and that he was safeguarding me against any troubles. Not that there were any," she hastily added. "But in your letter you mentioned vague fears about me being in danger, so I thought I should address those."

"Mmm hmm." Nic's ostensible agreement sounded more skeptical than anything.

As Nic also said nothing more after that, Alise plowed on. "I mean, some things did happen that I'll share with you and Gabriel as you'll need to know about them." She was digging herself into a hole. Nic would be upset by the entire truth—information she and Gabriel needed as Lord and Lady Phel—but wasn't it bad for a woman in labor to receive bad news?

"Eventually," she added, "after the baby is born and you've recovered."

"Don't do that," Nic warned, her tone falsely mild. They'd entered an orchard with tiny, bright green leaves starting to unfurl on the gracefully twisted limbs of the ancient trees. "I'm pregnant, not addle-brained."

Alise belatedly recalled Nic's letter mentioning her threat to stab Gabriel with a fork for calling her emotional. "My point is that, to answer your question, no, I'm not romantically involved with Cilli—Wizard Harahel. He's a friend. And mentor. Only."

"I see," Nic replied amiably. "So, despite the difference I sense in your magic, which includes a wealth of feeling that's quite palpable, you didn't have—let's protect your delicate sensibilities, shall we?—ah, intimate relations with that adorable boy?"

"He's older than you are," Alise pointed out, irritated with both of them. How in the dark arts could Nic sense all of this in her?

"Is he?" Nic sighed rubbing her belly. Alise side-eyed the substantial mound, checking for more ripples. "I feel so much older than you lot these days, so much has happened."

Alise understood that feeling, very well.

"But," Nic continued in a brighter tone, "I observe that you have twice dodged this question and therefore conclude that you *did* have sex with the delightful librarian wizard and I of course happen to know this was your first sex, so… How was it?"

Wonderful. Amazing. Soul-shatteringly intimate. She'd never felt so loved and adored as when Cillian had made love to her. And now it was gone. "I think I liked our relationship better when we weren't speaking," she griped.

"That good, huh?" Nic murmured, squeezing her arm.

"Does the fact that you're here—clearly surprised to discover I'm in labor—without your beloved and smelling like a five-day old slaughtered pig mean that—"

"Enough with the stink remarks already." Alise extracted her arm and stepped a good two arm's lengths away. "As a matter of fact, no I haven't bathed in several days and I'm covered in muck because the roads here in Meresin, if you can dignify them with that title, are actually shallow bogs. I travelled here from House Harahel after *Lady* Harahel—who just happens to be Cillian's *grandmother*, a fact that adorable librarian boy *forgot* to mention—threw me out for being a filthy, stinking Elal, and I don't know if Cillian is even all right because he found the hidden Phel texts in the Convocation Archives and it nearly killed him to extract them and carry them to House Harahel where they'll be safe because House Hanneil sent a spy wizard to try to stop me, which was *horrible*, and—" She dragged in a breath, finding she simply couldn't around the rock lodged in her chest.

Nic regarded her solemnly, both hands rubbing her belly. "That's a lot."

"I'm sorry," Alise managed to get out, pressing her fingers on either side of her nose, willing herself not to cry and discovering it was too late. "I'm not supposed to upset you."

"Gabriel can tough it out if I can," Nic said, her gorgeous emerald eyes welling with sympathetic tears. "You should have told me your heart was broken."

"It's not. I'm just tired and… And Cillian, he…" A sob tore out of her.

"Oh, honey." Nic opened her arms. "Come here you little

stinkbomb."

Needing the embrace, Alise let Nic hold her, weeping on her big sister's shoulder. "I'm sorry I sm—sm—smell bad," she sobbed.

Nic patted her back. "It's all right. Nothing a small herd of grooming imps can't cure. You must have been right out of your head that it didn't occur to you to summon some. Let's go back to the manse and you can tell me the whole story, including who at House Hanneil we have to kill for daring to hurt you."

"He—he's already dead. Or as good as. Provost Uriel took care of it. She wiped the floor with him. She's actually a terrifyingly powerful wizard. Did you know that? And Morghana Seraphiel tutored me in the dark arts and then told me to tell *you* that House Seraphiel stands ready to assist, and I'm forgetting more."

"Definitely a story we need to hear." Nic patted her back. "Unfortunately, it will have to be later."

"What?" Alise pulled back in alarm. "The baby?"

"It seems so. Help me back to the manse, sweetheart, or I'm going to drop this baby on her head in the orchard and I'll never hear the end of it from Gabriel."

~ 7 ~

CILLIAN WOULD HAVE gone after Alise immediately, except that his grandmother forbade it.

Correction: his grandmother clucked in sympathy and made him his favorite hot chocolate, while Lady Harahel informed him in no uncertain terms that he would remain at House Harahel until she released him. She gave instructions that no one give him transportation out of Harahel, and it wasn't as if he could snowshoe or ski out on his own.

"So I'm a prisoner," he said with bitterness no amount of chocolate could alleviate.

"You'll thank me some day," Lady Harahel replied equably. "And try to be less dramatic. You're hardly the first disgraced wizard to be safeguarded in the house of their birth following unpleasantness. Besides, it's not as if you need to return to Convocation Archives, since you are no longer employed there." She raised her brows at his surprise. "What—did you think Tandiya Uriel wouldn't communicate your removal from employment?"

"I thought you didn't care to use Ratsiel couriers," he answered sullenly.

"You are correct that I don't use them, but you're making a

careless assumption in that one must employ a Ratsiel courier in order to have timely communication. In addition, it's insulting of you to imply that my choice to abjure the use of House Ratsiel products is a whimsical preference or a capricious choice. Using goods produced by other houses gives them entrée to ours, creates alliances we cannot afford to indulge and remain objective observers of history. If you had ever shown any interest in governance of this house, I'd have explained this before. Perhaps now that you've put your tenure in Convocation Archives behind you, that might change."

Cillian didn't reply to that bit of bait. Lady Harahel had offered him several thinly disguised bribes to cheerfully capitulate to her wishes. Not that she needed his cooperation as she controlled his fate with an iron fist. It turned out his parents weren't even in residence—gone off to consult on library acquisitions for House Minerva—a coincidental absence Cillian found highly suspicious.

"Since you sacrificed your career and your integrity as an archivist to steal the texts regarding House Phel and bring them here, coding the folded archive to yourself alone, you may devote yourself to reviewing the materials." She held up a hand when Cillian straightened at this. "With certain restrictions," she added.

He'd thought she wouldn't let him near that project, refusing to even discuss it when he'd asked. Coding the re-folded archive to himself had been expedient in the moment, then a disastrous choice in retrospect because what if he'd been killed? The archive would have died with him, all those texts lost forever. Now he was glad of it, not only because he'd lived, but also because he'd inadvertently made himself indispensable.

"What restrictions?" he asked, wary. He was accustomed to working within strict or externally imposed protocols, but this new face of his grandmother had him leery of agreeing to anything too quickly or easily.

"First, you agree to give up this nonsense of working at Convocation Archives and agree to remain here at House Harahel where you belong."

"I thought I'd already sacrificed that career and irretrievably compromised my integrity as an archivist."

The look she gave him was sour. "I don't advise you be flip about your situation, boy. I'm not best pleased with you. I also know you. Even without reading your thoughts, I can predict that you will be scheming your way back to those archives you love so well, if you haven't developed a plan already. You can abandon that tack immediately. I was never in favor of you going off to Convocation Center, being exposed to the corruption there, not to mention the poor food. You belong here. If you wish—and if you show sufficient interest and commitment—I'll train you to be my heir."

That startled him. "Father is your heir."

She waved that off. "For now. However, I intend to live a good long life and when the time comes for my heir to take over heading the house, it will likely be better to skip a generation and install someone younger."

"I would have to discuss with Father."

"Do so. There's certainly no rush. But you *will* agree to stay here at House Harahel or you will not be allowed access to any sensitive projects, most especially not the House Phel archives."

She had him in a tight spot and she knew it. Though it wouldn't take a mind-reader to know that Cillian desperately wanted at those archives, in part because any unsolved riddle plagued him mercilessly, but also for Alise. *Alise.* Who had left him without a word. He had been unkind to her in the carriage, he vaguely recalled, as if through the distortion of a fever. Perhaps he'd been worse than he remembered, hurting her enough that she didn't care to speak with him again.

Where had she gone? Probably to House Phel. He wondered if he could find a way to message her, convince her to reconsider. Training as his grandmother's heir would give him access to whatever communication system she was using—and agreeing to her terms would maximize his freedom.

"For how long?" he asked, then clarified. "How long would I have to remain at House Harahel?"

Lady Harahel looked almost sympathetic. "Cillian, my boy, don't pretend to be dense. For the rest of your life."

"But other Harahel wizards work in libraries across the Convocation," he argued, "or in other related professions."

"You are not just any Harahel wizard," she replied calmly. "Even if you were not my favorite grandchild, eclipsing even my own children in my affections, I would be making this same decision. You are too soft, too sensitive for the harsh world of the Convocation. This is why the unprincipled are able to take advantage of you. Because of my affection for you, I capitulated to your wishes and allowed you to experiment with a career in the Convocation Archives. I had the idea that you might learn from the experience, gain a thicker skin, a more cynical understanding of life. That has not been the case, however, which is truly no fault of yours."

She softened. "This is not a punishment, my boy. This is protection. You are uniquely valuable, as precious as a single edition from a rare collection. You belong in *my* archives, cared for, beloved, far from the ravages of the world."

"So: forever," he said slowly. "You want me to agree to never leave Harahel ever again. We're back to me being imprisoned here."

"Harahel is a big place," she replied with impatience. "There are people in the Convocation who never leave their villages in all their lives, let alone a land as expansive and rich in varied ecosystems as all of Harahel."

"I don't believe it's the size or variety of the cell that determines the level of imprisonment," he countered.

"I disagree. Humanity is unable to leave this world. We gaze upon the stars, but cannot reach them. Does that make this entire wild and wonderful world a prison?"

"I would argue that we only currently lack the ability to leave, not that we are being arbitrarily deprived of the freedom to do so," he answered quietly. "Whereas you, Grandmother, are proposing to limit my freedom to live my life as I wish for the entirety of it. Or until you die, at which point I wouldn't have to abide by your rule."

"By then you will grasp the wisdom of my strategy. Do you see me leaving Harahel lands? No. That's not an accident and this decision is far from arbitrary, boy. I don't need to leave and neither do you."

"I disagree, regarding myself."

"Why?" she shot back. "Because you long to find yet another ambitious young wizard from a high house to trample your heart and abuse your trust?"

"No." He allowed a smile. "Just the one."

"The one who *left* you," his grandmother pointed out with asperity. "Have you so little self-respect that you wish to go running after her, panting like a desperate puppy?"

His smile faded in the face of that marked contempt. No arguing with that. And there was no point in planning his escape—for escape he eventually would—until he had the information that would be his entrée to an audience with Alise. Once he knew what the Phel archives contained, he would go to Alise and give her those secrets. That would open a conversation and they could decide where to go from there. Capitulation would be the better part of valor in this moment. He allowed his very real heartache to show through.

"I can't believe Alise left me like that, not even knowing if I'd recovered."

"I'm sorry, Cillian." His grandmother unbent, sliding him a plate of cookies. "She couldn't leave fast enough."

"I know she doesn't love me like I love her," he confessed, sticking to that painful truth. "But I thought we were friends, at least."

"This is what I'm talking about. She used and manipulated your pure feelings. A friend wouldn't do that."

"You're right," he agreed on a sigh. Then made a show of coming to a decision. "The work is important to me. I risked a great deal to locate and extract those archives, not for Alise—

no matter what you may think—but because I thought the importance of restoring the integrity of those texts, of the historical record, eclipsed any concerns about my job security. Because House Harahel, and all we stand for, matters more to me than anything else."

Lady Harahel eyed him shrewdly, no doubt reading his thoughts for the veracity of his words. He focused on the inherent truth of what he'd said. None of it was a lie.

"I *am* impressed by what you managed to do," she said at last, almost grudgingly. "And I admit some of my motivation in keeping you here with me, derives from that. You achieved a feat of library magic that my best wizards have been unable to comprehend or replicate. You have displayed hidden depths that make you an enormous asset to House Harahel. I'm proud of you." She smiled faintly. "I apologize if I failed to recognize that before."

"And yet you require a test of loyalty from me."

Her smile faded. "If you regard being asked to cleave to your house and homeland as a test of loyalty, then yes. You have abilities I hadn't guessed at, my boy, which is on me. I underestimated you and allowed you to take yourself and your skills to Convocation Center. Now I must make the best choice for the house I lead, which means protecting our assets."

"I'm a person, not an asset," he retorted, bitterness in his voice. So much of this hurt far more than he'd expected. He'd been granted permission to cultivate a career in Convocation Archives not by an affectionate grandmother as he'd assumed, but by the head of his house who'd weighed his value and found him expendable. It was an uncomfortable irony that finding Alise, that his love for her, had been the incentive to push himself to strive for more than he'd ever imagined himself capable of accomplishing. He also hadn't shared that Alise, herself, had literally made that feat possible. She'd inspired him, yes, but she'd also shared her magic with him.

"You are wrong, Cillian," Lady Harahel said, not unkindly and not without a hint of regret. "You will begin to understand this as I train you to be my heir. Some high houses count their assets in their trademarks, their warehouses of produced widgets for sale, the wealth they've accumulated and invested. At House Harahel, our greatest asset lies in the intellect of our wizards."

"Also in the libraries and archives we maintain," he countered, and she accepted that with a nod.

"But the true value of what we bring is our ability to catalogue, index, read, collate, and analyze that information. And to do whatever it is that you managed to do." She smiled again, this time warmly. "I know I'm placing difficult restrictions on you and, in time, we can revisit them if you truly wish to travel beyond Harahel. You should know that this is all because your grandmother loves you and the head of your house values you. I'm asking you to give me your time, your presence, and the gift of your wizardry."

He believed her—and that she firmly believed in her decisions and the motivations behind them.

"Agreed," he said, careful not to make his agreement too specific. "I'll work on the Phel archives and take training with you."

"And you won't leave Harahel lands?"

"I will stay here, yes." *For now.* He suppressed the though as quickly as it bubbled up, concentrating on meaning what he'd said.

She inclined her head, accepting his words. He wouldn't make the mistake again of underestimating her. Lady Harahel would be keeping tabs on him, no doubt about it. Time to plant some seeds for the future.

"You should consider this, however," he said, allowing himself to look as troubled as he felt. "What I managed to do with those hidden Phel archives… I did that by *undoing* what someone else did. Only a wizard with powerful skills and magic in Harahel proprietary archival tools would have been able to hide that volume of information and make it undetectable."

Lady Harahel drummed her fingers on the table. "I had already thought of that and those considerations factored heavily into my decisions regarding you and my requests."

Cillian raised his brows in mute question, not trusting himself to speak and be caustic about her choosing the word "request." Probably extortion sounded too harsh in her mind, however accurate it might be.

"The perpetrator isn't necessarily one of ours," she mused. "The library magic itself isn't damming, as those skills can crop up in any number of wizards." She held up a hand when he opened his mouth. "Though I concede the power and skill needed are unusual, as is access to our proprietary tools. Still— it could be an outside wizard operating with intelligence from someone within." She leveled a stern look at him. "Perhaps in this light, you will reconsider condemning me for declining to give unnecessary access to outsiders."

"You are wise, Grandmother," he replied, trying to sound rueful. Instead he could only think of House Phel and how they embraced everyone who came to their door.

Which made him think of Alise, wondering if she'd gone there and what she was doing.

And if she was thinking of him.

~ 8 ~

Alise held her infant niece in her arms and could think of nothing but the miraculous appearance of this whole new life. An hour before, there had been no Bria in the world; now Alise loved this baby, this child of her sister, this daughter of a dark wizard, with every fiber of her being.

"I am your Auntie Alise," she whispered to the red-faced baby, nuzzling the so-soft skin, the silky skein of black hair over the perfect roundness of her head. "And I will be there for you always. No matter if you are wizard or familiar. No matter what house you choose or what path you take. No matter who threatens you or even looks at you sideways. You call on Auntie Alise and I'll take care of everything."

"Big promises," Quinn teased, practically sitting on her hands. The Byssan familiar who lived at House Phel with her bonded wizard and sister looked on enviously as Alise held Bria. Nic was sleeping in the next room, Gabriel sitting in with her and glaring thunderously at anyone tending to her, including Asa, the Refoel healer. That meant the visitors got to play with the baby, Wizard Qaya overseeing them with far more benevolence.

"If anyone can fulfill promises like that, Alise can," Iliana said staunchly. The redhead wasn't being nearly so patient, her hands partly extended, fingers wiggling. "Han and I would be in Sammael chains if Alise hadn't saved us. She's the best fairy, I mean, wizardly, godmother a baby could have. Is it my turn to hold Bria yet?"

"Don't you try to take my baby," Alise warned, not entirely teasing. Holding Bria, feeling this amazing love that seemed to be born out of nowhere, soothed her strained heart like nothing she'd have imagined could.

"I'm pretty sure that's *my* baby," a new voice announced. Jadren El-Adrel—now Lord El-Adrel, Alise reminded herself, no matter how unlikely that sounded—deftly snagged Bria from Alise's cradling arms.

"Hey," Alise protested. Behind Jadren, Seliah rolled her eyes, tossing back her waist-length, shining black hair.

"You don't even like babies," Seliah informed Jadren, who indeed held Bria awkwardly. Wizard Qaya had already intervened to adjust his hold.

"I like babies," Jadren countered. "I like you, don't I?"

"Ha ha." Seliah glared at him, though she looked too pleased to make it convincing, and she tickled Bria's cheek before glancing at the closed door, then Alise. "How is Nic? And has my brother lost his mind in an overprotective frenzy yet?"

Quinn and Illiana tried to restrain their giggles and Alise shook her head. "Just about, though both Nic and Bria are strong and healthy, so he's backing down from full wizard meltdown." Thunder boomed above and Alise winced. It had been pouring rain nonstop since Nic went into labor.

"Everything is flooding," Jadren commented. "Slowed us down, which is why we're so late getting here. Someone needs to slap His Phelness upside the head and get him to control his feelings."

"Good idea," Seliah said, slipping Bria from Jadren's hold, using a very similar technique to steal the baby that he had. "You go do that."

"Really, Lady El-Adrel," Illiana said meekly, but with a pronounced whine, "it was my turn next.

"I'm not bearding the lion in his den," Jadren replied to Seliah, both of them ignoring the pouting Iliana. "I vote for Baby Elal here. She's not doing anything anyway."

The two of them exchanged a brief glance, then turned on Alise. "Aren't you supposed to be at Convocation Academy?" Seliah asked, frowning a little.

"She probably got kicked out again," Jadren observed, stroking his short, auburn beard, wizard-black eyes full of teasing glee. "Getting to be a bad habit. Baby Elal here is apparently going for the Convocation record on expulsions."

"Only because you never went," Alise retorted. "If you had, Lord El-Adrel, no one could have hope to beat your record of transgressions."

"Fair enough," he admitted.

"And," she continued before he could, "I've never once been expelled, only placed on probation. I'm absent from the academy at the moment with full knowledge and permission from the provost." That was mostly true, even if Provost Uriel thought she was at House Harahel with Cillian and the Phel archives. "I'm here for the same reason you are, visiting family and a new baby. Lastly, it's Phel now. Though I'm officially not the youngest Phel anymore, so you can't call me Baby Phel."

Jadren shook his head, making a sad face at Seliah. "They grow up and get mouthy so fast."

"You bring it on yourself," Seliah retorted.

"True enough. Always have."

Seliah handed the baby to Iliana who accepted the sleeping bundle with a quiet squeal of happiness. "Let's go in and see my brother and heart-sister." She glanced at Alise, not Wizard Qaya, which came as a surprise. "If it's all right to go in?"

Though not the highest-ranked person in the room, by any stretch, Alise realized Seliah was according her the respect of being the highest ranked of the Phel household, an acknowledgement of her place in the family and in House Phel that Alise sorely needed after the debacle with Lady Harahel.

"Of course," she answered Seliah, who she suspected knew exactly what she was doing. "Go ahead. And tell Lord Phel we're begging him to stop the rain."

"I'll tell him it's an order from you," Jadren replied with a wink. "You're scarier than I am."

THE NEXT FEW days were a bustle of visitors from near and far, their arrival assisted immensely by Gabriel banishing the rain and the myriad of House Phel water wizard minions bending their magic to the task of drying the roads again. With the re-emergence of the sun and warming spring in these milder climes, the orchards burst into bloom, echoed below by meadows of wildflowers. Alise took to long walks, partly to remove herself from notice, so no one would remember that she was supposed to be elsewhere, and also to practice her newly acquired skills.

Professor Seraphiel had been kind enough to teach Alise the basics of the dark arts, as a defense against Hanneil mind-control attempts. Though everyone in the Convocation seemed to swear by the dark arts, very few wizards at the academy actually studied them. Alise, in fact, had never even been to the dark arts wing until Cillian took her there to meet Professor Morghana Seraphiel. Whatever Alise had expected, the experience had been polar opposite of that. She'd learned a whole new way of seeing the world and the realm of wizardry during those few long hours with Professor Seraphiel.

Those lessons had stood her in good stead during that final confrontation with Gordon Hanneil—although she'd had to face the sobering realization that those skills that worked so well in self-defense could do nothing to protect Cillian. She bitterly regretted not being able to prevent Gordon from taking over Cillian's mind.

Also, those abilities had backfired somewhat with Lady Harahel, but Alise suspected Cillian's grandmother would have been suspicious of her regardless. More important, had Alise been more practiced at her defenses—especially the elusiveness Professor Seraphiel had emphasized—Lady Harahel wouldn't have been able to read what thoughts she had. Which meant that Alise needed to concentrate on practicing those skills. She was only partly motivated by the anticipation of Morghana Seraphiel's intense displeasure if she found Alise slacking.

Fortuitously, both the wild and the cultivated landscapes surrounding House Phel leant themselves perfectly to that practice, rooted as the dark arts were in the elements of earth, air, water, and fire. The first three could be found in abundance wherever she went in the area, and for the fourth, she summoned a little fire elemental and fed it whatever dry tinder she could find—which was frankly the greatest challenge.

She'd followed a path through the gloriously and sweetly blooming orchards and into a swampier area, cleaving to the much narrower, but at least consistently dry trail. Flowers burgeoned there also, but more subtly. Periwinkles peeped out between low rushes and exotic orchids dangled from spires amid the draping moss that hung in almost sinister curtains from the trees. Finding a relatively dry hummock, she took off her shoes—the better to dig her toes into the soil—and lit her small fire in a bowl she'd brought for the purpose.

Then she began the ritual Professor Seraphiel had taught her, calling in turn on the essence of the natural elements to cleanse and fill her mind. The dark arts operated in a totally different fashion from the more commonly used forms of wizardry, which was in part what made them so effective as a defense. It felt like using an entirely new muscle, but she was gaining facility with it. Practicing the novel, not yet familiar, and still unwieldy magics required all her concentration, which also served to keep her from thinking about Cillian.

Cillian, who hadn't messaged her.

The silence from his direction eroded the edges of her attention, making her wonder what he was doing, how he felt about her, what he was thinking. She'd considered sending a message to him, but felt divided. First of all, she wasn't sure a message would get through, which would leave her in the same position as now, except that she'd be even more on tenterhooks wondering if he'd not received her missive or if he'd elected not to respond. The possibility of the latter was truly what stopped her from taking action. She had her pride. She didn't want to be tugging at his sleeve to pay attention to her. Cillian was a smart wizard. He'd easily guess where she'd gone—it wasn't as if she had many options—and he knew where to find her.

If he wanted to.

Thinking that he *didn't* want to hurt like a grinding ache, a constant abrasion against her pride and her heart. She couldn't help remembering, how he'd rejected her in the carriage on the way to House Harahel. It could be that he couldn't forgive her for leaving him vulnerable to Gordon Hanneil. Or for dragging him into this whole cursed business to begin with.

So, she did her best *not* to think. Practicing the deliberately mindless rituals of the dark arts—mindless in the sense that the practitioner strove to relax conscious control—helped to dismiss those haunting worries. Not to mention the practice served to focus her attention on what truly mattered: the many enemies seeking to once-again remove House Phel from the Convocation. She and Nic hadn't talked again about all she'd confessed upon her arrival. Nic had been consumed with recovering from labor and learning to care for Baby Bria, but that day would inevitably arrive.

If Cillian, or House Harahel, hadn't contacted them by then with the results of their audit of the Phel archives, Alise didn't know what they'd do. But that was a question for another hour on another day. In the meanwhile, she immersed herself in the ritual practice of the dark arts.

After a while, she became aware of someone else present, practicing with her. A wizard who'd moved so seamlessly into the ritual chants and gestures, his magic effortlessly blending in with hers and that of their environment, that his arrival had felt no different to her from that of the birds in the trees, or the fish swimming below, or the small rodents busily harvesting tender shoots in the rushes. In her startlement, she bobbled the next phrase of the ritual, but he smoothly carried it through, his bass voice like the sustaining earth itself.

As she recovered, she focused on the dark-skinned, genial face of Wizard Asa, the Refoel healer who'd taken up permanent residence at House Phel. His wizard-black eyes sparkled with warm amusement at her surprise, and he continued the ritual with the ease of long practice. His healing wizardry suffused the magic of the dark arts with a green freshness that buoyed what she'd managed to draw, giving the defenses she wove a new and effervescent resilience. She found herself smiling and he grinned back, making her realize how rarely she'd seen him smile since he lost his familiar, Laryn. He was raising their baby, Cornelis, alone and seemed more or less content on the occasions she'd glimpsed him. But seeing this genuine smile reminded her of how fully happy he'd once seemed—and how that had changed.

They finished together, allowing the last note to hum in the soft spring air, the buoyant magic they'd raised together to settle again, filling the empty spaces in their magic reservoirs. As the magic and the moment of perfect communion quieted, then dissipated, Asa cocked his head. "I didn't think you were studying the dark arts at Convocation Academy."

"Professor Seraphiel took me on as a special case," Alise answered judiciously. Asa was firmly on the side of House Phel, but she didn't know how much Nic and Gabriel took him into their confidence.

"Ah, I see." Asa nodded knowingly, perhaps seeing too much, then squatted and opened a pack, extracting an apple and tossing it to her.

She caught it automatically, bemused, and suddenly hungry. "Thank you."

"I have several." He bit into one. "From last autumn's harvest, but all the sweeter for that. Water?"

Accepting the water bottle—one of House Phel's special brand of flasks that never ran out of clean, cool water—she drank, handed it back, then bit into the apple appreciatively, *hmming* in pleasure at the sweet flavor. "Is it standard in the training for healing wizards to study the dark arts?" she asked, probing as she normally wouldn't, but figuring he'd given her license.

"Not in the least," he answered with a chuckle, then tipped his head back to look at the overarching limbs, trailing moss and orchids, perhaps to the sky beyond. "But I was always drawn to the dark arts. I received permission from my house to take courses as electives, so long as I maintained my standing in the healing tracks." He glanced at her. "I studied quite a bit with Morghana Seraphiel and remember her fondly, if with a wince for those grueling sessions."

Alise laughed with him. "Oh yes."

"That's part of why I wanted to come to House Phel, you know," Asa said, stretching out his long legs, "when Lord and Lady Phel issued the invitation to fill out their staff. I knew Meresin would give me ample opportunity to be out in nature, to practice my hobby." His half-grin let her know the practice meant far more to him than that. It faded, and he shook his head. "I knew Laryn didn't want to come here. She loved Convocation Center and everything to do with society there. We bonded as wizard and familiar because of the Betrothal Trials, did you know?"

Alise nodded, though she wasn't entirely sure why he was telling her all of this. Asa sighed heavily. "It's a cursed system, those trials. I don't know why I went along with it except that I wanted to be able to choose my placement at a high house, largely so I could practice the dark arts untroubled. To have that freedom of choice, I needed a powerful familiar. I was an arrogant, self-involved fool in many ways, but the greatest one was this implicit belief that Laryn and I matched because it was meant to be. That we'd find our way into being harmonious partners and parents. Looking back, I can see now that I mostly didn't want to be bothered with courting a familiar. I liked the idea of the trials deciding for us, so I could then go on to focus on what *I* wanted from life."

"You wouldn't be alone among wizards, feeling that way," Alise suggested. How much of her own resistance to even the concept of bonding a familiar came from not wanting to deal with a similar courtship?

"No, but that's hardly flattering, given the attitudes of our cohort toward familiars," he replied wryly. "Laryn was, predictably, miserable here. She was miserable before that, frankly. We turned out to be compatible fertility-wise, but in no other way. From the beginning, we made each other unhappy."

"From what I recall of Laryn," Alise offered, "though I was younger, she ran in the same circles as Nic and visited House Elal a few times, she was never a happy person. At least, not after she manifested as a familiar."

"Many familiars are not and who can blame them? It's a raw deal, the life of a familiar in the Convocation." He gazed at her steadily. "I want you to know, Wizard Alise, that part of why I agreed to having you sever the bond between Laryn and me was in the hope that she might be able to move on and find happiness with another wizard, or in living unbonded. It wasn't all vengeance."

Alise gazed back at him, beyond surprised—and realizing that this confession had been the aim of this conversation all along. Perhaps of him joining her in the dark arts ritual to begin with, establishing trust and all. He regarded her steadily, seeming to acknowledge her thoughts.

"Even after all Laryn did?" She asked. "Betraying Nic so profoundly…"

"I'm not saying she didn't deserve consequences for her reprehensible actions, and Lord and Lady Phel were absolutely justified in meting out any justice they found appropriate."

"But with Laryn being pregnant with Cornelis?"

"Even so." Asa stared off into the distance. "I wouldn't have blamed them and I was resigned to losing them both—the familiar I'd tried to love and the unborn child I already loved without reservation. So you see…" His gaze returned to hers. "When you offered to sever the bond between us, I leapt at the opportunity. And, as a healing wizard, I could forecast the potential risks. I was up front with Laryn about those risks, and she agreed to it, too, remember."

"And died anyway," Alise pointed out bitterly. Along with Maman. Alise might as well paint her hands with their blood.

"That's my point, Wizard Alise," Asa said with quiet authority. "Laryn lived to deliver Cornelis, for which we were both grateful beyond measure. Laryn said as much to me before she passed, that at least she'd brought him into the world. I think she regretted, in the end, how she'd let bitterness and misery consume her."

Alise nodded, too choked up to speak.

"You gave us all three a great gift," Asa continued soberly. "Your ability to sever the wizard–familiar bond can change the face of the Convocation."

"And kill a lot of familiars in the process."

"It's a new technique. Do you have any idea how many new healing techniques employed through desperation end in killing the patient rather than saving them? You'll work it out. Don't reject this revolutionary ability because you're afraid of the damage it could do in its unpolished state."

She nodded, slowly, turning that thought over. "I'll think about it."

"Good. That's all I ask." Asa stood, slapping his hands on thighs muscular from his long hikes. "Ready to head back to the manse? The naming ceremony will begin soon."

"Yes." She stood, chucking her apple core into the water. "Thank you."

"No thanks necessary. I have Cornelis because of you. Which is good, as I'll never bond a familiar again," he added darkly, "even if I forgive myself for the role I played in Laryn's self-destruction, in my pride, arrogance, and self-involvement."

"Thy name is wizard," she offered ruefully and he grimaced in agreement.

Once off the narrow bog trail and on the wider path through the orchard, they strolled side by side. "You know," she told him, coming to a decision, "wizards can share magic with each other."

Asa slid her a curious glance. "Of course. They just rarely do."

"Competition, pride, self-involvement, arrogance," she listed on her fingers.

He laughed. "Thy name is wizard. Yes, I get you."

"I practiced magic sharing a fair amount with Wizard Cillian Harahel at Convocation Archives. I can't tell you too much about the particulars," she added hastily, to fend off the inevitable questions.

Asa laid a finger alongside his nose. "I can guess, but enough said. Did you find it worked as well as receiving magic from a familiar?"

"Well, I've obviously never had a bonded familiar, but... yes." The experience of giving and receiving magic had been transporting, intimate, even sexual. "It's something for you to consider, since you don't want another familiar, for which I don't blame you."

"Hmm. I've received magic from wizards from time to time, but it wasn't as… effortless as drawing from Laryn. Tell me, do you think it's necessary to be emotionally and physically involved with the other wizard?"

Alise tripped on a root, glancing quickly at Asa, who watched her with a canny sparkle in his black eyes. "Oh, ah, no. You see, Archivist Harahel and I… We did not have that kind of relationship." Her face grew hot at the lie. "It was a matter of exigency."

Asa nodded, dark lips curved in a knowing smile. "If that's the position you wish to claim, I won't gainsay you."

There was nothing to say to that, Alise decided, so she simply inclined her head in acknowledgement, keeping her mouth firmly shut, as she should have done in the first place.

THE NAMING CEREMONY wasn't as grand as some of those Alise had attended at House Elal. Pretty much everyone who lived at House Phel wanted to attend the naming of the first of the new generation of Phels, however, so they held the ceremony in the grand ballroom, lavishly decorated with spring flowers. The weather had turned chilly as evening came on, with a soaking, naturally formed drizzle falling, so the windows had been closed and fires lit in the grand fireplaces.

Gabriel's parents held young Bria, up on the dais, while Gabriel performed the ritual according to Nic's whispered prompts. "I name thee Gabriella Phel, treasured child of House Phel. I also name the magic of your rightful heritage. Water." He anointed the infant's forehead with water he'd purified.

"Moon." He laid moonlight in a shimmering band across her brow. "And the spirit world." Drawing on Nic's Elal magic, he summoned elementals to represent that part of her heritage, too. He nodded to Alise, who had changed into the one formal gown she'd brought. At least on this frenzied escape to House Phel she'd packed outfits suitable for a variety of occasions, if only because she'd thought she'd need them at House Harahel.

She stepped up to Gabriel's beaming parents, exchanged a smile with them, and set a gentle hand on Bria's forehead. "I bestow upon thee a guardian spirit to watch over and protect you." She'd summoned and tamed the spirit for Bria, tasking it to interfere as it was able, should the child stumble into danger, and also to alert Nic and Gabriel if anything unusual happened. Alise, Nic, and their brother, Nander, had all had such protectors when they were little. The efficacy of the guardians tended to fade over time, especially as the child grew more mobile and unpredictable, exhibiting more complex behaviors and motivations. Certainly Alise and her siblings— especially all being sensitive to spirit magic—had learned how to duck their protectors at a fairly young age.

Children possessing spirit magic quickly figure out who is tattling on them and spirits as a rule aren't that bright. No one could say yet whether Bria would end up with magical potential scores in spirit magic, or any magic at all, but the guardian would serve to look out for the child in her most vulnerable years. Knowing that, Gabriel and Nic gave her grateful smiles, and Alise felt the warm embrace of truly belonging to a family. Bria's unfocused gaze followed the spirit and she blew bubbles at it as it flew around her head and nestled by her cheek. The affinity boded well for Bria's potential in spirit magic.

Seliah and Jadren were next, presenting Bria with a clockwork doll made with El-Adrel magic that looked lifelike and was so stunningly lovely, with shiny, soft copper skin, that the child immediately reached for it with wide eyes and grabby hands.

Wizard Asa stepped forward, adding a gift of healing magic to keep Bria strong and vital through her early years. One by one, other wizards, familiars, and mundane family, stepped up with gifts tangible and magical, tears and laughter intertwining at the celebration of Bria's fresh new life and limitless possibilities.

It was an event of pure joy and celebration. Until it wasn't.

Alise sensed the breach in the spirit-patrolled boundaries around House Phel at the same moment the voice rang out.

"Did someone forget to invite me?" Piers Elal inquired.

~ 9 ~

Piers Elal, Lord of High House Elal, posed in the center of the room for effect. He'd dressed for the moment, too, wearing a deep violet velvet cloak over a fitted Ophiel suit of the same material, which took on black lowlights as it shifted, giving him a sinister cast. The effect was amplified further by the gold metal eye-patch he wore, affixed to his head with matching buckles that fastened to black leather straps.

He smiled at them, malevolent and triumphant, unmoved when Gabriel hurled a silver spear formed of moonlight at his head.

"No!" Nic shouted, lunging to stop Gabriel, even as the invisible shield of spirits surrounding their father deflected the spear, sending it spinning wildly away into the gathered guests, who scrambled out of its path. "You can't," Nic urged Gabriel, hanging onto his arm, even as he tried to put her behind him. "Jadren, help me!"

"Lord Phel," Jadren said in a carrying voice that caught Gabriel's attention. "Lady Phel is correct. You cannot take action against her father at the naming of his grandchild. It's against Convocation etiquette."

"Watch me," Gabriel snarled, his magic billowing in the

air, intensifying into water and silver.

His father, GF, tucked the baby securely into his wife's arms and put himself between them and Lord Elal, standing squarely beside Gabriel. "Agreed," he said in his deep voice, clasping together work-roughened hands. "This old farmer may not know Convocation pretty-quette, but I know a murderer when I see one."

Nic cast a pleading glance at Alise, reflecting her own inner conflict. This could go very badly. Would go very badly, regardless, but they could at least protect Bria. Alise faced Gabriel and GF, feeling not unlike a mouse confronting two angry bull elephants, the men towered over her so, but she was a wizard, and she possessed the grounded strength of a practitioner of the dark arts and those aspects outweighed physical stature.

Beyond glad that she'd filled herself with the magic of the dark arts—but feeling like a traitor at the same time—she locked gazes with Gabriel, the wizard who'd become more of a brother, more of a father to her than either of her biological ones.

"Gabriel," she said, speaking wizard to wizard, as aunt to father of this child they already loved beyond life itself. "This is about Bria. Convocation law supports primacy of blood. You cannot prevent a grandparent from having contact with a direct descendent or you will give them legal grounds to take custody of the child."

"The hell you say," Gabriel ground out. "That would happen over my dead body."

"It would," Alise insisted, "and then my father would still

be able to take custody of Bria. Think about it. This is what he's wanted all along." As she said the words, she realized the truth of them. Their father had somehow engineered the match between Nic and Gabriel, wanting to bring that water and moon magic in combination with spirit magic into House Elal. "Don't let him play you."

"Alise is right," Nic said in a quietly strangled voice. "We wondered why he was staying so quiet. This is the moment he has waited for, knowing that either way he'd win access to our child. Our only path toward maintaining control is to cleave to Convocation law and etiquette."

Gabriel never glanced at Nic, fiercely glaring at Alise instead, as if she had somehow instigated all of this. "Asa, Wolfgang, Quinn—what say you on the boundaries of the legal requirements here?"

Alise didn't relax enough to release a breath of relief. She held her stance, hoping to transmit through the firmness of her physical and magical posture just how serious this was. The two wizards and familiar that Gabriel called for briefly consulted. They'd all been champions of their debate teams and mock trial events at Convocation Academy.

Wolfgang, the Ratisbon wizard who, with his familiar Costa, produced furniture and other carpentry goods for the house, spoke for the group after a hurried, whispered discussion. "Lord Phel," he said with a bow, at the edge of Alise's peripheral vision, "we agree that Lord Elal must be allowed to approach his grandchild and to inspect the infant's health. He need not hold her to do so. The law is very clear on this, that the infant can remain in the physical control of one or both parents, but the grandparent must be allowed to touch the infant."

Gabriel set his jaw, a bright chiming echoing through the vast and silent hall as silver pinged in a soft rain onto the marble floor. At last he tore his gaze from Alise and turned to Nic. "What say you?" he asked.

Behind Alise, Lord Elal scoffed. "Some wizard and supposed lord of a house, asking his *familiar* for an opinion."

Everyone ignored him.

"We stick exactly to the requirements," Nic said, too softly for anyone beyond those right there to hear. "We get through this moment, then regroup."

Gabriel nodded, the silver rain halting abruptly even as his magic intensified around them. Behind Alise, her father's Elal magic similarly burgeoned, blazing like a furnace against her back. "Don't let him provoke you," Alise warned Gabriel. "He's seething for a fight. Don't give it to him."

Gabriel gave her a sharp dip of his chin in acknowledgment. "I'll hold Bria for this." His mother, Daisy, looked like she might refuse, her pressed lips wobbling, but she let Gabriel take the infant, gazing up at her powerful son in beseeching trust. He whispered something to his mother that Alise couldn't hear and Daisy turned to bury her face GF's chest. Bria, who'd been happily clutching the clockwork doll, gleefully tasting any part she could fit into her mouth, gave an unhappy warble, subsiding when Gabriel kissed her forehead.

"Nic, Alise, by me," Gabriel said, and stepped off the dais.

Gratified to be included in the triangle, though uncertain why he wanted her there, Alise flanked Gabriel a half-step behind, able to see her sister's coldly composed profile. Nic had always loved their father more than Alise had—probably because he'd loved her the most to begin with. Until Nic shocked and devastated everyone—including herself—by manifesting as a familiar instead of a wizard, she'd been the House Elal darling, their father's heir-apparent and golden child. In truth, Nic had enjoyed such privilege as their father's favorite that she'd been blind to his darker nature and more egregious behaviors. When she'd fallen from grace and later discovered just how awful their father could be, Nic had been blindsided.

Alise could see it in her sister now, that vulnerability to the wizard she once worshipped and who'd wounded her more deeply than could ever heal.

For her part, Alise had forever been a disappointment to her father and so felt at most cold hatred for him. It was so much like him to pull this stunt, so in keeping with his grandiose ambition and vainglorious decisions that they should have predicted this would happen.

They should have known.

As if hearing her thoughts—though she knew he couldn't read minds—Piers Elal fastened his mocking black eyes on hers. "Shouldn't you be in school, Daughter?" he asked silkily.

"I don't answer to you anymore," she replied in the same tone.

"Rumor has it that you think you answer to no one. I've heard of your troubles keeping enrolled at Convocation Academy." He tsked, shaking his head. "A pity. But then, you were never what anyone would call a star student, were you?"

"You're here to see the baby," Gabriel inserted, standing close enough to Lord Elal to tower over him, "not taunt Alise."

"I can do both," Piers replied with a smirk, but he reached out for Bria.

Gabriel held her close. "You may touch her. Not hold her."

"I'm her grandfather."

"Nevertheless."

Piers didn't like it, casting a reproving glance at Nic who looked on with that stoically remote expression she assumed when she was trying to hold herself together. "The doll is in the way," he complained.

Nic didn't move, didn't seem to be able to, so Alise eased the doll away from Bria, having to unwind the small chubby fingers from their surprisingly strong grip on the toy. Immediately, the infant began to wail in protest and sorrow. Nic instinctively reached for her baby and Gabriel turned his shoulder just slightly to block her. Nic made a small sound of despair, a quiet echo of her daughter's. Gabriel flinched at the sound, as did Alise, clutching the doll to her chest. Bria's wail grew in volume and intensity.

"Get on with it, Elal," Gabriel ordered, his magic tightly contained.

Piers, seeming not quite certain of his moves at the moment to Alise's eye, put tentative hands on the baby, touching the soft skin of her forehead, the perfect round of her cheeks. No doubt he sampled her magic, too, which remained much like Bria's young mind: brilliantly present but as yet unformed and without the clear resolution into particular directions that would later distinguish her as an individual.

"That's enough," Gabriel decided, lifting Bria away from the shorter man's reach.

"I've barely begun," Lord Elal protested with a thunderous frown.

"Advisors?" Gabriel called over his shoulder without taking his gaze off his much-loathed father-in-law, his magic like molten silver in the air, steaming with fury. Alise wondered if he regretted not killing the wizard when he could have, taking only the eye. It might be some small comfort that Piers Elal hadn't reached a Refoel healer in time to save or restore the eye. The metal eyepatch looked to be of enchanted El-Adrel devising and Alise suspected he could use it for some form of seeing, if not actual vision.

"No time requirement, Lord Phel," Wolfgang called back. "A good faith effort at allowing contact is sufficient."

"This is hardly 'good faith,'" Lord Elal complained.

"You can argue it in court," Nic bit out. "Now go. You're not wanted here."

Their father eyed Nic craftily and Alise's stomach tightened. She knew that look well. Lord Elal had a card up his sleeve, a way to win he'd yet to exploit. "Then I suppose it's time to bestow my gift on the child," he said in an oily pretense at sounding paternal.

"No," Gabriel said.

Lord Elal smirked. "Advisors?" he called, clearly mimicking Gabriel.

"Lord Phel," Wolfgang said, pointedly speaking to the lord he owed allegiance to, rather than answering Elal's question, "I should add that the grandparent is allowed to give the infant one gift of their choosing."

Alise shuddered internally. Seeing it, her father smirked in satisfaction. "I see my heir has already attached an amateurish attempt at a guardian spirit." He scrutinized her very sweet and simple spirit, which cringed away from his wizardly poking. Alise had to restrain herself from leaping in to defend it. Her father turned his gaze to her. "Not terrible work, but nothing that could withstand a wizard of any caliber in spirit magic." In the next moment, he annihilated the guardian spirit which vanished with a pained wail and a flicker of apology to Alise. Bria sent up new cries of distress.

It hurt her heart. She'd spent days selecting, binding, and teaching the spirit, crafting it to grow with Bria and learn with her. That the spirit felt so bad failing her was a testament to how well Alise had embedded its mission. Bria sought the vanished spirit, bereft of both it and her new doll. Nic had closed her eyes and fisted her hands by her sides, clearly unable to bear it either. Their father had taken this day of joy and celebration and shattered it for all of them. Worst of all, he knew and savored their pain, relishing this cold and delicately plotted vengeance.

"Since the child is in need of a guardian spirit now," he said, "let me provide one." He drew forth a meticulously crafted spirit of such malicious intent and inestimable power that Alise gasped in horror. Her involuntary cry caused Nic's eyes to fly open and she whimpered deep in her throat, well able to see exactly what their father had planned, even with her familiar's magic.

"Please," she whispered. "No."

Gabriel glanced back and forth between Nic and Alise, able to sense the powerful magic being held at bay like an avalanche stopped in time, but without the necessary expertise to know what it meant. It was a mark, of what a very different wizard Gabriel was that he followed Nic's lead with perfect trust and no questions.

"I will not allow this," he informed Elal, silver daggers manifesting in the air to surround the older wizard. He tucked the disconsolate Bria against his chest, muscular arms wrapped in a firm shield around her.

"Then I take custody of the child," Elal crowed with sparkling delight.

"That remains to be seen," Gabriel replied with such eerie menace that Alise didn't know how her father withstood it. "In the meanwhile, I can take your other eye, and then begin carving off pieces until there's nothing left of you. I defeated you before, Elal, and I will do it again." The daggers spun silently, several aimed at Lord Elal's remaining eye.

"I'm in the prime of health this time," Piers replied with easy confidence, "and in the fullness of magical reserves. And I have nothing and no one to protect while you have..." He made a show of looking around the ballroom. "Why, I suspect that every soul that matters at all to you is in this room right now. How many of them are you willing to sacrifice? Perhaps I should start with your sweet mother."

Daisy screamed and it was all Alise could do not to look. Gabriel visibly shuddered with holding himself in place.

"Stop this," Nic shouted, the order lashing out, garnering her father's immediate attention. Daisy stopped screaming, though Bria still wailed against her father's chest.

"Excuse me," Lord Elal said, giving Nic a blank, polite smile. "Do I know you?"

Nic's upper lip curled in contempt. "You just love to dis-own your children, don't you, *Papa*? It's the last bit of your crumbling control you try to exercise and it just kills you that it doesn't work. That you have to resort to this horrific charade."

"It's no game," he warned her in kind. "I will see this through. I *will* win."

"Is that all that matters to you?" she asked, almost wistful-ly.

"It's all that matters, period," he answered with conviction. "You'll learn that someday."

She shook her head. "No, I used to believe that—because you taught it to me, to us," she added, glancing at Alise. "But I've learned better. You could have been invited here, could have had contact with your grandchild, been part of her life, by simply being human. But that's beyond your ability isn't it? You have to control everything and everyone."

"I'm a wizard, not a human," he spat at her. "If you hadn't utterly failed to become the wizard you were meant to be, you'd understand that."

"I am a wizard," Alise inserted, surprising herself—and having to straighten her spine when her father's ire turned on her. "And I don't understand why you're such a monster. How could you summon a malevolent spirit to fasten onto your granddaughter like that? You would ruin her life before it even began."

"True," he replied thoughtfully. Too mildly. Something

very bad was coming, verified by her father's spreading smile. "Because you've raised such a salient point, Daughter, I'm willing to entertain a third option. I'll withhold my gift in exchange for a favor. My daughter—my *wizard* daughter—will return to House Elal with me, to be trained as my heir."

A stunned, fraught silence thickened the already dense air of the now stuffy ballroom, pierced only by Bria's increasingly frantic wails.

Then: "No," Gabriel and Nic said in unison.

Alise had known they would because they were just that good. And because they were, she knew her own answer had to be just as easy, firm, and nearly as fast.

"Yes," she said.

And her father smiled in such triumph that she knew this, too, had been part of his plan all along.

~ IO ~

DAYS FLOWED BY seamlessly while Cillian devoted his entire attention to untangling the folded archive. Though he still smarted at the personal sacrifice asked of him by his house and family, he was ultimately grateful to be the one to do this investigative work.

Though he'd never admit as much to his grandmother.

Not that she inquired or seemed to care. Appearing satisfied that he'd meekly knuckled under, that he was making no attempts to even bend the limits she'd set, that he was not even so much as mentioning Alise in passing, Lady Harahel went about her usual business. Which meant that most of the time, she assumed her persona of doting grandmother, clucking over her seedlings in the greenhouse and her grandchildren equally. The only difference, really, was that Cillian recognized the persona for what it was. It was particularly diabolical in that her cheerful grandmotherly ways were absolutely sincere and authentic. They simply masked the ruthlessness she generally disguised.

So, on the surface, House Harahel returned to the quiet, scholarly peace that he'd known all his life. Like his grandmother's layered persona, that gentle rhythm of days spent reading, writing, and contemplating was real. None of it was a lie. But it concealed other realities like a gilded mask. Cillian learned his lesson from it all, and showed only his own surface persona: dutiful, scholarly, content to be in the bosom of his house, entirely focused on the academic problem set before him.

Learning from his grandmother's example, he disguised the raging beast Alise had brought to life within him. Though he longed for her with such profound need that he felt as if part of him starved into nothingness, he never said her name or truly allowed himself to give her much thought. Only at night, when he lay in his childhood bed under the quilts his grandmother had made by hand, did he allow himself to embrace the aching loneliness her absence created.

He craved her sexually, of course, fantasizing that her hands and mouth pleasured him, evoking memories of their intimate times together so often that the moments grew thin and tattered, like pages rubbed too many times between eager fingers, blurring the type and fraying the paper to transparency, eventually ripping holes in the text. He began handling those precious memories like rare manuscripts, touching only the edges and saving the best parts for when he most needed them. He also found the House Harahel copy of *The Saga of Sylus and Lyndella*, reading that to soothe his aching heart, finding over time that he read it less and less for research and more for the sheer romantic escapism.

Thus he partitioned his nights and days, his private and public selves. By night, a bereft lover, beset by unrequited longing and heart-rending doubt. By day, he conducted himself with calm certainty, unraveling the web of enchantments binding the archives, picking apart the strands with meticulous tenacity. In both cases, he remained almost entirely alone. Lady Harahel determined that the twisty enchantments binding the folded space to be a potential danger to House Harahel, decreeing that Cillian would be the only one to work with it and only in a room shielded for that purpose. When Cillian had arrived unconscious, carrying the immense and invisible burden of the folded archive, the other wizards of House Harahel had been able to take it from him and place it in a shielded salon, but no one had been sure what it was, so they'd isolated and left it. Now, with the door warded and keyed only to himself and Lady Harahel, Cillian spent his days alone.

He supposed he was fortunate his grandmother hadn't made him live and work in a barn.

The process turned out to be even more laborious and time-consuming than he'd predicted. As difficult as locating the folded archives and extracting them from their hiding space had been, it was only the first step. Whoever had done the work of moving the extensive library of texts relating to the centuries of House Phel's existence, had been beyond thorough. As Cillian worked the problem over long days, absorbing himself completely, he began to realize that the original feat hadn't been accomplished in one fell swoop as he'd—in retrospect, quite foolishly—assumed.

Instead, in a progression so logical that he kicked himself for missing it before, it seemed that the tomes had been hidden one by one. He couldn't be certain yet, but he theorized that originally a single book or set of documents had been slipped into that enchanted fold of space, which had probably been a relatively simple and small pocket to begin with, one just big enough to disguise one or a few texts. It could be that the first step had been an attempt to disguise or remove specific words or passages from that original book. He wouldn't know until he found it.

Ultimately that meant getting to the core of a fantastically layered package. Likely, long, long ago, a second text had been added to the first, with the spell expanded, reworked, and repowered. Then, sometime later, a third, a fourth, a fifth, and so on. With each addition, the null space had been stretched and revitalized. It reminded Cillian of packing figures for one of his game sets, where he'd wrap one in a layer of cloth, then add another and wrap the cloth to include that, creating a layered bundle of the figures to set in a crate. He'd have to do that at some point—or have someone do it, if he never escaped Lady Harahel's edict—go remove his belongings from the faculty apartment at Convocation Academy he'd occupied since graduating.

The prospect gave him a pang. He'd loved that little apartment, that admittedly little life. It hadn't been glamorous, but it had been all his. And Alise had—

Don't think about her.

Firmly setting those thoughts aside, he focused on the problem of unwrapping the archive. That's where his analogy failed, because it wasn't simply a matter of loosening the outer layer, liberating the books within that, then going to the next layer, as he would unpack his game figures. No, instead the enchantments had been woven together, the threads of magic deliberately tangled so they knotted in and out of intersections. Rather than a neatly packed set, Cillian began to envision the archive as an enormous spider's nest, the hundreds of thousands of strands of silk cocooning the entire bundle, swathing it in threads he was forced to pick apart one by one.

It didn't help that the entire thing remained in the null space where it didn't quite physically exist. All of the work of picking apart and untangling, of extracting the enchantments by following a single thread to the nearest knot and extracting it from that tangle was mental.

The salon remained cozy enough—the archive obviously occupied no physical space, so they hadn't needed a large room—with windows and a fireplace, a comfortable chair and desk. It had also been lined, floor, ceilings, walls, and windows, with a containment spell that was a variation on the silencing spell most wizards could employ to have private conversations. This one operated to contain all that metaphysically folded magic within the four walls, just in case. It had the happy side-effect of muffling all sound as well, and preventing anyone from entering without Cillian's assistance, which allowed him to sink deep into the patient concentration required to unwind the mess one strand at a time.

At first he'd been tempted to cut the threads, but that initial impulse ended badly. The enchantment resisted that kind of violent treatment, actually flexing like something alive and responding to pain. It lashed out, sending a white noise wash of magic in all directions—and knocking Cillian ass over tea kettle. Apparently Lady Harahel had been prescient in storing the archive in the shielded room. Though it might have been nice for her to warn him. When he mentioned as much over dinner, she simply smiled, close-lipped and knowing.

After diligent and meticulous work over time—he frankly lost track in the timeless round of muffled days and lonely nights, the sameness of the work and the endless snowfall outside—he finally extracted a single book. It came free from the cloying enchantments, the sticky web of the whole resisting the loss of that single piece. But it gave, relinquishing the tome with a palpable *pop!* The book hovered improbably midair, spinning and shivering as the last shreds of resistance frayed, then completely released. It fell to the thick carpet with a gratifying thud.

Overwhelmed with excitement at a tangible result of the grueling effort that had yielded nothing until now, Cillian grabbed his notebook and leapt from his chair, though not without gently withdrawing his mind and magic from the folded archive, more practiced now at getting in and out without triggering a metaphysical explosion.

He approached the book carefully, as if it might be hot from a fire or liable to trigger another wave of blistering wizardry to singe his senses.

But nothing happened. Outside the globe of his magically isolated workspace, snow fell silently, in thick lacy flakes. Inside, the fire crackled, the smoke from the real wood tinging the air. Out of an abundance of caution, he knelt, examining the tome visually only, not touching it. When nothing seemed out of sorts, he probed it with his librarian-wizard senses, using his indexing skills to assess the publisher and age. It had come out of House Calliope, but centuries before. It lacked the indexing information that modern archivists applied to collections to make retrieval easier. A good Harahel wizard could find a relevant text from the content alone, no matter how poor the client's description of what they were looking for, but having the spellwork embedded in the physical book to identify it made it locatable by lesser wizards and even mundane librarians with access to the right tools.

All of the older books in Convocation Archives had been retroactively tagged with this indexing, which was applied as a matter of course to new additions to the collection as part of the standard processing. That had been one of Cillian's responsibilities on the quieter night shift, and he'd always enjoyed the orderliness of classifying the new books and formally adding them to the archives. So he knew full well that much older books than this had been indexed. The only reason this one hadn't been was because it had been secreted in that folded space. Not that this told him anything he didn't already know, but it added another data point and they might need all the data they could produce. Thus, he carefully noted the missing indexing.

Gingerly, he touched the embossed cover with light, questing fingertips. His wizard senses identified that it was bound like any other book from the era. Nothing else seemed unusual about it. Finally, he picked it up, noting down the title on the spine—*Flora and Fauna of the Meresin Wetlands*—then opened it and began copying down the publication information. Nothing about the book popped as unusual. It obviously was related to House Phel, if only tangentially, as the Phel lands were located within the larger area known as Meresin.

Not every high house named the lands they owned after the family. Elal did. Refoel did, as did Hanneil, Sammael, and El-Adrel. But others like Harahel, Uriel, and Ratsiel did not. In those latter cases, the high houses focused on intellectual property rights rather than land acquisition or in governing populations. For House Refoel, the land itself was relatively small, and they had set their closely guarded boundaries long ago to protect their neutral sovereignty and the vulnerable who took refuge there. In Contrast, Elal occupied a vast territory and seemed to be eternally looking to acquire more. People liked to joke that House Harahel had never expanded their ancestral lands because everyone there had their nose in a book and that wasn't far wrong.

Naturally, the second, third and lower tier houses didn't have eponymous lands—unless they'd once been a high house that had degraded to a lower tier, and even then their territories generally shrank, often by so much that their "land" comprised only a small area around the living quarters, sometimes no grander than a mundane farm.

Regarding House Phel and Meresin, however—especially given that Phel had been one of the original high houses—it was passing odd that the land was called Meresin and not Phel. With their traditional combination of magic specializations in water and moon magic, Phel didn't seem to have an emphasis in the non-physical realms, like Harahel with knowledge and Uriel with administration, that would distract them from land ownership. Indeed, from what Cillian had observed, the denizens of Meresin regarded themselves as beholden to

House Phel, even generations after the house itself and family ceased to be.

At any rate, a perusal of the table of contents didn't reveal anything that waved a flag saying "this is dangerous information regarding the fall of House Phel and should be hidden away so no one can see it!" Neither did a more thorough assay with his library magic. It hurt his librarian's heart to consider the likely truth: that this book might've been hidden away categorically and entirely because of its association with Meresin and House Phel, and not because it contained any specifically damming evidence. The author who'd labored over the research and writing, the editors and publishers who'd made sure it would be this beautiful volume, all of their effort had vanished into the nothingness of that folded space. Instead of taking its rightful place in the archives, the book had fallen into a nearly eternal obscurity. And for what?

Well, that was the question.

Or, one of them. The next question was whether a copy of the same text existed in the House Harahel archives, as there should be, since they were intended to be identical.

After that came the monumental task of reading the books for clues. This was but the first book of possibly thousands. Cillian hadn't been able to tell how many nestled inside the vast cocoon of sticky-threaded enchantment.

He set the book aside for someone else to pursue the verification in the Harahel archives and went back to his chair, clearing his mind to extract the next book, hoping the process would begin to go faster. When he'd first envisioned this project, he'd imagined Alise beside him, with her serious mien and deepwater calm presence. They'd have shown each other fascinating tidbits and shared kisses and hot chocolate.

But Alise was gone, and no doubt happier for being away from him. Allowing himself one more nostalgic moment to miss her, he then bent mind and magic to his never-ending task.

~ II ~

ALISE AND HER father rode in his carriage to House Elal. It was even more elaborate than the Elal carriage that had been stored at Convocation Academy that she'd taken without permission. Her father only commented on that theft by saying he'd arrange to have it returned to Convocation Center, in case Nander had need of it.

Lord Elal's personal carriage was grand and large enough that they each could pretend the other didn't exist for some time. He'd traveled to House Phel under an invisibility veil made by his cadre of spirits. That, and his superior ability—not only to Alise, but preeminent over all wizards wielding spirit magic—had allowed him to slip through the guardians she'd set to alert House Phel to intruders. She'd been a fool, not predicting her father's next move in their cold war.

Nic and Gabriel had objected to her departure, of course, as had all the minions at House Phel, quietly or loudly offering to fight for her. All it had taken, however, had been the smug, triumphant look on her father's face for her to refuse them all. He'd expertly arranged it so that either Bria or Alise would return to House Elal with him, to be molded into a dutiful heir. At least Alise had some chance of withstanding the molding; she'd never subject an infant to the man, let alone her beloved niece.

For quite some time, Alise refused to speak to the man who called himself her father. That bit of spite satisfied her until she realized her silence suited him just fine. He sat in his section of the carriage, tended to by various servile spirits, steadily working through correspondence brought and taken away by an unending stream of Ratsiel couriers. He was probably delighted that she'd elected to keep her mouth shut. Well, enough of that.

"Why not Nander?" she asked abruptly.

"Uh?" he grunted, not looking up from the missive he was penning. He put a hand out as if expecting a Ratsiel courier to land on it, clearly thinking the unusual sound of her voice had been an alert from an incoming message.

"I *said*," she didn't bother to hide her anger, her hate, "why do you want me for your heir? Nander is eager to lick your balls or ass to have the dubious honor. In fact, when last we spoke, if you can call it that, he'd seemed convinced he had the job." Her younger brother had, in fact, preened and taunted her over his elevation and her disgrace, an effort that would have landed far more solidly if she'd given a flying fuck.

Her father lifted his gaze and attention from the letter he'd been writing, studying her with the one depthless, wizard-black eye. The gold metal patch on the other eye seemed to also stare at her, unwinking, baleful, and swirling with a condensed knot of spirits that no doubt enabled him to see, possibly beyond what physical human eyes could.

"It speaks," he observed sourly.

She glared back, unamused.

"I'd come to the conclusion that my sole remaining daughter, chief among my ungrateful progeny, condescended to speak only to the lowly, the renegades, familiars, useless 'high' house minions, and mousy librarian wizards without true magic."

Oh, so that's how the wind blew. Despite her concerted efforts—and an intensive magic-working that had all but drained her to her very soul—he'd apparently managed to keep spirit-spies on her. "Are your feelings hurt?" she cooed in a falsely sweet voice.

"My feelings?" He barked out an incredulous laugh and set aside his lap desk. "I can see I went very wrong with you, Alise, allowing you to grow up with such sentimental ideas. You don't have Nic's hard-headedness. I never had to teach her to ignore the puny mewlings of the flesh that are our so-called emotions. She understood that much from birth—and managed to turn it against me, all out of bitterness because she failed to become a wizard."

"Failed? She couldn't control that she manifested as a familiar."

"Couldn't she?" He scratched his temple under the gold-buckled, black leather strap that held on the eye patch. Alise had seen him do it before, thinking that it probably didn't itch so much as he'd developed the habit to stop himself from messing with the patch. The missing eye had to pain or at least gall him. She hoped it hurt like a burning coal in his brain.

"That's debatable," he declared. "What are the origins of failure? Some say they derive from a weakness of will."

"Ah." She nodded sagely. "So, your failure to acquire the House Phel arcanium and take that magic for yourself, not to mention nearly perishing at Gabriel's hands and being sent home, spanked and maimed—that came from a weakness of will?"

His pressed lips twitched, one eye glittering like volcanic glass while the other swirled almost idly. The effect disconcerted her, but she didn't let it show.

"This is where your inexperience shows itself so embarrassingly, Daughter. I didn't fail. They cheated and my allies failed, yes. I, however, triumphed—as you witnessed at House Phel. All that matters is the long game. I won this battle and I will win the war. And you, Alise, are a weapon in that war, one to be molded and tempered into the service of our family's cause."

Alise suppressed a chill of foreboding. Talk. It was only talk. He couldn't make her do anything she didn't want to do. "And what, exactly, is our family's 'cause'?" She loaded the question with scorn. "Accumulating wealth? Crushing dreams? Oppressing the masses? Ruling the known world?"

"Ruling *all* the world, not just the known world," he corrected, black eye glittering with unsettling avariciousness. "Once the world becomes known, it too will become ours. As for wealth, that's a pathway to power. Crushing dreams and oppressing the masses is just a fun side-benefit."

He seemed to be utterly serious, not in the least sardonic in adding that last. With new worry worming deep in her heart, she thought he might actually believe that.

Piers Elal shook his head slightly at her, mouth curving in

sordid amusement. "You will learn, Daughter, to find joy in life where you can."

"In the suffering of others?" she spat.

"Why not?" he countered. "It's pure propaganda that's shoveled down our throats that we should be sorry if others suffer. Why not savor the sweetness that *we* prosper instead? Their debasement exists as a contrast to our exaltation, else our supremacy wouldn't be as sweet. That's all that matters in life. Nature teaches us that. It is devour or be devoured. Why not enjoy being the apex predator? Do you think the crippled prey, the weak, the starving, those who exist only to feed you, that they wouldn't change places with you in a moment? Be sure they would, my daughter. When you have your teeth buried in their throat, they will fear and loathe you—but they will also admire and wish with every fiber of their being to be *you.*

"There is no shame in giving yourself the same regard. You were born to rule the world. Bred for it. Gifted with the power and the ability. You possess even greater talents than I realized. If you squander those abilities, that's where the shame lies. What would we say of the tiger who refuses to kill, who only wastes away nibbling grass until it dies, mangy and skeletal? Would we admire and glorify that pitiful creature or do we celebrate his brother, strong and sleek, muscled, radiantly gold and terrifying as it prowls through the territory it owns utterly?"

Alise found her convictions blurring. He made a compelling case, though she knew the principles he espoused must be wrong. Still, the image he painted of the starved tiger denying itself food compared to the glorious, well-fed one… She didn't want to be the pitiable, starving tiger. Her father saw it in her, too, that shared pride, the desire to be the best. All this time she'd worried about becoming like him—had the struggle been in vain, for no reason?

"We are not animals," she said, knowing that to be true and important.

"Correct. We are *better* than animals," he shot back. "As wizards, we are also better than humans. Everything that applies to those lower tiers of beings, applies to us, but magnified. We have a manifest destiny to better ourselves, to rise ever higher."

"My point is that the tiger knows not what it does. There is no morality, no question of compassion. It knows it must eat to live and its instincts drive it to kill. There is no deciding not to. The tiger lives in the moment. It cannot predict the future or plan for it. It has no abstract thought."

"Exactly," her father said with approval, even a kind of pride that could become intoxicating. "*Now* you are thinking and you understand my point. Humans improve over animals in just that aspect. Because of our ability to predict a future that has not yet occurred, to plan in the abstract, to concoct a strategy and see it through, humans have risen to dominion over animals. Despite our lack of claws and fangs to rend and tear, we puny creatures have triumphed because of one thing." He tapped his temple, stirring the spirits in his glass-domed patch to swirl like snow in a decorative globe. "Our minds. By employing magic and wizardry in addition to that intelligence, we possess more formidable weapons than mere claws and fangs.

"Alise, you and I, like most wizards stand at the apex of all the world. With magic, we are gifted with metaphysical fangs and claws. They allow us to win every fight, to put down the weaker prey, and feed on them. With the ability of our human minds to plan, to strategize, even centuries ahead, we ensure our place as the most powerful beings in all the world. More important, among wizards, you and I are at the very top of even that rarified group. *This* is your legacy. This is what I want for you."

"What if I don't want it?" She lifted her chin, but her resolve wavered in the face of what seemed like irrefutable logic—and so her voice trembled too.

"You don't fool me, Daughter," he replied, not without a strange form of compassion. "You *do* want it. You'd be an idiot not to recognize that in yourself and you're no idiot. You only question yourself because you've been too long among the prey, the losers, the ones pretending they enjoy their lives as is to console themselves over the brutal truth, that they lost before they even began. I left you too long in the contamination of small minds and little lives. I seek to correct that now, to both elevate you and help you to cherish what makes you so very special."

He was making too much sense and Alise looked out the carriage window as spring once again yielded to winter, growing whiter and harder as they crossed into the high altitudes of the Knifeblade Mountains, traveling at the speeds of luxury. The landscape became sterile without the gentle blossoms and fuzzy new leaves. Was it still snowing in

Harahel? Probably. And Cillian would be cozied up inside, buried in books, as he was happiest. And she was in the cold and bitter world, once more alone, as seemed to be her destiny. Special? Maybe. But she'd never asked for that.

"Nander craves all that," she said quietly. "Give it to him, because I don't want it."

Her father laughed and picked up his lap desk again. "Yes, you do. I can see it in you. And that's why it's always been you and never my wastrel son. He lacks your pride, your drive, your determination, your acute intelligence, and your sheer ability. I know it was you who took the bonds of the spirit spies attached to you. All of them, at once." He laughed with every appearance of utter delight. "When I felt you do that, I felt such a burst of pride, Alise. Only my true daughter could accomplish such a feat—and at such a young age! With time and training, you could eclipse even me. You could well be the one Elal has waited and bred for all these centuries, the one to put House Elal forever at the pinnacle, after which all the world will be known simply as Elal."

She returned her gaze to him, curiously. "Me? I thought you wanted this for yourself."

"Of course I do," he acknowledged, "but I labor for a greater goal. There is a selflessness required in laboring for the good of the family, of our house and name. None of this is truly about me. I am carrying forward a strategy formulated long ago, as passed to me by my father, and as I will pass along to you. That should help to clear your conscience, should you retain doubts. This is not about you raising up your own interests; this is about you ushering in a new world order."

"With Elal at the top."

"Of course." He smiled and unfolded the letter he'd been writing. "Would you choose to elevate another high house? Sammael? Hanneil?" He snorted. "No house is more worthyor better equipped to rule than Elal. Believe me, *someone* will win this war. It is a choice between being the oppressed or the oppressor. Which would you rather be?"

When she didn't answer, he chuckled drily and surveyed his missive so far. "Think on it. You'll have plenty of time, now that you've agreed to study with me."

"What about my degree—I still need to graduate from Convocation Academy."

He looked up again, his one eyebrow climbing into an incredulous arch. The other must have been destroyed along with the eye because that quadrant of his face didn't move, other than the lazy swirling of the spirits in the glass dome. "Now you pretend to care about your education? After repeatedly ditching school on various errands where you pretended to save people."

"I did save people," she retorted, stung into indignation.

"Temporarily, which means nothing. If you can't make something last, you've failed. All that matters is the long game," he repeated. "Those little lovebird familiars you think you spared their fate at House Sammael? They will inevitably be bonded to wizards, as is their rightful destiny. The librarian wizard will retire into his well-deserved obscurity along with the rest of his sorry excuse for a house. House Phel will be House Fell again, this time forever. They have served their purpose."

Alise knew better than to ask what purpose that was, letting the silence fall as her father wound down and returned his attention to his letter. He'd changed, she realized, replaying the conversation, more than he knew. The missing eye was the outward manifestation, but something in his mind had destabilized. In the past, he'd never have been so garrulous nor divulged so much. He'd dropped many clues, however. A centuries-old strategy that had to do with the disastrous dissolution of House Phel. And why did he seem to think Nic could have overcome being a familiar? As far as anyone knew, including centuries of research on familiars, willing and unwilling, familiars simply could not become wizards. A neurophysiological connection failed to form, rendering them unable to wield magic, only to generate it.

"Speaking of familiars doing their duty," he mused without looking up, adding something to the letter, "I have need of a new one. I'm considering engaging in the Betrothal Trials—or possibly offering a pre-empt. I understand Brinda Chur will be up for the taking soon. Adding fire and sun magic to our arsenal would be brilliant, indeed."

That shocked Alise out of her musings. "Brinda Chur?" she echoed. Brinda had approached Alise at Convocation Academy, offering generous portions of her bright and brilliant magic in exchange for information on how to manipulate the Betrothal Trials. Surely she hadn't been thinking to snag Lord Elal? Although she had expressed high ambitions. The prospect turned her stomach. "She's my age."

"A year older, I believe," he replied absently. "Though you are in the same class, aren't you? By all accounts, she's rich in magic. And an alliance with House Chur could be very well timed, indeed. Besides, I need a young familiar. Your mother had grown old, her magic withered. I had to wait days between major workings, it took her so long to recharge. Yes, a fresh young familiar for the arcanium and a nubile young body for my bed will be just what the Refoel healer ordered. I'll be like a young man again." He looked up suddenly, grinning at what was probably an aghast expression on her face. "And she can breed me more heirs, as a backup to you, in case you falter. Though I'll also have the Phel infant."

"You agreed to leave Bria alone if I came with you," she fired at him, heart thumping.

"Peace, Daughter. I will abide by my word. I'm aware your… compliance rests on me leaving the child alone. But, when House Phel once again sinks into the swamps from which it came, your pretty niece will need a place to go. Would you leave her an orphan, alone in the world to fend for herself, or adopt her into her rightful house?"

"Her rightful house is Phel."

"No. Phel is only the seed. Elal is the source and the soil. Why do you think I allowed your sister to quicken with a rogue wizard like Gabriel Phel? Elal needs that child. And perhaps Seliah Phel's to round it out. We could stand to recharge our portion of El-Adrel magic."

"Seliah isn't pregnant." And Jadren would never allow her to be in jeopardy, or for anyone to take their child if she were.

He shrugged, pen moving across the fine stationery. "If she isn't yet—and I'm not sure you're correct, given the information I'm privy to—then she soon will be. But there's time to let that one ripen, as it were."

Alise dearly wished to be able to tell Cillian all of this. The pieces of the puzzle, as he would put it, seemed to be all laid on the table, only awaiting the right mind to assemble them into the big picture. Perhaps she could figure out how Nic had used the confidential Ratsiel courier to send him a message. Or bind a spirit to take a missive to Cillian. They were still friends, more or less, weren't they? And even if he never forgave her for leaving him without a word, he wouldn't be able to resist a riddle. Yes, she'd get a message to him and another to Nic and Gabriel. Also to Jadren and Seliah, warning them all.

"If I'm to be your heir, Papa," she said, returning to her childhood name for him, "I should complete my degree." Being back at school would give her the freedom she needed. "It shouldn't take long at this point. A few more months at Convocation Academy and—"

"Out of the question," he interrupted without raising his voice, a wreath of spirits encircling her throat and squeezing with light, but inexorable pressure. "Do you think I would share all of this with you and allow you the option of communicating with any of *them*?" He sneered the word. "No, until I'm convinced that you are firmly on the side of House Elal, I will complete your education in isolation. I think the tower where Nic spent her Betrothal Trials will work admirably. You will live there until I am certain of you."

Aware suddenly of the reality of her imprisonment, Alise looked out the carriage window at the valley below, House Elal proudly situated in the middle, in the curve of the river. Several towers spiraled up from the ancient, rambling structure, the tallest holding at the top the circular room Nic had occupied for months without leaving, sequestered so that the identity of the father of her child could not be in doubt.

"You might consider using the time to good effect," her father added. "Conduct your own fertility trials."

"Fertility trials?" she echoed, too aghast to do otherwise.

"You, too, will need a familiar."

"I don't want a familiar," she replied without thinking, still consumed with the horrifying prospects of being sequestered in that tower room, entertaining male familiars in an attempt to become pregnant, and having Brinda as part of House Elal. Her father had forced breeding on his brain and it was ugly.

"Nonsense," he snapped. "Any wizard of worth has a familiar. That's the entire reason for their existence, to bolster the careers of wizards. You know what they say: behind every great wizard is a great familiar. You must simply set aside those foolishly romantic notions of that bookish boy you dallied with—I'm sure he was fine to learn on, but that's in your past now—and realize that in a male familiar you can have everything you need. Magic, companionship, support, sex, children."

Her face had grown hot, though from embarrassment or anger, she didn't know. Her father didn't notice, or if he did, didn't care, not even looking up from his letter.

"The more I think about this," he continued, "I'm certain it's the ideal situation. We can kill several birds with one stone. I'll arrange for a parade of suitable candidates to visit you, for you to choose from. It's good for a woman to have her babies young, while her body is fresh, leaving her later years to build magical skills."

Lady Harahel had said almost the exact same thing, though she didn't have a familiar. Cillian had said that most Harahel wizards didn't. Familiars provided reservoirs of magic for workings that required massive power, or in case of emergencies. And there was no such thing as a library emergency.

Except for when they'd needed to extract the Phel archives from that folded space, and then she had given Cillian the power to do it. That had felt like such a triumphant moment, when they'd finally succeeded, defying the odds. *That* had felt like the ideal path, not this. Somehow she'd been navigating a labyrinth of conflicting choices, dodging monsters and worse, gradually finding her way out—and then had hit a dead end. Neatly cornered by her father and fate, finding herself back exactly where she'd started. Where Nic had started.

Depression settling over her like a dense fog, Alise stared out the window at her tower home for the foreseeable future and wrapped herself in silence again.

~ 12 ~

CILLIAN NEEDED A familiar. Possibly several. His eyes gritty, his magic reservoir drained to the dregs, books piled around him, he had to confront the fact that this was not a one-person job.

Rather than growing easier, extracting each book from the sticky web of enchantment embedding them grew more difficult the "deeper" he went. Though he knew it was a fallacy to think of the folded space in terms of physical dimensions like depth, he couldn't help envisioning the layers of books as being like nuts or raisins studded throughout a giant, insubstantial cinnamon roll he was gradually unwinding. The image amused him as much as the grueling process did not.

As he worked, he'd become more and more convinced that the key texts, the critically important ones with the information that had caused them all to be hidden, lay at the gooey center. There didn't seem to be a discernible pattern in the books he pulled out like wrenching teeth from the hardened jaw of a fossilized mastodon. They came from different eras regarding different topics by different authors, randomly shuffled together. The only consistent theme was, of course, that they all had to do with Meresin and House Phel in some way. Whoever—the multiple whoevers over the centuries—had stowed in them in the archive had done so by rote, he imagined. Someone had started it all with the key incriminating texts, then others had followed behind, probably obeying instructions by rote, wedging books in with no regard for order.

Although it could be the nature of that folded space that made establishing and maintaining order impossible. Still, whether as a result of his library magic operating subconsciously or flights of fancy taking over, Cillian began to form an idea of how the folded archive had been first created and then added to over the years.

The initial enchantment had clearly required a librarian wizard of immense skill and power, but after that, various minions probably had been assigned the task over decades and centuries. There had been at least a hundred of them, judging by the magical remanence they'd left behind on the books they'd hidden. For a time, Cillian had considered indexing those actors, along with the other data he was collecting, but it seemed like a wild-goose chase. These were not major players, but lackeys lobbing books willy-nilly into the folded space, ensuring that they stuck, but otherwise leaving them to randomly settle.

He couldn't decide which sort he loathed more: the initial traitor to the sanctity of the Convocation Archives who set up the elaborate spell to hide these books from existence or the shitty flunkies who'd blithely and unquestioningly followed along all those years. It was especially galling to know that so many had been willing to simply comply. It deeply offended him that *any* librarian wizard would violate the historical record this way; that there had been so many heaped insult upon injury.

The one he most wanted to identify was that long-dead initial culprit, the deeply unethical wizard who'd colluded with the enemies of House Phel centuries ago. They were well past punishment, but Cillian wanted their identity anyway. The world should know what had been done and by whom. And why.

Just as soon as he figured it out.

Which wasn't going to happen with him sitting there on the salon floor, surrounded by towers of books like a kid building a fort, his eyes so gritty he couldn't blink without pain and his magic so threadbare he couldn't even feel the folded space, much less consider extracting one more book. He hadn't begun the task of comparing the extracted books with their counterparts in the Harahel house archives.

That phase was complicated by the quarantine on the texts from the folded archive. He couldn't take those books out of the shielded room and he could hardly bring the entire Harahel archive to them. Probably what he needed to do was index everything regarding Meresin or House Phel in the Harahel archives, make a comprehensive list, then compare it to the list he had yet to make of the books piled around him. Eventually.

"Cillian." The sound of his name came as if from a great distance, and with the tenor of having been repeated more loudly. It occurred to him to look up, gaze traveling over the neatly aligned titles of the tomes in the nearest tower. His grandmother stood there, lips quirked in amused irritation,

peering at him over that teetering pile. "What in the dark arts do you think you're doing?" she demanded.

He blinked—ouch—and considered how to answer that. "Working on extracting books from the folded archive. You told me to."

She snorted inelegantly. "I gave you the assignment, yes. I never said to kill yourself doing it. When did you last eat? You haven't been to a family meal in over a week."

No, he hadn't wanted to take the time, or face the questions, or be made to engage in conversation of any kind. He'd been grabbing snacks from the kitchen or trading on his meager sway as a scion of the house to have plates sent up to his room. Unfortunately, especially in the evenings, those plates of food went cold and congealed when he passed out before remembering to eat.

"You're too skinny and your magic is whisper-thin," she observed. "And you look like a demon scraped you off the pavement then put you through a washing wringer."

"I love you, too, Grandmother," he replied wryly, realizing as he said it that he did love her. Still. Despite everything. He sighed. "I just want to get to the bottom of this riddle."

"You never could resist a puzzle," she noted fondly. "You were just like this as a boy, glued to whatever riddle-game you'd found, refusing to eat or sleep until you solved it—or we forcibly pried you away." She paused meaningfully. "Do I have to forcibly pry you away?"

"No," he said, capitulating to the fatigue so intense it nearly hurt. "I'll go sleep." It looked to be nighttime anyway, the windows black, not even a reflected glow from the wintry landscape outside.

"And you'll eat first."

"Yes, Grandmother."

"Don't 'yes, Grandmother' me, boyo. I'm wise to your tricks." But she offered him a hand up, steadying him when he swayed. "You'll sit at the table and eat while I watch," she decided.

"I had no idea that fell under the aegis of Lady Harahel," Cillian mused. "Should I add it to my list of techniques to learn? 'Badger junior wizards into eating and sleeping. Personally observe when necessary.'"

"Very funny," his grandmother replied, sounding not at all amused now as she steered him out of the salon—barely preventing him from colliding with the door frame as he stumbled—and locking it behind them. "In general, junior wizards are *not* difficult to pry away from work. Keeping them from indulging in side-projects, pleasure reading, and eating their weight in cinnamon rolls and hot chocolate is the primary challenge."

"This project is important," he said fuzzily, knowing that much to be true. Even in his current state, the need to get to the core of the archive, to solve the riddle, burned like an unquenchable flame. "Alise needs these answers."

His grandmother came to such an abrupt halt, he rocked on his heels and nearly staggered. "I knew it," she swore, making the words sound like a curse. "You're doing it for that *girl*. Even after she abandoned you, just like Szarina. What will it take for you to wake up and realize these wizards are using and discarding you?"

He considered a dozen responses, but his head ached. "I'm too tired for this conversation," he admitted.

She blew out a harsh breath and recommenced steering him down the hallway. "You'll eat first."

The manse, always quiet, had the midnight stillness of everyone else being asleep. "What time is it?"

"Well past time for me to take this situation in hand. I'm shutting down this project, for your own good."

Oh, he wasn't so far gone into his own version of folded space as to agree to that. "All right, then I'll plan to depart in the morning." In the family dining room, a lone place setting had already been laid out for him, several steaming platters nearby under old-fashioned silver domes to keep them hot. "We should have asked Alise for a couple of fire elementals to warm food," he noted, just to needle his grandmother. Now that he'd slipped by mentioning her name, he might as well go all in.

"All I need is more Elal spirit spies," she snapped in a retort. "Besides, your erstwhile wizard girlfriend was in too much of a hurry to leave to give us anything."

"So you've said." Though he wondered about that story. He knew Alise, better than she knew herself, in some ways, and she was loyal to the bone. She might have other flaws, but she genuinely cared about people. Sometimes despite herself. More than that, she cared about *him*. Szarina had manipulated his feelings for her, he could see that now. Alise simply didn't have it in her to do that, not to anyone, but especially not to him.

As he ate, his mind sharpened and cleared. Amazing what a

little food would do. His grandmother sat, watching him as promised, sipping her tea.

"I need help," he told her, making it sound like an admission. "I'll stay, but I want to finish this project. Also, I need a familiar's magic, and some clerical assistance wouldn't go amiss, either."

She drummed her blunt fingers on the table. "Because of *her*."

"Because of me," he corrected coolly. "You said it yourself: I've never been able to let go of a riddle until it's solved. I found this hidden archive, I extracted it, and I want to follow the mystery it represents until the end."

"I still don't want any of my people exposed to this potentially deadly information," she replied. "This is House Phel's problem, not ours."

"Is the integrity of the historical record not our problem?" he countered.

She sat back. "We already had this argument."

"The clerical help wouldn't have to know the implications of the work," he told her, having given this subject extensive thought in his clearer headed moments. "I've established an indexing system where I record pertinent information as I extract each book, assigning them a number according to my own system. I could continue to establish that number and record the information that only I can detect and understand. Information like when I extracted it and other factors about the folds of the archive that may prove useful. But if I could then pass off that information for further evaluation, any Harahel wizard could evaluate what's in our archives and add data using that index number."

His grandmother continued to watch him thoughtfully. She hadn't said no yet.

"I don't think we need to take the step of performing a textual analysis against the Harahel archives," he continued. "Not yet, anyway. For now I want to know *if* we have copies of the texts. Maybe later comparing the contents will become important, but my impression so far is that these books weren't altered—they were eliminated from circulation."

"To what purpose?" she asked, sounding jaded and weary.

"Why, to disguise the original reason for the conspiracy against House Phel. There has to be some reason why a number of suspect houses colluded to cause the utter collapse of that high house."

"Have you considered that the house simply fell on its own?" she suggested, not ungently. "It happens. Magic wanes over generations, especially if scions are allowed to breed indiscriminately, without care to ensure their progeny will add to the robustness of the bloodline. There are countless examples of this exact pattern in the Convocation. There's an entire system built to handle this exact phenomenon. This is why we have second and third tier houses, to provide a deep bench for potential advancement to high house status should one of those fail. Because fail they do."

"Then why conceal all these books related to Meresin and House Phel?"

She spread her hands in disavowal of any knowledge—or concern. "If they meant to hide a conspiracy, why not eliminate only the pertinent texts? The disappearance of almost all Phel-related texts created suspicion. If your purported conspirators were so clever, so subtle in engineering this conspiracy to destroy a high house that no one noticed enough to write down, and they're powerful enough to perform such a feat as to hide this archive, then why draw attention by hiding all of the books instead of only the necessary ones?"

"I have a theory about that," he answered with excitement, having wondered that too. "From what I've excavated so far, I think that was the original plan, with only those most dangerous texts hidden away. But, over the ensuing centuries, books were added more haphazardly, with less finesse. Because of lack of skill, I extracted those texts first. I suspect less proficient flunkies were assigned to maintain the hidden archive, to monitor it to ensure it remained hidden, and to add any new texts that came to their attention. These people didn't know the full story, however, so they couldn't discern the dangerous from the innocuous, so they just threw anything Phel or Meresin-related into the fold as extra insurance."

She considered that and Cillian took pleasure that she had no immediate counter-argument. "Why not simply destroy the books?" she asked softly. "That would be most efficient. And thorough."

He knew the answer to this one. "Because librarians did it, Grandmother." Before she could interrupt, indignation bright in her expression, he continued. "You know this. We discussed it before, that only a Harahel-trained librarian wizard could have pulled this off. And, no matter how corrupt or compromised—and I do think that's a possibility—that wizard was, I think they could no more bear to destroy a book than you or I could."

She let out a sigh, looking weary. "Then why did this ancestor of ours comply at all? That's the part that bothers me. What did they know about House Phel that concerned them so much that they'd go to this extreme? For you and I both know that removing these books from Convocation Archives is a short ethical step from destroying them full stop."

"I have two theories." Cillian had considered whether to share these thoughts, but she was the head of his house, after all. And despite his differences with her high-handed ways—a definition that could be applied to the heads of all houses, let alone high houses, and Lady Harahel was probably among the least autocratic of them all—he did owe first loyalty to the house of his birth. She needed to know if he'd brought danger to their doorstep.

"I still don't know why the conspirators went to so much effort to bring down House Phel." He regarded her steadily, though she hadn't tried to interrupt. "I don't believe for a moment it was part of a natural progression. If the Phel family magic had declined, why did it appear again in such strength in Gabriel Phel and in his sister, Seliah? I checked and I've seen no other instances of spontaneous reoccurrence of a family's exact magical potentials suddenly bursting forth like that. It's as if the magic in the family had been suppressed and escaped those constraints."

"If these purported conspirators of yours are still active, as you seem to be indicating, why would they allow the suppression of magic to fail?" she asked cannily.

"I have a theory about that, too." He finished shoveling the last of the food on his plate into his mouth and signaled no when she moved to offer more. His stomach strained with fullness, reminding him that he really had failed to eat as he should. *No more of that.* He needed to be strong for what was to come. For Alise. "But let me stick to this wizard who made the folded archive. Either they believed in the conspirators' cause—which I am certain will be revealed when I find the root texts in the archive, the one or ones that began it all—or they were psychically manipulated."

His mind-reading grandmother's face tightened. "You think House Hanneil is involved."

"I *know* House Hanneil is involved," he corrected, "because they sent an agent to stop Alise's research into the missing archives. He very nearly succeeded, too."

"House Uriel could perform the same level of manipulation you suggest," she pointed out.

"Yes, but they're too principled. *And,*" he added when she looked dubious, "Provost Uriel has been helping us. She neutralized the Hanneil agent. She assigned me to assist Alise. I believe House Uriel is invested in uncovering this conspiracy."

"A lot of suppositions," Lady Harahel noted thoughtfully. But she'd also stopped arguing.

"True, but I'm working on verifying what I can. I need to get to that root book or books and you're right, Grandmother, my magic is too low. I need help. A familiar or two. Someone I can trust."

She gave him an impatient look. "You know full well House Harahel doesn't employ or house familiars. They're of no use to us here. Never mind one or two you can trust; I don't have anyone of sufficient strength to assist you. Any familiar potent enough to be useful gets sent off to the other houses."

Like a commodity to be traded. Cillian didn't voice the thought, however. That was a core tenet of the Convocation and not something he could change by arguing with his grandmother, especially when he needed her to agree to this request. "I have an idea."

She narrowed her usually warm wizard-black eyes. "I'm not going to like this, am I?"

"Probably not," he admitted. "But I think it's a sound one. At House Phel there are two unbonded familiars, Han and Iliana. Both are exceptionally powerful and owe fervent loyalty to Lord and Lady Phel. They would assist me and be discreet."

"I know about those two." Lady Harahel pointed an accusing finger at him. "You think I'm an ignorant bookworm living in the backwoods, but I know those two escaped agreed-upon contracts with House Sammael to become bonded familiars. And Alise Elal is the one who helped them."

"All true," he replied evenly. "Which is why those two would sacrifice anything to repay the asylum House Phel gave them and what Alise did to set them free."

"Need I mention that our relations with Sammael are already sour due to your shenanigans with Szarina?"

"All the more reason to ignore their wishes," Cillian pointed out. "In addition, Han is particularly skilled with weapons, both wielding them and teaching others to use them in pitched fighting."

Lady Harahel raised her brows. "Do I want to know why

you think weapons skills are something I should care about?" She swept a hand at the quiet manse around them. "Do you expect our books to suddenly attack?"

"No," he answered, though his amusement drowned in the seriousness of his gut-deep fears. "I expect that House Hanneil will."

~ 13 ~

A LISE REFUSED TO fuck the familiars her father sent to her. Even though it made them sad, sulky, bitter and, with one memorable young man, outright angry. She made each candidate sleep in her bed alone, while she wrapped herself in a blanket nest by the fire. They were locked in together, which wasn't their fault, but no way would she sleep in the bed where they could crawl in to join her.

Beyond having to argue with these hopefuls—and dashing their hopes in the process—she grimly reminded herself that at least she enjoyed the privilege of being able to refuse them. Unlike Nic, who'd had no choice but to accept those wizards that won the monthly lottery and arrived to spend a night attempting to impregnate her.

In that circular room in the tower where Nic had been sequestered while Alise was happily off at Convocation Academy, Alise spent time surveying the slices of the view through the slanted metal shutters meant to prevent the occupant from escaping via the window—or throwing themselves to their death. Alise, as a favor to Brinda Chur, had written to Nic about her experience in the Betrothal Trials. Lines from Nic's reply kept circling through her mind like her own pacing within those walls, the single door locked and warded against her escape.

It was awful.

I didn't think it would matter to me so much, letting those men have me, attempt to impregnate me, but… it did.

It hurt me inside in ways I can't describe.

I would have agreed to anything, to anyone, to any level of treatment to escape the extended torture of boredom punctuated by rape.

Because that's what it is, no matter how they dress it up as informed consent.

Even if Alise hadn't been resolved not to lay a finger on the familiars sent to her—or for them to lay a finger on her—those remembered lines would have stopped her. Though several of the familiars, most in fact, attempted some form of seduction, believing her to be shyly virginal, she had no trouble setting them back on their heels. Unlike Nic, Alise had neither agreed to cooperate, nor did she lack the power to enforce her will. And, sadly, the fact that the familiars had all been trained to reflexively obey a wizard worked in her favor.

Though she recognized many of them from classes above her at school, and though others were even older, they all deferred to her, once they got past their initial confusion at her determined refusal. A couple mentioned that her father had told them she was shy and needed a man to take the lead, so she quickly learned to disabuse them of that notion right off. In the end, though, she found her greatest strength and certainty in knowing that—no matter how eager they seemed to be— none of them could be considered to be truly consenting. Like all familiars, they had one pathway, which was to be subservient to wizards in one way or another.

It grimly amused her to witness her father's persistence and how clever he imagined himself to be. As time went by, with one disappointed familiar after another leaving in the morning after a night alone, it occurred to her that the men he sent to entice her had begun to resemble Cillian more and more closely.

She reached her limit with a bespectacled familiar who could have been Cillian's brother, with dark curls and an earnest, intellectual mien. It turned out, however, that he'd never read a book in his life that wasn't for school. And that he didn't even need the glasses. As the guard unlocked and opened the door, she called out. "Tell my father that he doesn't know what I want, so to stop trying."

The familiar, whose name she'd barely registered and had already forgotten looked confused and apprehensive. So much so that she waved the words away. He'd never summon the courage to speak so impudently to Lord Elal and it had been wrong of her to take out her frustrated ire against him.

Once the door closed and locked behind him, she went to test it, another of her newly acquired habits. The Iblis lock had, of course, been coded for the door guards to operate, not her. With time—of which she had plenty—she could probably wizard her way through breaking the lock. In addition to the lock, however, and the minor-wizards serving as guards, her father had stationed a particularly vicious set of spirits on the door. Not on the shuttered windows, however, which made her wryly aware that, while he expected her to try to escape, he figured she wasn't desperate enough to choose plummeting to her death.

None of it was absolutely necessary as what truly kept Alise from leaving was the knowledge that Bria would have to take her place as his heir. She had spent her initial days of imprisonment binding and training a new guardian spirit for her niece. It had taken a bit more work to imprint the spirit on Bria from a distance, but—again—Alise had nothing but time. When she sent the little spirit off to Meresin and felt the snap of connection upon it finding Bria, Alise at least was able to savor that small victory.

She found it overkill that her father went to such lengths to lock her in when he'd already chained her with her love for her niece. Telling, she supposed, that he thought he needed insurance beyond that. Piers Elal might be savvy enough to use emotional extortion to manipulate her, but he could never understand basic compassion. Just as his transparent attempts at finding a familiar with a physical type similar to Cillian's betrayed her father's utter lack of understanding for what real connection between two people was about.

Yes, Cillian's face had become dear to her, with his intelligent wizard-black eyes and sexy librarian look with those spectacles. His black curls framed an exquisitely boned face, with his narrow chin and sweet, bow-shaped mouth that kissed her with such tenderness. Those elegantly long-fingered hands that had caressed her body with the same care he showed a delicate and fragile, rare and ancient tome. That was key: Cillian cherished her as if she were precious. He understood her, amused even by her flaws and foibles.

She realized with a sudden crystalline clarity that a person like her father would never in a million years comprehend what she loved about Cillian. He'd built his entire understanding of relationships around manipulating people, so he'd never know how it felt to have someone come to him out of true regard and real feeling, with actual trust. He'd arranged his life so that he was surrounded by people forced to cater to him. Not one person in the whole world wanted to be with him for himself. He could trust no one at all.

Alise had what her father never could. Not just Cillian, though he lived closest to her heart, but also family like Nic and Gabriel, her many friends at House Phel, and even—bizarrely enough—at House El-Adrel now. Her father could weave a web of words about competition and power, but she had experienced for herself the immense rewards of true connection. No amount of wealth or status could compensate for the richness of knowing someone took joy from being around you, even from simply knowing you existed in the world.

She understood that now because knowing Cillian was out there, cozied into House Harahel, reading his books, perhaps poking at that archive, made her happy. Imagining how Bria would be growing day by day gave her joy. Han and Iliana enjoying their forbidden love, Asa practicing the dark arts, Quinn scheming to get her hands on the baby for a while, Nic and Gabriel growing and protecting their house and people … All of that rested like a glowing sun at the core of her, mitigating the cold isolation of her imprisonment.

Nic had written:

Had I been sequestered in that tower much longer, had Gabriel not come along to change my entire world, I'd have succumbed to both despair and the overwhelming need to escape that monthly and harrowing night with my suitors.

Alise knew exactly what Nic meant in saying that. Familiar or not, Nic would've found a way to escape that room, probably via those shuttered windows and the horrible drop to the courtyard far below. But that glowing certainty that Alise loved and was loved in return, kept her from considering any such thing. Her father need not shutter the windows or even lock the door. Alise would stay put and see this through, not out of fear, but for love.

The door flung open, Piers Elal's stocky build filling it from side to side, though his head reached nowhere near the lintel. Alise got her diminutive height from him, along with her magical gifts, and possibly some of her more irascible personality quirks. She would take nothing else of his. If it lived in her—and as much as Cillian claimed otherwise, Alise knew the corrupt tendrils of her father twined around the empty, insecure holes in her heart—then she would root it out.

"Oh, hello Lord Elal." She pretended to consult the nonexistent El-Adrel clock. Probably the inability to track the passage of time precisely should bother her. "Apparently you received my message after all."

"Yes." He smiled, and she didn't care for the look of it. "Come with me."

ALISE FOLLOWED HER father through the familiar halls of her childhood home. House Elal was by far the largest of all the high houses, something Elals long before her father had insisted upon. They laid claim to having the biggest house—in physical size and in population—although that was a claim difficult to prove. House Hanneil, for example, had an architectural profile that blended innocuously with the landscape above but purportedly extended below ground in an immeasurable warren of caves and tunnels. And they never disclosed their actual population.

In a similar fashion, House El-Adrel couldn't be precisely measured in size as the clockwork, semi-sentient structure changed itself routinely, hiding away rooms—sometimes with the unwary trapped inside—and producing entire wings that hadn't been seen in centuries. Conversely, House Refoel had no single structure, but instead spread over an entire fertile valley of hot springs and dwellings from spare single-person huts to the multi-roomed main facility.

But House Elal did take the prize for appearing to be the largest manse. It looked like a castle out of fairytales with its towers and turrets, the actual portcullis and drawbridge that lowered over the "moat" created by the near circular bend of a river. If the house hadn't been built in that serpentine curve—completed by a spike-filled chasm to bridge the distance on the narrow spit of land—and therefore constrained in horizontal sprawl, it would no doubt be even larger. As it was, in their zeal to expand and place their personal stamp on the manse, the generations of Elals had managed to fill their self-made island from bank to bank, with expansions added mostly upward in the more recent eras.

Inside, this made for a confusion of hallways and staircases. One almost always had to ascend and descend several sets of stairs to move from one side of the manse to another. Having played in this house from her earliest days, Alise knew every twist and turn, every tower and cellar, and even those odd semi-secret rooms created by the access being mostly walled off by some desired addition and the resulting bottleneck making it too inconvenient for anyone to use on a regular basis.

Even so, trailing behind her father, Alise discovered herself in a part of the twisting manse she'd never before seen. With dawning realization, she began to think he was showing her the House Elal arcanium, a truly shocking development, especially given her obnoxious message.

She'd known that her wizard father used an arcanium, of course. Every high house, and some lower tier houses, boasted an arcanium. They were kept secret, as far as the wizards using them could contrive, and warded against intruders. Alise and her siblings had so feared their father's many dire warnings should they intrude upon his sanctum sanctorum that they'd never even tried to find it. Now, as they traveled through one of those apparently unused bottlenecks, through a secret doorway so invisibly sealed Alise had never suspected its existence, though she'd—ironically enough—played prisoner in a tower with her friends there more than once, she decided they never *could* have found it.

They descended a short flight of steps that ended at a landing, which curved in a hairpin loop, went through another invisibly sealed doorway, up a wrought iron spiral staircase in an otherwise empty column to nowhere, ended up on a circular balcony overlooking open air. And then her father removed a curtaining veil of spirit matter unlike anything she'd seen before.

It was old, incredibly ancient, and comprised of spirits that had been combined and somehow retrained to have lost their individuation. Alise didn't know that could be done, but her father brushed aside the barrier with an ease he'd use to push past one made of silk. Beyond it, a door with a huge wheel inset glowed with magic. Piers Elal put his hand to the lock, then gave her an impatient glance. "Your hands, too, Daughter. It's meant to be opened by two people. Usually a wizard and familiar. The only other time I've opened it with another wizard is when my father showed me."

She stood there dumbly a moment. "Why are you showing me now?" Surely he didn't trust her.

"Because you are obstinate beyond belief and I've come to the conclusion that *showing* you what can be yours, along with the critical importance of having a bonded familiar, will be what it takes to convince you to cooperate with me."

"I *am* cooperating with you," she pointed out, not moving. "I am here in House Elal, fulfilling the terms of our agreement."

"And yet there you stand," he bit out, barely containing the fulminating irritation practically leaking from his pores. *"Not cooperating."*

He had a point. Biting back a sigh, Alise went to his side, wishing she could feel about this moment as she'd fantasized as a little girl. Back when Nic was the favorite, the obvious heir, the apple of their father's eye, Alise had nursed a secret and jealous longing to have what Nic seemed to have. Everyone had been so certain Nic would manifest as a wizard, not a familiar, that Alise had been sure of the reverse: that she would be a familiar or, in the very best case scenario, a minor wizard forever in her brilliant elder sister's shadow.

But she'd still imagined this exact scenario: being at her father's side in his arcanium, which in her childish fantasies, looked more like a toy-filled playroom than a wizard's workshop. Now she disliked having to be in such close proximity to him, his magic an unappealingly lurid mix of churning colors, an unpleasant smell emanating from his body. Why he smelled like rotten fruit, she didn't know, but it turned her stomach and she had to hold her breath as she laid her hands opposite his, in the grooves obviously made for them in the big wheel.

"Invoke your spirit magic," her father instructed on a grunt, mollified but far from pleased.

She nearly asked for more information than that, but then her wizard senses came alert to the spirits embedded in the wheel. No, not embedded but... forming the wheel. Like the surprising spirit curtain, these entities had somehow been condensed into an even more solid form, though these remained more aware, a living substance inquiring as to her blood and identity. Before she could think what to do, the material of the wheel gave the sense of a sigh beneath her hands, huge locks turning deep in the walls, releasing.

A door that hadn't been there a moment ago appeared in the curve a short walk away. The magic of their wizard ancestors seemed to far outstrip anything they could do today. The set of her father's face as he gestured her to precede him through the doorway made her wonder if he felt the same.

Or he could be just generally disgruntled, which was more likely.

Inside the door—surprise—another set of stairs spiraled up, daylight pouring through a circular opening at the top. Alise climbed all the way to the top and stepped into a place more wondrous than any fanciful playroom her childhood self could have conjured up. The top of the tower lay open to the sky, allowing in the pour of sunshine from one direction and the seething vista of yet another winter stormfront approaching from the north. It took her a moment to realize there was a barrier, this one formed of a transparent, almost undetectable film of solidified spirits, a combination of those in the door mechanism and the disguising curtain. Below, the manse sprawled in all its iconic glory—including her own tower not that far away, a bit lower, a twenty minute walk and a short hop for a crow.

She had never seen the tower in which she stood. Hidden from sight. Fascinating.

"Hello, Wizard Alise," a politely quiet voice said, and Alise spun, torn from her enraptured contemplation of the spectacular view and even more transporting wizardry that had made it all possible.

"Brinda," she blurted, then felt stupid, managing to pull back anything more foolish like asking Brinda Chur what she was doing there in the House Elal arcanium, instead of in class at Convocation Academy. As Brinda was currently bound to a transparent apparatus, her once long locks cut ruthlessly short, it was obvious what she was doing there. It was all the other questions that needed answering.

"Ah, I forgot you two know each other," Lord Elal said, lying outrageously, and strutting over to the young Brinda and pinching her chin to make her look up at him. Which she did, utter worship in her brown eyes. "Meet my new bonded familiar, Brinda Elal."

Alise took in a careful breath. "I thought Familiar Brinda planned to undergo the Betrothal Trials."

"Yes, well, I put paid to that idea, didn't I, Precious?" Piers said, nearly cooing, and Brinda responded with a radiant smile.

Alise shuddered at the sound of the nickname her father had once used for her maman. Not out of any kind of nostalgia, but more out of a realization of how cloying and condescending the nickname was—and out of a low-grade horror for what lay in Brinda's future.

"Being Lord Wizard Elal's familiar is all I ever could have hoped for," Brinda said in a reverent tone, her eyes shining. "I have no doubt I'll bear his child in time."

"Throw enough money at a problem and people are happy to solve it for you," Piers advised Alise. "That approach will always stand you in good stead. House Chur was most obliging. I wanted my new familiar now and, to my delight, she wanted me. Didn't you, Precious?"

"More than anything, my Wizard," Brinda responded promptly.

"Well," Alise said brightly, ignoring the sick feeling in her gut at Brinda's display of meek adoration for a man she couldn't possibly admire. "Welcome to the family, Brinda. I offer you best wishes for success here at House Elal. I would shake your hand, but…" She nearly added that Brinda seemed to be tied up, but she'd accomplished annoying her father already, so it felt superfluous and she simply shrugged.

"Thank you, Wizard Alise," Brinda replied, ever so sincere. She beamed at Piers. "This is more than I could have hoped for."

And far more than she bargained for. A strange circle had been completed here and Alise wasn't sure how to interpret that cycle of events. She'd severed the wizard–familiar bond between her mother and father in order to free Maman from his tyrannical control. Yes, it had been to save Maman's life, too, but fundamentally what she and Nic had most wanted for their mother was to escape being Piers Elal's familiar.

Now Brinda—who was far from a friend, but also not someone Alise wished ill—had stepped into Maman's chains. Though Brinda had attempted extortion, threatening to spill secrets about House Phel, Alise knew the familiar had done so because she was following instructions from the house of her birth. She couldn't hate Brinda for it. And now Alise possessed the power to break the chains binding Brinda. If Alise could find a way to do so without killing the familiar, as Asa had suggested.

Regardless, Brinda didn't want that and would never thank Alise for it. Well, maybe not *never*. Eventually, when Piers had used, broken, and drained Brinda as he had their mother, then Brinda might see the light and regret. But for the moment, Brinda embraced her metaphorical chains, not even struggling against the physical ones that currently bound her. A lesson in that.

"Let us begin the lesson," Piers said, following hard on the heels of that thought. "I want you to observe, Daughter, how a bonded familiar can catapult a working from adequate to ultimate."

"Why is she tied up?" Alise asked, unable to restrain the question any longer, but trying to make it sound like genuine curiosity and not an accusation.

"If you'd bedded those familiars I sent you, then you'd know the answer to that question," her father retorted instead of answering, then peered at her. "Did you even properly bed that librarian boy? Is that the issue, that you're still a virgin?"

Brinda made a sound very close to a giggle, though she swallowed it in an appearance of deference, avoiding Alise's gaze and fastening her worshipful brown eyes on her wizard. "Cillian Harahel isn't terribly masculine, sir, if you know what I mean. Not like you are."

Her father raised his brows at Alise. "I wondered about that. So there *was* a problem."

Alise kept her posture relaxed, refusing to rise to the bait. She'd defend Cillian to her dying breath, but only if it mattered and this ridiculous, juvenile taunting was far beneath both of them. Brinda was too innocent and her father too cruel and jaded for either of them to understand what she and Cillian had shared. Passion, yes, but also that emotional intimacy, that longing that would burst through her skin if she gave into it. Which she could not. She'd given that up forever.

So, she shrugged. "That's in the past, isn't it. I'm here to learn from you, Father. Perhaps as you demonstrate the advantages of a familiar to me, I'll overcome my… hesitancy over those you've sent to me."

He bought it, his ego and certainty too large to allow for the possibility that she was playing him. Lord Elal smiled, his magic billowing with an unnecessary flourish. "Then pay attention, my child. This you will never learn at Convocation Academy."

With an internal sigh and full-body resignation, Alise set herself to watch and learn. She might be there under duress, but there she was and she might as well extract whatever useful information she could.

After all, she'd need every advantage just in case she some-day must face her father in a duel.

$$\sim 14 \sim$$

C ILLIAN WAS DEEP into the folded archive with a mental image of himself head-down and mostly submerged in a massive trunk of tissue paper, ass in the air as he scrabbled blindly around for books hidden in the bottom. He just knew more books must occupy the null-space, but they were getting more and more difficult to locate and extract. Especially as he reached those original, meticulously crafted inner layers where, he felt sure, the first books had been hidden.

His continued work over the days following that conversation with his grandmother—while going slowly, preserving his magic, pausing to take breaks, eat healthy, blah blah blah—had only further convinced him of his original suppositions. The first librarian wizard to create this folded space to hide the House Phel books had been diabolically clever and fueled with immense power. Possibly they'd had the help of familiars, which Cillian found deeply ironic at this point. There might not be library emergencies, but clearly there existed tricks and twists in the use of their magic that House Harahel had lost over time by devaluing the power of their art. Not that Cillian ever wanted to have a bonded familiar, but the magical assistance clearly made a difference.

He missed Alise. And not just for her rose-infused, wine-rich magic that she'd gifted him so generously, but for her insights and her acerbic wit. Was she still at House Phel or had she gone back to Convocation Academy? He hated not knowing and could only hope that his compliant behavior and successful completion of this project would soften Lady Harahel enough to give him to permission to at least message Alise. But he couldn't do that without concentrating on the task at hand.

Mostly, it would be really nice to have a magical boost from someone.

On the heels of that thought, he heard something. Voices? Surely not. Even if his grandmother had intruded on his secured salon again, there'd be only one voice. A hand crisply collided with the back of his head and Cillian groaned, rubbing the smarting spot as he unwound his wizardry and conscious mind from the sticky beehive of the folded space.

"I was already—" he began and yelped. "Han? Iliana!"

The pair of familiars grinned at him, Han extending a hand. "Sorry, mate, that was me that smacked you. We spoke to you several times, but you were that far away."

Dazed, Cillian shook the hand of the tall blond man, while Iliana bounced excitedly next to him. When he next extended a hand to her, she squealed and threw herself into hugging him. With her exuberance and red hair flying, embracing her felt like holding onto a fire elemental.

"We're so happy you sent for us!" she exclaimed.

Of course, he hadn't, since he was interdicted from sending for anyone. "Did you… meet with Lady Harahel?" he asked cautiously.

Iliana nodded with enthusiasm while Han looked a bit more jaundiced. "She's lovely, your grandmother," Iliana answered, then poked him in the ribs. "Why didn't you tell us you're the scion of a high-house family? You outrank all of us. Well except for the Elal sisters, but they don't count. I can't believe Alise kept it a secret, too."

Cillian barely managed to avoid wincing. He'd meant to tell Alise. Eventually. But it ranked so low in matters of importance in his mind that he hadn't quite gotten around to it. Now, observing Iliana's reaction, and Han's new reserve, Cillian began to wonder how Alise had taken that news. Was that part of why she'd left? Could she be that angry with him?

"Being a grandson in a family like House Harahel's hardly ranks in anyone's estimation," he said ruefully, wishing he could explain that reasoning to Alise. Good idea in hindsight, as so many were. "I haven't heard from Alise recently," he tendered, wondering how strange that would sound to these two, but needing to know something, anything about her. "Is she still at House Phel or...?" He trailed off as they exchanged looks, a shared expression of grim worry that immediately alarmed him. "What?"

"You don't know then," Han said slowly, and Iliana elbowed him in the ribs hard enough to make him blow out a breath and slide her a glare.

"Of course he doesn't know." Iliana threw her hands in the air. "He wouldn't ask if he knew."

"I was gathering my thoughts," he protested to her. "It's not easy news to give."

"Well, nothing you're doing is going to soften the blow."

"Oh, you think that there's something we can say or do to soften this blow?" Han gestured sharply at Cillian. "The man is in love with her. He's going to be devastated."

"Han. That's their personal business and—"

"With all due respect," Cillian interrupted sharply, far enough out of his usual mild-mannered behavior that they both looked shocked, "the suspense is worse than anything. Please tell me immediately, and as succinctly as possible, where Alise is." He braced himself, knowing that hoping they'd say she'd gone back to Convocation Academy would be asking too much.

"Elal," Han said briefly, then clasped him on the shoulder. "Alise went back to House Elal with her father."

ONCE THE PAIR had settled down, they made a decent tag-team, telling Cillian the story of little Bria's birth, the naming ceremony, and all that ensued, all while interrupting each other with salient details and agreeing on some points, amiably bickering on others. As awful as the story was—or perhaps because their byplay lightened the darkness of the tale—he found himself watching and enjoying their back and forth.

Han and Iliana had been friends for years, certain that they could never have more than that, as two familiars destined to have their mates and fates decided by someone else. Alise had told Cillian the tale of their escape from Convocation Academy. Though Han was the warrior of the pair and Iliana the gentle-hearted, inherently sweet one, it had been Iliana who determined they would defy the Convocation and find a way to be together. Theirs was a love that had overcome the greatest of obstacles and their deep connection shone through clearly.

Cillian rather envied that, telling himself he was learning from their example, even though he knew he was focusing on that to distract himself from the dawning dread and gnawing worry for Alise.

Alise.

At House Elal.

Trapped there with her father, whom she loathed and feared. All alone.

And all this time he'd been more than half angry with her for deserting him. A lot of that anger came from hurt, that she could be so callous, so uncaring, so easily leaving him without even a goodbye. And then she'd gone and nobly sacrificed herself to save her newborn niece.

According to Han and Iliana, there had been a number of discussions at House Phel on how to retrieve or rescue Alise. There seemed to be no legal recourse. The bargain had been fairly struck and exactly walked the lines of Convocation law. As a scion of House Elal and the obvious heir, regardless of what the Convocation would regard as standard family squabbling and drama, Alise was where she belonged. The only wiggle room they'd found was that House Phel had paid for Alise's education through graduation, which meant they had some leverage with Convocation Academy. But that would only manifest if Provost Uriel really wanted to confront Lord Elal and that seemed unlikely, especially given that the provost had informally suspended Alise.

And given that Uriel seemed to be aligned in a cold war against the Elal-Hanneil conspiracy—or however many houses were involved—with outright war looming on the horizon, the provost was unlikely to tip her hand or compromise their strategy to recover one young wizard who'd only caused her trouble.

Which meant that they were at an impasse, with Nic and Gabriel alternating between talking each other down from storming House Elal to forcibly extract Alise. Neither wanted the other to make the attempt, and they had the added complication of little Bria to care for. As Lord Phel, Gabriel had categorically ordered everyone at House Phel to stand down, though more than a few of them had considered disobeying. From the way Han and Iliana fell into arguing about it, they and others would have staged a rescue—if only they could have devised a strategy that had a hope of succeeding.

Even Jadren and Seliah, still assimilating their roles as Lord and Lady El-Adrel—a house that likely was part of the conspiracy before their coup d'etat—had considered going after Alise, before eventually agreeing to wait. Jadren had extolled the virtues of simply formally approaching House Elal as another high-house head, with Seliah rolling her eyes and demanding if he planned to simply knock on the door, and Jadren retorting, why not, it had worked to rescue *her* from House Sammael. Han and Iliana even partially acted out the two roles in their recitation, which had Cillian laughing despite himself.

Which, he realized, had been their aim.

In the end, no one knew what to do and so no one had done anything. The solace they all clung to was that Alise should be safe. Lord Elal wanted to subvert her, to bring her into alignment with his cause, so he wouldn't hurt her. But there had been no word from her either.

Cillian listened to all of this, nodding along in apparent agreement, his thoughts delving deep. He might be giving in to romantic delusions to imagine that he knew Alise better than any of them, but he believed he did. Alise kept that cool reserve around her like an impenetrable wall, allowing others to see only what she wanted them to see. And Alise wanted to be seen as capable, intelligent, in control of her magic and her destiny. Which she was. But she was also a deeply sensitive and caring individual who'd been starved of love all her life. Though she'd found a sense of belonging and family at House Phel, it was still new to her.

How would Alise feel that no one had come for her? She would assume they had written her off, that everyone was preoccupied with their own problems and concerns. And she wouldn't be wrong. After all, Cillian had accepted his grandmother's edicts and buried himself in the archives, believing the worst of Alise without attempting to see if she was all right. And he was the one person she'd finally trusted, that she'd allowed inside that careful reserve.

For the first time, he considered that she perhaps hadn't left him without a word of her own free will. His grandmother wasn't above lying to protect him and House Harahel, or simply slanting the perspective on what had happened. She'd clearly indicated she felt Alise was a threat.

Regardless, the ultimate responsibility lay with him. He could have chosen to rebel against his family and house instead of knuckling under in his usual meekly accommodating way.

Angry at himself, he fulminated over his lack of action. If he wouldn't go against the rules for Alise, then who would he do it for? This was a test of character and so far he'd failed miserably. His grandmother, so-called friends, and pleasant-voiced enemies, they all gave him shit for being bamboozled by beautiful, sweet, lithe-limbed Szarina, saying he sacrificed his integrity for her. They liked to mock him for thinking himself her savior, for fancying himself a white knight charging to the rescue, but he'd had good reasons. Honorable reasons. Yes, he'd violated his personal integrity for Szarina, but he'd had the noblest of intentions.

He would stoop to far worse for Alise. She wasn't fine and safe at House Elal. She was in the gravest peril, even worse than what she'd faced from Gordon Hanneil. That vile wizard, at least, had been clearly her enemy. She'd known from the first moment that he posed a great danger to her, and she'd had the wit to be justifiably afraid, finding ways to fight back.

With her father, as much as Alise feared becoming like him, as much as she hated him, she also still loved him in that indelible way of a child for their parent. Cillian knew that some part of Alise, the girl who'd been perceived as less than and had been neglected by her father, still longed for his approval.

And Piers Elal might be a loathsome toad of a wizard, but

he was far from stupid. He knew how to manipulate people and he'd clearly set his sights on winning Alise over as his heir. He'd pull out all the stops to convince Alise that she could be happy embracing whatever it was he wanted her for. Alise was a powerful wizard, possibly more powerful than anyone who hadn't swum in her magic as he had could know. The opportunity to exercise that power could be terribly seductive. Especially if she believed that no one cared about her. It had taken diligent effort on his part to convince her of his love for her. She might not return his intense feelings, but it would harm her to think he hadn't been sincere or that his feelings had changed.

How could she believe otherwise when he had effectively abandoned her? He'd promised her once that he'd never let her down, that he'd always be there for her, and when it had come down to it, he'd failed her. Well, no longer. If no one else could think of a way to extract Alise, then it should be left to a librarian. He would develop a foolproof strategy that wouldn't require might or the law or the assistance of any of the high houses, including his own.

Also, he possessed a secret weapon. He patted the pocket where Alise's favor rested, always over his heart. Such antiquated Convocation customs transcended law, dating back to the days of outright war. Lord Elal would abide by it. So would Alise, whether she wanted to or not.

Cillian became aware of the silence in the room, broken only by the crackle of the fire, now dying low. He should add some wood to it. Han and Iliana sat still, arrested expressions on their faces. He rather thought the three of them might have been sitting in silence for some time.

"Cillian?" Iliana ventured, a worried line between her fiery brows. "What's in your pocket."

"A key to open a locked door," he answered, not intending to be inscrutable, but liking the way it sounded. Heroic.

"I told you he'd go after our Alise," Han said with satisfaction. "I'll go with you."

"Lord Phel forbade it," Iliana reminded him, almost absently, her gazed focused on Cillian.

"Thank you, Han," Cillian said. "Thank you, both. But the plan I have in mind will work for only me to go to House Elal. I promise, though, I'll get her out." By hook or crook.

"Well, all right." Iliana sighed. "Though we only just got here and I thought you needed our help. Magical help."

"Oh, I do," he assured her. "And I have to do that first, so let's get to it."

~ 15 ~

ALISE SPENT DAY after day with her father and Brinda in the arcanium, the light passing over and around them in sun and storm, moon and night. Without those cues—and her regularly scheduled escorted sojourns to her locked room to sleep—she might have forgotten about the passage of time entirely.

She was both exhausted and bursting with magical energy. True to her father's word, he'd taught her how to take full advantage of Brinda as a power source. Even with Brinda bonded to her father and not her, Alise had discovered that the pure inhalation of that magic, especially amplified and intensified by her ancestral arcanium, intoxicated her to the point of losing reason. She finally understood why wizards, especially the most powerful, had succumbed to various levels of madness working their enchantments in their arcaniums.

In that space, she exceeded the boundaries of her own skin, becoming mightier than she'd dared imagine she could be. It had never occurred to her that the Elal arcanium would feel as if she'd slipped her hand into a glove. No: into an armored gauntlet. But the place had been built by wizards like herself, sharing her same blood and her same magic. Over the ensuing centuries, they'd imbued the arcanium with their magic, storing it there and creating channels for more. Alise could open a gateway with a drop of her own magic and receive an ocean in return.

She had to give Brinda credit where it was due, also. Back at Convocation Academy, the familiar had been arrogant in her confident assessment of her own magic, over the edge into unbearable, despite her otherwise charming ways. Well, her charming *mask*, which had given way to an inner ugliness when she threatened to expose Gabriel and Nic for using a fertility spell to game the Betrothal Trials, strictly against the rules. But now that Brinda had what she wanted—or what she thought she wanted—she was back to being delightful company. And her magic was exactly as robust and adaptable as she'd bragged about.

The House Chur fire and sun magic burned bright and hot, indeed. Brinda had referred to it as the universal donor and that hadn't been an exaggeration. Her magic folded seamlessly into Alise's—and, she assumed, her father's—making Alise feel like a sun herself. She understood now why the ancient and reclusive House Chur had survived centuries of challenges by upstart houses even though they brought few direct products to market, and why the powerful magics they supplied worked so well to fuel countless other manufacturing processes. House Chur didn't need to play the political games to amass wealth and power. They could simply rest easy on their already massive, old-money coffers, kept healthy and vigorous with a steady stream of passive income.

All of that was beside the point, however. What mattered

was those boundaryless days in the Elal arcanium, working magic with her father, learning proprietary techniques and tricks she couldn't have guessed at. Looking back at how she'd struggled to hold a dozen spirits at once, she almost pitied her past self and that striving. Powered by the arcanium and quickly mastering what her father demonstrated, Alise could now handle ten, a hundred times what she could before. She understood why her father scoffed at her insistence on graduating. Yes, she'd need that certification at some point, but it really was superfluous. Even Professor Cixin couldn't teach her what Piers Elal had.

Of course, Professor Cixin had been a House Elal wizard before he left to take the teaching position at the academy, but not family. He'd never learned what she now knew.

"Excellent work," her father said, giving Alise a real smile as he untied the sagging Brinda from the framework that served to channel magic directly from her body and into the very structure of the arcanium. His familiar gazed at him wearily, though no less worshipfully, allowing him to sweep her into his arms, then laying her head against his shoulder. He kissed her on the forehead, the picture of a loving... something.

Alise looked away, her feelings too mixed to consider. She'd been doing a lot of that lately. Cillian would probably call her out, saying she was in some kind of denial, but Cillian wasn't there, was he? No, Cillian was ensconced at House Harahel and too busy—or too pissed at her—to send a Ratsiel courier. Probably he didn't even know where she was. More likely, he didn't care to find out, which was fine. Their relationship, such as it had been, had always been about the intimacy of the moment, the time and place and project. She'd known from the beginning and every step along the way that the liaison with him would go nowhere. Where she'd tripped up was forgetting that essential truth and getting attached.

And, as much as she hated to admit it, her father might be right about her getting a familiar. If she found one she liked, and that didn't have to be right away—and she definitely didn't want babies anytime soon, if at all—she could see now the benefits of bonding a familiar. It wouldn't have to be a predatory relationship. Look at Nic and Gabriel, Jadren and Seliah, too. They were bonded and they worked together as a team, a loving partnership.

It was something to aspire to. She could find a male familiar with the qualities she'd enjoyed in Cillian—bookish, intelligent, gentle, a nurturer—plus she'd have his magic to boost hers in this truly delicious and exhilarating way. There was a compelling aspect to the adoration with which Brinda regarded her wizard master. With a bonded familiar, Alise would never need to worry if he was angry at her or disappointed in her. Her familiar not only wouldn't abandon her, he wouldn't *want* to leave her, full stop. He *would* want to take care of her and that sounded pretty wonderful at this stage, too.

Nic and the other familiars at Convocation Academy liked to make a joke out of some of the classes teaching familiars how to best support their future wizards. They called the classes "Care and Feeding of Wizards 101," which was funny, but also contained a grain of truth. Familiars were perfectly suited and positioned to provide for a wizard's needs. Feeling the hunger and exhaustion set in from the hours spent in the arcanium, Alise could easily envision the pleasure of having a loving partner to put a meal before her, to run her a bath, rub her shoulders, perhaps make love to her in the way Cillian had taught her to crave. Would that be so wrong?

Having someone look at her the way Brinda regarded Piers, too, well… Cillian had also taught her to value that, to cherish that feeling of being cared for. She couldn't have Cillian, that much was obvious, was water under the bridge, but she *could* have a familiar of her own. It was her birthright. No one would blame her for bonding one.

Familiars were relegated to their station in life regardless. Alise couldn't change that. Even though she could sever the wizard–familiar bond, she couldn't do that without killing the familiar. And if she didn't bond her familiar, someone else would, and they very likely wouldn't be as kind as Alise planned to be. Maybe she was, as her father insisted, being stubborn about refusing all the young familiars he'd sent. Any number had been pleasing to look at and eager to win her favor. She could have at least talked with some of them, gotten to know them a little.

She could discuss this with her father, she decided, as she followed him out of the arcanium. He'd listen to her as she explained her thinking, that she didn't want babies yet, and he'd be mollified, encouraged by her interest in courting a familiar on her own. Yes, he'd be happy that she'd begun to see the validity of his argument.

Because he carried Brinda, now sleeping trustingly in his

arms, Alise handled locking and disguising the entrance, something a solo wizard could do and a task her father had begun trusting her with a few days ago. Or was it a week? She was seriously losing track of time. Their relationship had changed over the past... while. Whatever. He was a good teacher, quick with praise, precise with critique for improvements. She'd begun to think that she—all of them—had perhaps judged him too harshly.

Yes, he'd been angry at Nic, but looking at it from his perspective, as he'd asked her to do, Nic had shamed him and House Elal by attempting to escape. She'd made them all look bad and then refused to even have a conversation with him about it. Instead Nic had demanded her dowry and more, having the temerity to expect Elal vines to grow her own grapes, which meant she could compete with House Elal wines in the future.

Piers had been deeply hurt by that, he confessed to Alise one night after their regular father-daughter dinner. At first those dinners had been stilted, Alise sitting in sullen silence, refusing to converse. But her father had determinedly kept up a one-sided discourse, explaining how difficult it had been for him to be abandoned by his eldest daughter, and then his heir, to have lost his wife and familiar of nearly thirty years—only to have no one to comfort him in his grief.

Though he'd hinted in the past that he suspected Alise's role in the severing of his wizard-familiar bond with her maman, he couldn't know anything more than that the bond had broken and she'd eventually died. Maman had been weak when he was forced to leave her behind at House Phel. He'd been injured, unconscious, packed into a carriage by Gabriel Phel and forcibly separated from his lifelong familiar, who then died. And then to have everyone treat him as a villain instead of as the bereaved widower… Well, it had been devastating.

Then, to heap insult upon injury, none of them had thought to give him the barest courtesy of notifying him of Bria's birth, much less inviting him to the naming ceremony. Yes, he'd been angry and he was ashamed of himself in the wake of it all. He'd always had a temper, as Alise knew, and he'd let it get away from him, in his hurt, offense, and ongoing grief. He'd never expected his entire family to turn on him and, well, it had injured his pride. All of it had made him take a good long look at himself. Still, he couldn't regret the outcome as it had brought him this: this one, golden and unique opportunity to get to know Alise, and to teach her all he knew.

One of his greatest fears had been that he'd never be able to pass on the Elal secrets he alone had known. All due to his foibles, may their ancestors curse him. Ferdinand had his place and his uses, but he wasn't the wizard Alise was. Piers deeply regretted, he confessed one night, when they'd both had a fair amount of a truly excellent vintage of Elal Summer Red, on top of a very long stint in the arcanium, that he'd taken so long to bring Alise under his wing.

What if something had happened to him—as when he'd very nearly died during the battle at House Phel—and the location of and access to the Elal arcanium had died with him? He'd actually brushed away a stream of tears from his remaining good eye. That had been a real wake-up call, when he emerged from the worst of his grief and found himself alone. And he'd known he needed to do whatever it took to make Alise his heir. Not for his own sake, but for the sake of the Elal legacy his foolishness and pride threatened to destroy.

And now, he'd found so much happiness with her—and Brinda—and it had become the greatest wish of his heart for them to continue to work together. Alise was everything in a wizard and heir he could hope for. He wanted her to know that, how exceedingly proud he was of her, of her natural talent, her power and proficiency. In truth, he predicted that Alise would someday exceed himself, that she'd lead House Elal to even greater heights. Mostly he wanted her to know how very proud he was of her. He didn't expect her to forgive him anything—he didn't deserve forgiveness, not after how badly he'd behaved—but he hoped she'd understand if he clung to a dream that she'd finally believe, in her heart and mind, how very much she meant to him.

For a time—quite a while, really—Alise had clung to her cynicism, her memory of all that had happened, the things that she knew to be true. There was no alternate perspective to her father penetrating the House Phel arcanium, attempting to steal that magic for himself. That confrontation had led to Gabriel taking his eye, and only because Nic asked him not to kill her father outright.

When Alise mentioned that, her father acknowledged that it had been a terrible time for all of them, but gave it no more weight than that. Hadn't *he* paid a terrible price, he wanted to know? He had and paid dearly. An eye for an eye, and all when his greatest crime had been to fight for House Elal, for all the people beholden to House Elal, and the hundreds of thousands living in Elal proper. He'd been doing his duty as Lord Elal, battling for his life. He was sorry that Nic couldn't forgive him, but he wondered if she didn't bear him some love in her heart somewhere still, as she obviously hadn't wanted him dead. At what point could it be considered that justice had been served and he should be, if not forgiven, at least allowed to go forward without prejudice?

Alise didn't have a good answer to that. As the days wore on, she felt she grew to know her father as a person in a way she never had before. He agreed to let her move out of the tower, admitting that he'd put her there out of fear that she, too, would leave him. As she'd hoped, he enthusiastically agreed to her proposal that she court potential familiars outside of a bed-or-be-bedded scenario. He'd been laboring under false assumptions and truly only wanted the best for her, had hoped that the old adage that the best way to get over someone was to get under someone else. He'd added a bawdy wink that had her laughing, surprised to find herself unexpectedly in sync with him.

Which described the entire experience of being back at House Elal, not as a prisoner or a child or a probationary heir, but as a fully acknowledged heir and… appreciated partner. Every time she earned praise from her father, every time he told her how proud he was of her, of her accomplishments, she felt as if she grew a little taller. He showered her with gifts: more beautiful clothing than she'd ever owned, various fancy tools and instruments to use in the arcanium and out, gorgeously bound books fresh off the Calliope printing press. When she moved out of the tower room, expecting to go to her old rooms, she instead found he'd given her an entire floor of the newest wing.

She didn't know where the various wizard minions who'd occupied those rooms had gone, but no one complained. In truth, everyone she encountered at House Elal greeted her with a new and gratifying deference. After being a social pariah at Convocation Academy, an unwelcome and quickly evicted guest at House Harahel, and always feeling like an extra with no permanent place at House Phel, being treated like a queen at House Elal was, well, kind of nice. Perhaps she *could* make her place there. After all, Jadren had become head of the house of his birth without compromising his values.

It hadn't seemed possible before, but she could see a path forward now. There could be an ongoing conversation with her father, reaching across the differences that divided them and finding mutual consensus. She could be the one to do that. She understood now what her father had been saying to her in the carriage about having the courage and fortitude to lead House Elal forward. He wasn't telling her what to do, simply asking that she accept her birthright and heritage. Once she became Lady Elal, at some point in the future, she'd be well-positioned to ally with House Phel. She could take her revenge against House Hanneil. No one would laugh at her then, or exclude her from their social circles. She'd be too powerful to shun.

And, if she bonded a familiar, she'd never be lonely.

So, she moved into the grand suite of rooms with large windows paned with the finest Byssan glass. Her father encouraged her to decorate and furnish it as she liked because, as his heir, she should have the best of everything and her apartments at the house should reflect that. It was immensely gratifying to return to her own grand suite after a long day in the arcanium, to be greeted by her private staff of servants, and to witness all the changes that had been made in her absence, all to please her. She'd devoted an entire room to housing her nascent library, with comfy reading chairs.

Catching herself wondering how Cillian would like it, she set that thought aside. If Cillian had truly loved her, as her father had pointed out one night as they lingered over a lovely dessert wine, he would have at least sent her a message. Actions spoke louder than words, Piers reminded her with a sad and thoughtful sigh. He might be late to the game, but he was doing everything in his power to show her how much he loved her, how high she stood in his regard.

Alise selected five of the familiars from the ones her father had suggested, the ones she'd liked best, or at least felt some affinity for, and they came to live at House Elal, on the floor below hers. Any leisure time she had—other than the now regular, nightly dinners with her father, when it was only the two of them—she spent with the "boys," as her father liked to call them. They were sweet, attentive, and showed flattering interest in her. For a girl who'd barely even kissed a boy before Cillian, it made for a heady experience. They were all eager to win her, bringing her small, thoughtful gifts, even showing off skills like the one with a lovely tenor voice who sang for her or another who composed charming poetry.

It wasn't a terrible way to live. In truth, other than the long arcanium sessions, which left her rejuvenated with power and preening with pride over her accomplishments, it was leagues better than her grueling schedule at Convocation Academy. No one expected her to prove anything at House Elal, or to make up for past errors or live up to some exacting standard. She could be herself, which turned out to be plenty to earn the admiration of all around her.

In the fullness of time, she'd forget she'd ever thought to want anything else.

~ 16 ~

I T TOOK LONGER than Cillian had estimated or wanted, to get to the bottom of the folded archive. Or the side pockets or twisted-up middle, however you wanted to envision the non-space. Iliana and Han were tirelessly generous, taking turns supplying him with magic, for which he was immensely grateful, even though receiving magic from them was nothing like sharing with Alise.

The invidious comparison kept running around and through his mind to the extent that he had to bite down on the impulse to blurt it out. He was tired, that was all, that was the only reason he was tempted to articulate such an ungenerous observation. He was tired on a level beyond physical weariness, though that was a component. Even after he slept, he woke up unrefreshed. But, more, he felt emotionally exhausted, wrung out from worrying about Alise.

He didn't trust the devious Piers Elal in the slightest, no matter the repeated reassurances from Han and Iliana—the pair sensing his restless anxiety—that Lord Elal wouldn't harm his daughter, that he wanted her for his heir. There were more ways to harm a person than physically. In truth, the physical injuries the world inflicted on a person were the most easily healed and the most transient. Alise's father didn't need psychic ability to get in her head. She was vulnerable to him in ways she possibly didn't realize. If her father figured out to shower her with the love and praise he'd always denied her in the past, she would—

"Is that all of them, Wizard Cillian?" Iliana asked, breaking into his morose fretting. When he focused on her earnest face, she raised her brows. "You've been searching that folded space for a long time without extracting any more books."

She gestured at the shelves of neatly stacked and categorized books that had once occupied the null space. One advantage of having the tag team of the pair of familiars was when one ran low on magic, they could sort the books already recovered, taking over recording the information and indexing that Cillian had been doing before. There were nearly a thousand books recovered, from points all over the last several centuries—including well before the abrupt fall of House Phel—but nothing had jumped out at them as a reason for the house's reversal of fortune. Nor had they found anything that seemed so terrible that a coalition of other high houses had decided to conspire to destroy House Phel and erase their historical record.

"I can't shake the feeling that there's more," Cillian answered Iliana's question, after a long hesitation. "I don't have any good rationale for it, but I'm just sure I haven't found them all."

Iliana scrunched up her nose. "It could be that you feel that way because we haven't identified a particular book as the culprit for all of this, but maybe it's interwoven throughout all these texts."

"*Or,*" Han said from an armchair where he was skimming one of the texts they'd identified as being potentially more relevant than others, "it could be that Cillian's wizard senses are alerting him subconsciously to the presence of more books. We know wizardry works that way sometimes and wouldn't library magic be especially sensitive to something like books?"

"Well, of course it would," Iliana agreed, her forehead still pinched in worry as she side-eyed Cillian, as if he wouldn't notice, "but at some point you have to concede—"

"Defeat?" he filled in when she broke off, abashed.

"That you've done everything you could," she countered with a defiant lift of her chin. "Some tasks, like searching for something you aren't certain exists, are so open-ended that they become infinite. You have to apply your own ending, decide upon a point at which you have diminishing returns for your effort. Otherwise you trap yourself in an endless quest for something you may never find."

Behind Iliana's back, Han lifted his eyes to the ceiling and shook his head.

"But I am certain this thing exists," Cillian argued.

"Are you?" Iliana pounced on that. "Or are you wishing it's so—fastening your hopes on it?"

"Iliana," Han began, a cautionary note in his voice, his striking aqua eyes lingering on Cillian's face with concern.

Cillian lifted a hand in acknowledgment, but he didn't need Han to protect him. He didn't need Iliana to do that either. "I believe some quests are important enough to see them all the way through," he answered. "This is worthy of my effort, no matter how long it takes. If you don't want to continue to provide me with your magic, then—"

"It's not that," Iliana interrupted with exasperation. "I'm not convinced you're being entirely reasonable about this. I worry that you think you're going to find some magical solution that will solve everyone's problems and make you the hero, so you can take it to Alise and she'll…"

Iliana trailed off and Han snorted into the awkward pause. "Neatly trapped yourself with your big mouth there, didn't you?"

She tossed him a glare over her shoulder. "I do not have a big mouth!"

"Loose lips?" he suggested.

"You have reason to know my lips are wonderfully tight," she retorted, then blushed. "Sorry, Cillian."

He pretended he wasn't blushing, too. One day he'd feel more comfortable taking part in the more ribald exchanges of those comfortable in their sexuality, but for now those feelings remained too tied up in the wondrous, almost painfully raw intimate moments he'd shared with Alise that he couldn't manage his reactions. Grief, hope, longing, anger, bitterness, need, love—they all surged against the meager rational control he maintained.

Iliana was right about one thing: Cillian was clinging to hope, probably against all reason. But he could no more let go of it than he could of his love for Alise. That probably made him a fool in anyone's estimation, even his own. "You're not wrong, Iliana," he said, abandoning any pretense at dignity. "And neither are you, Han. I know I'm not being logical."

"No one expects wizards to be logical," Han replied lightly. "You lot are renowned for your dramatic passions. Like Sylus destroying all the world for love and hate."

"Not so much librarian wizards," Cillian pointed out drily, feeling a bit of starch go out of his spine. What in the dark arts did he really think he could accomplish? He'd finished *The Saga of Sylus and Lyndella* and the ending truly had been heartbreaking and romantic in an utterly tragic way. Even though he'd known how it ended, he'd been affected, sharing Sylus's rage over Lyndella's pointless and painful death. "We mainly get fussed if someone dog-ears pages."

Han laughed, but came over, bringing the stack of unusually raggedy-looking bound papers with him, and gracefully lowered himself to the floor beside Cillian and Iliana. Cillian rather envied Han his dancer's athleticism, and his prowess with weapons, and his blond handsomeness that had more than a few of the younger folks—and some older ones—at House Harahel abuzz with delight. Han never seemed to notice, his attention all for Iliana, who now leaned into him as he put an arm around her, cuddling her close.

"Love isn't logical or rational," he said, brushing his cheek over Iliana's shining hair. "We two know that better than anyone. Or we should," he added, setting the stack of documents down and using both arms to squeeze Iliana so she squeaked. "We defied Convocation law because we couldn't bear to give each other up."

"And because we really hate Sabrina Sammael," Iliana put in darkly.

"You would have made the same choice, even if the loveliest wizard in the world wanted to bond me," Han told her.

"Depends on *how* lovely," Iliana retorted with an impudent sniff. "I might've been willing to share."

Han ignored her quip, focusing on Cillian. "I, for one, don't think you should give up." He didn't specify on whether he meant the quest or Alise, but Cillian rather thought he meant both. "There was a time when I thought I'd resigned myself to fate, when I thought I was too tired to keep fighting, that what I wanted had become so impossible that I told myself the smart, wise, *rational* course of action was to give up."

Iliana, leaning against Han's shoulder, had closed her eyes. All pert attitude fled, her face held a quiet pain as she listened.

"Giving up, however," Han continued, gazing down at her and placing a soft kiss on her forehead, so she opened her eyes and smiled at him, "is defeating yourself before you even engage the enemy. Like plunging the dagger into your own heart rather than face your opponent. It could be they'll win, that they'll strike to your heart, wounding or even killing you, but you don't need to do the job for them."

Iliana nodded a little against his shoulder. "I think that's what decided it for me, back when it looked like Sabrina would win. If we went along with her plan, we'd suffer. If we rebelled, there was a chance we'd lose our bid for freedom and suffer—but knuckling under ensured we would. It was worth the risk—and now look what we have."

Han smiled at her fondly, but looked to Cillian, frowning at whatever he saw in Cillian's face. "No?"

"I worry that..." Cillian said slowly, plucking at the documents Han had brought over. The pages weren't finely cut, but slightly uneven, and bound with tape. Not House Calliope printing, but something done by an archivist, possibly even at Convocation Archives, given the meticulous work. Judging by the age of the paper, the documents had been bound a couple of centuries before, but the tape had held, looking only somewhat brittle and lifting barely at all. Of course, the null space tended to preserve texts better, being somewhat timeless. Usually, however, documents like these—often committee meeting minutes and similar records—were only temporarily perfect bound like this. After a sufficient accumulation, they were sent to Calliope for a more permanent binding into a collection. Likely this little batch hadn't made it in with its brethren because it had been secreted away.

"You worry what?" Iliana prompted.

So much easier to think about all things archival than his deepest fears. Maybe he should ditch thoughts of romance and stick with books. No doubt his grandmother would be delighted. But he made himself face the painful truth. "I worry that, even if I find something to take to Alise, that she's... happier—" He almost couldn't say the word "—at House Elal. That, for her, this isn't some choice between a dire fate and supreme happiness. Arguably, she's where she belongs, where she shines. She's always been meant to be Lady Elal."

"But you're in love," Iliana protested.

"I am," Cillian said on a sigh, "but Alise isn't."

"Just because she hasn't said so, that doesn't—"

Han interrupted Iliana with a quiet shushing sound.

"I think that, if she knew, she would have said so," Cillian explained to Iliana and to himself. "But our relationship is so new and we both understood it to be temporary, an alliance of the moment and circumstance. She's young and she shouldn't have to know what she wants yet."

"But—"

"No, Iliana," Cillian felt more certain now, Iliana's arguments solidifying his own. "Alise is a generous, warm-hearted person. I don't want her to feel she needs to accommodate my feelings."

Both Han and Iliana sat silent, the mood glum. "So, how do you want to proceed?" Han finally asked. "Do you want to declare the search of the folded archive done with? We can complete the inventory of its contents and make decisions from there. Begin the comparison list to the Harahel archives. You don't have to go to House Elal and use the favor to make contact with Alise."

No. No, he didn't have to go to Alise. Giving that up might be the most generous move he could make for her. He could ask his grandmother to let him send a courier to Alise with the inventory. If he swore to give Alise up forever, Lady Harahel might lift her sanctions. And then perhaps someday they could return to his original fantasy, the one where he visited her at House Elal, her trusted friend and advisor. As Lady Elal, she would welcome him and they'd talk fondly over their escapades back in the day and exchange news over Bria and other children. Perhaps Alise's children, too—though he couldn't bear to think of that, so he firmly banished that image. He would bring her interesting books, discuss archival trivia, and…

His gaze focused on the bound documents he'd been idly studying. *Committee meeting notes.* Why would those have been hidden away? Cillian always got a tingling sensation when he hit upon what he'd been searching for. Whether plain old intuition or his wizard senses, when he used his magic to index books, looking for the text a patron had described in terribly vague—or horribly incorrect terms—he'd get that feeling that he'd found it, even before he verified.

That tingle roared into excitement as Cillian flipped open the text. *Minutes from the Committee for Verification of Research Results.* This was it. This had to be it. "Dark arts," he whispered.

"I was about to shelve those," Han commented, sounding uncertain. Maybe sounding like he thought Cillian might be losing his mind. "They're minutes from some committee meeting two-hundred and fifty years ago. Lots of Wizard Bumble-Dumble opining on control groups."

"Not just any wizard," Cillian murmured, paging through the notes, his wizardry racing ahead to search for the terms he hoped to find. "The one suggesting that experiments were conducted without proper controls is Wizard Moore Elal. And here." He stabbed at a point on a page, heart racing. "Here is Wizard Anciela Phel's rebuttal. She…" He trailed off, reading. "Dark arts," he whispered.

"What?" Iliana nearly screeched, tearing herself out of Han's loose embrace and bouncing with excitement. "What did you find??"

Cillian looked up at them, in wonder and horror. "House Phel had been conducting independent studies with familiars. They'd found a way to trigger the change in familiars."

"Change?" Han asked, with marked urgency.

Cillian nodded. "To make them into wizards."

<h1 style="text-align:center">~ 17 ~</h1>

T HE THREE OF them sat in stunned silence for a very long time.

"But…" Iliana breathed the word, then licked her lips. "That means—"

"That means they knew hundreds of years ago that familiars weren't doomed to be this this way," Han filled in, a deep and long-buried rage in his voice. "That our inability to wield magic isn't a natural state of being, but instead a correctable malfunction. Do I have that right?"

Aching for them, Cillian nodded. "According to the data Wizard Anciela Phel presented to the committee, yes."

"And they buried it," Iliana said, face and voice hollow.

"They contested the results," Cillian corrected, feeling pedantic.

"The control groups," Han spat.

"Yes. I mean, they're not wrong, but," Cillian added hastily, "that could have been corrected. That's what Anciela brought to the committee. She wanted trials run in the various high houses, to expand the experimental groups and see if they could replicate results. The problem with the scientific approach was that the technique could trigger the ability in a familiar to wield magic, to become a full wizard. There wasn't an obvious control for that."

Han and Iliana stared at him in smoldering rage, as if he'd been the one to decide that. "I'm not defending the committee's debate," he clarified, "just explaining it."

"But, they could have—" Iliana burst out, cheeks bright red, usually warm brown eyes glittering.

"The other houses didn't want to conduct the experiments," Han interrupted, sounding resigned.

"It appears not," Cillian agreed. "I have to read more, but it seems they implemented a number of delaying tactics. Anciela planned to return to House Phel to create a new experimental paradigm. The minutes are quite dry, as you can imagine…" He cleared his throat aware of descending into pedantry again to avoid the extreme emotion of the topic. "But it seems clear that Wizard Phel was exceedingly upset with the committee."

"Good ol' Anciela," Iliana murmured. "And no one even remembers her."

"Erased from history," Cillian agreed. "Along with her research."

"Did they destroy it all?" Han demanded, sliding a look at Iliana.

And Cillian became abruptly and painfully aware of the keen-edged presence of hope in another. Did he nurture that hope, only to risk having it dashed forever at a later point—or kill it now out of mercy and in the expectation that they might find something eventually? *What would you want?* he asked himself. *The truth.*

"We don't know," he said. "It could be it was destroyed as

too dangerous to the status quo."

"What would wizards do without familiars?" Iliana asked bitterly, of no one at all.

"They would be less powerful," Han answered thoughtfully, though they all knew she hadn't been seeking an actual answer. "Converting familiars to wizards would double the population of wizards."

"More like quadruple," Cillian put in absently, skimming the rest of the committee minutes. At their fraught silence, he glanced up. "Is that not well known? The number of familiars has been regularly three to four times as many as wizards, closer to four in the last fifty years or so."

"No," Iliana said. "At school they made it sound pretty close to one to one."

"At least in the classes for familiars," Han added. "No wonder they keep floating the idea of changing the laws so wizards can bond more than one familiar."

"Though with the practice of keeping in-house familiars for general use, like House Sammael planned for me," Iliana replied, "they effectively have that setup but without the bonding."

"I wonder how many wizards have bonded more than one familiar?" Cillian mused aloud, then nearly laughed at their shocked expressions. "Oh, come on—surely you can't be surprised by the suggestion that the high houses might bend or break the law within their own hallowed halls? It's practically Convocation custom to do so."

"I wonder if that's what Sabrina had planned for me." Iliana looked at Han. "That would make a certain sick sense."

"It would," he agreed grimly. "But I want your opinion, Wizard Cillian."

At the sudden formality, Cillian straightened and met Han's gaze. "On whether the experimental design and data were destroyed?"

"Yes. You've been talking about how you believe a Harahel wizard had to create this folded archive and that they might have done so in order to avoid fully destroying the texts. What if it had been a bonded pair? A wizard-familiar partnership might have worked together to subvert the destruction of the data, maybe thinking they'd be able to get it out again, once the conspirators weren't watching so closely."

"Harahel wizards don't work with familiars," Cillian replied automatically.

"*Ever?*" Iliana pressed. "Never ever in all of House Harahel's storied history?"

Cillian gave her a dry look for her exaggeration. "All right, not never ever, but not typically. Let's say rarely."

"And if there was such a pairing, maybe they were in love," Iliana continued, warming to her subject. "The wizard would have wanted the best for their familiar, the same freedom and social status. They could have planned the hidden archive and saved the information, for someday." She cast a longing glance at the middle of the air where Cillian focused when accessing the folded space, as if she could see it for herself.

Cillian didn't point out the flaws in her romantic story, unwilling to rain on her parade—and dash her hopes. "What we can postulate is that these minutes were certainly hidden first or early on. And that House Phel was destroyed by a coalition of other houses in order to suppress this information."

"The Phel library was only partially sunk, though," Han pointed out. "Why not destroy all of it, if they wanted to be sure?"

"A good question," Cillian allowed. "Another question is *how*. How did they manage to suppress magic in the Phel family to bring down the house?"

"And why did it suddenly pop up again in Gabriel and Seliah?" Iliana wondered. "We're always speculating on that."

"Maybe we can answer those questions," Cillian said, thinking. "Han, when did I pull out those bound minutes—today?"

Han uncoiled gracefully to his feet and went to check his ledger. "About two hours ago. Since then you extracted a booklet on wasps and the effect of their larvae on young peach trees, a book of recipes for using dried fall fruits, and a record of the ball gowns worn by the last Lady Phel to various Convocation functions."

"It makes no sense that they hid away such banal stuff," Iliana complained. "Or that any of that information was in Convocation Archives to begin with. Who cares about Lady Phel's ballgowns?"

"Lady Phel did, along with her friends," Cillian answered, unable to help himself. "It was a common practice in that era to note what was worn to society functions so as not to repeat outfits or inadvertently wear the same gown as a friend. They stopped after House Ophiel took over the trademark for all formal wear and, as part of their service, they began tracing style, color, etc."

Iliana gazed at him for a long moment. "Sometimes I worry about how you've spent your life so far, Cillian."

"In the library, nose in a book, thank you." He gave her his version of her impudent nose-wrinkle. "You should try it sometime. You'd be amazed at what you learn from gaining a general knowledge of even what you call banal records. They can give insights into the lives of the people of the time, illuminating that history, revealing layers of meaning that..." He trailed off as the significance struck him.

"Layers of meaning," Han echoed, raising his pale brows.

Iliana looked between them. "What am I missing?"

"It's a code," Cillian said with rising excitement and the certainty of intuition. He seized the slim book of ballgown records, which included sketches of the designs and listing of fabrics used, embroidery, jewels, and other accessories. Even as he scanned the pages with their meticulous detail, he fumbled blindly for another. Iliana put one into his outstretched hand.

"Experimental data on wasp larvae," she said, practically vibrating with hopeful excitement. "Do you think this is code for Anciela's experiments on turning familiars into wizards?"

Cillian tried to train his own wild and hopeful speculations into a rational and clear-headed analysis. "If we go with the theory that the archive was initially created to hide documents out of a desire to protect the Phel records rather than out of malice, then that could make sense."

"Anciela went back to House Phel," Iliana mused, picking up the story thread, "to prove that the other houses needed to test this widely, gathering her data."

"Meanwhile, House Phel became aware of enemies moving against them," Han filled in. "They couldn't have been so naïve as to imagine this discovery would be widely embraced by the Convocation, especially after the committee's reception."

"But Anciela might have believed the committee, at least, would be more invested in knowledge and sharing information than in suppressing it," Cillian added thoughtfully. He would have been like her, blithely trusting his colleagues.

"House Phel would've been a fully staffed house at that time," Han said. "Even if Anciela had been immersed in the research and knowledge side, Lady Phel and her support staff would have been thinking in terms of conflict and how to manage that. They'd have accessed their allies and determined who would support them. Even if they couldn't predict that this would result in the demotion of the house and the destruction of Phel to the point of sinking the manse entirely, they would have known this information had to be preserved and protected. And hidden, just in case."

"Phel took a risk allowing the research in the first place," Cillian agreed, holding up a hand. "I'd have to think they'd have planned for the eventuality that the Convocation would move to destroy the information and suppress all knowledge of it."

"Uriel and Harahel would have helped preserve knowledge," Iliana said staunchly. "Those two high houses have always believed in that."

"And in fairness," Han agreed, holding Cillian's gaze.

"House Harahel would have helped."

Cillian appreciated their faith, and that they took the time to express their confidence in House Harahel. It had bothered him deeply, maybe more than he'd acknowledged, to contemplate some Harahel archivist ancestor working on the side of the conspirators to conceal the books that rightfully belonged in Convocation Archives, violating their sacred charge. This new spin, that the clever and powerful maker of the folded archive had been acting to help House Phel to preserve this crucially important knowledge, instead of working to destroy it. He wasn't sure about Iliana's fanciful tale of the wizard and familiar working together. It seemed a little *too* romantical.

"It makes sense this way," he said slowly. "Though that might be because I want it to. If Phel and Harahel worked together to codify and hide Anciela's data, we still have to account for a few facts we're unsure of. One is that House Hanneil had to have erased memories of all this, especially as they've been actively working to prevent anyone from knowing about this archive. But Hanneil wizards couldn't have continued to add to the folded archive over the ensuing years. You need a librarian wizard for that, and that means Harahel. So why did they continue to hide everything Phel related if they weren't on the side of those protecting the knowledge?"

"I know why," Iliana inserted, nodding so that her fat, fiery braids slithered over her shoulders. "Once things like that get started, they're perpetuated. Who knows what happened to your unknown Harahel wizard, Cillian? They set up that archive, hid the coded information, then maybe had to go into hiding themselves."

"Or were killed," Han said bleakly.

"It sounds like maybe a lot of people died, the memories of their existence erased, and no one left to save their stories," Iliana agreed sadly. "But the Hanneil conspirators could have embedded an instruction in a Harahel archivist of the time to continue the work, since they couldn't be sure if more information had been encoded in books that hadn't been hidden away. I don't know if a Hanneil wizard can do that, but—"

"They can," Cillian assured her, thinking of the compulsion Gordon Hanneil had embedded in Alise's mind. If not for her powerful will and wizardry, she wouldn't have been able to resist it as well as she had. A lesser, milder librarian wizard might not even have been aware of the compulsion. "And that would make sense that they simply stowed everything that came across their desk—or that they found in the stacks— regarding Meresin and House Phel until there was nothing left."

They were all quiet a moment. Then Cillian shook himself. "All of this speculation is worth only so much. What we need is to break the code."

"Don't look at me," Han said. "Iliana is the smart one in this relationship."

Iliana was already shaking her head. "Not that kind of smart. I'm not good at puzzles and riddles. We need someone who is."

"You are, Cillian," Han pointed out.

"Not in the way we need." Besides, Cillian couldn't devote the extended time it would take. More urgently than ever, he needed to get to Alise and tell her what they'd found. "We need someone who can find the key in here."

"Key?" Han echoed blankly.

"A legend," Iliana explained. "There has to be a document—also in code—that explains how to unlock the rest of it, like the letter A means the number one, though it won't be that easy."

Cillian nodded. "And that indicates which texts contain the relevant information to decode, along with a guide for assembling it all back together into one picture."

They looked at the nearly one-thousand texts Cillian had painstakingly extracted from the folded archive. "That will take weeks," Han said. "Maybe months."

"More likely years," Cillian corrected, feeling the same weariness as showed in Han and Iliana's expressions. "And that's if we can find an expert codebreaker."

"You won't like this," Han said, "but I'm worried that we don't have that long."

"House Hanneil." Cillian said it half question, half sigh.

"And the others in the conspiracy. They won't wait to move on House Harahel. I'm surprised they waited this long."

"Do you think it's possible they don't know you've extracted the folded archive and brought it here?"

"It's a possibility," Cillian agreed judiciously, "but I hate to rely on us being that lucky."

"Maybe they thought we wouldn't be able to figure out why these texts were hidden," Iliana suggested.

"Maybe they don't know," Han pointed out with excitement.

"Maybe," Cillian agreed, though doubtfully. "They could be waiting on something else." An uncomfortable thought wiggled to the top of his mind. "House Elal is in the thick of this, too. It could be that Piers Elal is holding them off until…" Until Alise was firmly in his pocket. "I have to go see Alise. I can at least tell her all we've discovered."

"I suppose we can continue the cataloguing and guard these texts," Han said.

"And make copies," Cillian instructed firmly. "I'll get my grandmother to clear it, but I think we can recruit in-house help for that. Also, I'd lay down good coin that many of the texts first hidden away are *not* in the Harahel archives. Those would be the ones to start analyzing for coded information."

"And we need to look for that key," Iliana added, a frown line between her brows. "Do you maybe have any books on codebreaking that I can reference, to see what I should be looking for?"

Cillian laughed. He was far from happy, but the amusement felt good. "Iliana, you are in House Harahel. We have books on *everything*."

~ 18 ~

CILLIAN'S CARRIAGE CAME to a halt at the Elal border. The journey through the Knifeblade Mountains had been riveting, their unusual spires twisting sharply against the sky, the road between them so narrow at times that the precipitous peaks seemed to lean overhead, crowding in and making jagged stripes of the light. He'd never before come this way and had brought several books along that described the history and unique geography of the region, but the scenery was so spectacular, he sometimes forgot to read, the books lying open on his lap while he gazed out the window, enraptured.

The distractions were just as well, as it definitely helped to have something to take him out of his head, pull him out of the endless cycle of worry, dread, excitement, anticipation, and back to worry. He couldn't wait to see Alise again, to see her face light up as he told her of their discovery. But she also hadn't responded to the message his grandmother finally allowed him to send. Lady Harahel had eventually relented in the face of his arguments, though it had taken hours of intense debate to wear her down. He considered it his first real victory where she was concerned.

In her capitulation, Lady Harahel, gave him one of the

Harahel carriages, which—like everything in the house of his birth—was an antique. The leather on the seats had faded from a once rich crimson to a splotchy brown and odd pink, deep creases having cracked in places to reveal the cotton padding beneath. Rather than the stout and flexible specially made Byssan glass windows the Elal carriage had boasted, this one had thick curtains, the velvet threadbare in patches. Despite the cold, Cillian kept them tied back most of the time, in order to enjoy the view and because the carriage smelled strangely of old soup when closed up. He availed himself of lap blankets and the fire elemental in a floor-mounted brazier, which he tried coaxing to greater warmth using Alise's wizardly tricks, with minimal success.

Now that he'd stopped at the notoriously well-guarded border, Cillian wondered what he'd do if they turned him away. His message had given the estimated day and time of his arrival, but with no reply he couldn't be sure if he'd be admitted—he didn't hope to be welcomed—or repelled, perhaps violently. And what he'd do in the latter case? He supposed he'd find out. With his newfound resolve—no more meekly going along for Cillian!—he found the prospect excited, rather than frightened him.

Stepping out of the carriage, he studied the invisible barrier with his wizard senses. Texts on Elal indicated the barrier had first been conceived and erected some several centuries ago, though around a much smaller territory comprising the river valley where House Elal itself was situated. Over time and with strategic land grabs, Elal had expanded to the size of a small kingdom and then to a large one. How the invisible barrier operated remained proprietary information. Given the Elal specialization in spirit magic, however, scholars speculated that it had been extruded from and remained fueled by spirit essences captured and harnessed to the task. So interesting. Maybe Alise would be able to tell him more.

A moment later, a wizard appeared from a cloud of fog— except that Cillian easily saw that the cloaked woman had used a spirit to create that appearance, much as Alise had done before. Alise had managed the trick far more neatly, though, rendering herself invisible rather than having to disguise the spirit as fog. Cillian felt a surge of pride in Alise, so much younger than this Elal wizard minion. Of course, being the equivalent of a doorkeeper at the Elal border wouldn't be a plum job by any stretch.

"Wizard Harahel." The wizard, sporting a gold pin on one shoulder, the House Elal crest of spirits intertwined in a braided circle, tipped back her hood, and scornfully raked Cillian with her wizard-black gaze. "I am Tyrna, wizard to House Elal. Welcome to Elal."

"Am I?" Cillian inquired mildly. "I received no word on whether I was expected."

"You are." She smiled mirthlessly. "Though you are correct that you are not exactly welcome. Lord Elal, however, is interested to interview you, so you may proceed onto our lands. Do not stray from the main road. It will lead you directly to House Elal. You should have no reason to diverge from that path."

"Shouldn't I?" Cillian mirrored her smile, though with far more amusement. "Diverging from the direct route often leads to the most interesting discoveries."

"Spoken like a Harahel," she replied with contempt, black gaze sweeping over the antique carriage. "I recommend against making any discoveries, interesting or otherwise. Also, the roads in Elal are heated and dry. You'll want to exchange those sled runners for wheels. If you have them."

Cillian had been able to see for himself that the snow-packed road ended at the border wall and continued dry from there. "Not a problem, Wizard Tyrna," he replied genially. He raised his brows when she didn't move. "I'll wait until I cross. Wouldn't want to get mired in this snowpack." Indeed, the snow on this side had melted somewhat from the radiant heat that clearly could cross the barrier screen, making it mushy and sloppy. He gave her a little bow that he hoped came across as ironic and just ever so slightly mocking. "Whenever you're ready."

With a hint of an annoyed scowl, Tyrna yanked off her glove and held out her hand in an impatient gesture. Her familiar stepped forward, placing his bare hand in hers. While every wizard needed to touch their familiar to access their magic—with the salient exception of Gabriel and Nic, who were exceptional in so many ways—it surprised Cillian that Tyrna needed her familiar for such a minor magic-working.

Harahel might eschew familiars on the grounds that library work rarely required massive or immediate amounts of magic, but the family also took pride in not relying on a familiar for wizardry. A wizard should be able to function independently, particularly performing magical duties that had become routine. Cillian allowed himself a bit of disdain for the dour

Tyrna who'd tried to look down on him and who couldn't perform this simple task without her familiar.

Tyrna made a complicated gesture with her free hand—another indicator of lazy wizardry, as she shouldn't need physical movement to express her magic—and an opening in the curtain formed.

Cillian, without moving a muscle, directed the air elemental in the carriage to proceed across. "Thank you, Tyrna," he said, then smiled at her familiar. "I don't think I caught your name."

The young man looked startled to be noticed, much less addressed, and smiled back shyly. "I'm Feny, Wizard Harahel."

"Good to meet you both." He tossed off a salute, enjoying Tyrna's scowl as she slammed the barrier shut behind him and swallowed Feny and herself in the fog again. Cillian would bet that parlor trick consumed more magic than opening the barrier had. He took a few moments to trigger the mechanism to convert the runners to wheels—the carriage might be antique, but El-Adrel mechanisms worked like a charm for a long, long time—and then rode on into Elal.

In only a few hours, he would see Alise. Or, at least, he'd be in the same building with her. He could only hope he'd get to see her. And convince her.

CILLIAN HAD, OF course, seen multiple illustrations of House

Elal itself. He wouldn't be *him* if he hadn't done his research. Seeing the manse in real life, however, eclipsed all of his preconceptions.

In the first place, you could easily fit five of House Harahel inside the house at Elal. That became slowly more and more apparent as his carriage drew near. Situated as the manse was in the river valley, its size was initially deceptive, seen from above, but as he descended, the edifice seemed to grow, until it towered overhead. It wasn't graceful and lovely like House Phel, or gothically old-fashioned like House Harahel, but it sprawled, wing upon wing and tower after tower, in a glamorous avalanche of architecture that transcended mere aesthetics.

The carriage trundled across the drawbridge spanning the moat. The fact that it was down and the portcullis—an actual portcullis, like out of fairy tales—up, seemed to be encouraging signs. At least he wasn't physically locked out of House Elal. He patted his shirt pocket, reassuring himself that the favor from Alise remained accessible. He had a feeling he'd need it before this had played out.

As anticipated, more liveried servants silently escorted him not to see Alise, but into what was clearly an office belonging to Lord Elal, the sort where guests would be formally received, particularly of the unwelcome variety. The servants waited for him to choose a seat—he picked a chair where he could study the room—then set a tray of refreshments before him. Shutting the door, they left him alone.

Cillian poured himself tea, eschewing the wine, though it was no doubt an excellent Elal vintage, and nibbled on the cookies provided. They were too dry and a bit on the stale side. No wonder Alise rhapsodized over his baking if she'd been raised on this sort of thing. He did pause, giving thought to whether he should eat or drink, but Lady Harahel had endorsed his visit and Cillian doubted even mighty House Elal wanted to get into a feud with Harahel by poisoning their scion, even a humble one.

Lord Elal kept him waiting over an hour. By then Cillian had formed more of an opinion of Alise's father from how he chose to furnish and decorate this receiving room. Most notably, there were no books. Cillian knew he was odd that way, as was House Harahel, in that he expected all unused wall space to be lined with bookshelves and stuffed with books. Not only that, however, and even more telling, none of the chairs had reading lights situated nearby. Arguably, a room like this wouldn't be used for reading or study, but he found the lack unsettling. In fact, the room contained no reading material at all, or even any interesting art, almost as if it had been designed to torture visitors into boredom.

Fortunately, Cillian was never without. He dug through his book satchel, putting back the texts on the Knifeblade Mountains and Elal countryside, along with the booklet on the ballgowns of Lady Phel long past, which he'd brought to show Alise, after having it copied by an expensive House Xerograf gremlin. At least his conservative grandmother had relented enough on her technological isolation to have one of those creatures on hand. He settled in with a history of House Elal, partly because he hadn't finished it, but also to tweak Piers Elal's nose.

Sure enough, when Lord Elal strode into the room, his one wizard-black eye went immediately to the book Cillian set aside as he politely stood, the man's lip curling in distaste before he studied Cillian, making no pretense of doing otherwise. "So you're the archivist who thought to woo my daughter," he declared without preamble, going to sit behind his desk and indicating the chair in front of it.

Cillian had no intention of sitting there to be interviewed like some supplicant. Instead, he remained standing, folding his hands nonchalantly behind his back as he returned the perusal with interest. Cillian had never had occasion to meet Lord Elal, but he'd been very interested to discover if the wizard's magic would feel like Alise's and Nic's. It did and didn't, the florid rose notes not nearly so predominant, the scent of wine much stronger. Nic and Alise both got their coloring from their mother, so Lord Elal's blond good looks were nothing like his daughters', but something in the haughty lift of the man's chin, the strong cheekbones, reminded him very much of Alise.

"I served as Alise's mentor and independent study project supervisor at Convocation Academy," he said agreeably, as if that had been the question asked. "I understand Wizard Alise is in residence." Or so he hoped. He didn't know what he'd do if that turned out to be incorrect. "Lady Harahel messaged ahead, requesting an audience for me with Wizard Alise." Much as she hadn't wanted to. Another victory for him, convincing her that she had to give him the freedom to prove he'd changed.

"How is Órlaith, that old battle axe?" Elal inquired. The metal patch over his missing eye seemed to be swirling. Some sort of wizardry, no doubt having to do with spirit magic.

"Lady Harahel is in excellent health," Cillian answered politely. "Thank you for asking."

That lip curl again. "Órlaith always did have more balls than any man."

No doubt that was true, but Cillian simply stood, attentively waiting.

Lord Elal huffed out an annoyed breath and stabbed a finger at the chair before his desk. "Sit, sit already."

"I'm comfortable standing," Cillian replied. "Is Wizard Alise on her way?"

"She doesn't want to see you."

Cillian absorbed the stab of pain, acknowledging that it could be true but that Elal had more reasons to lie than not. "I'd rather hear that directly from her."

"Oh, would you *rather*?" Elal questioned, mimicking Cillian's Harahel accent, exaggerating the roll of the R. "Well, I would r-r-rather you ceased wasting my time. If you don't wish to sit and converse like civilized wizards then you can crawl back into whatever dusty tome you crept out of. My heir is a busy wizard and has no time to waste on the likes of you."

Rather than being daunted, Cillian breathed in relief. Alise was here. "Naturally, I await her convenience. I don't wish to impose on her no doubt demanding schedule. When would be a better time for me to meet with her?"

"In the dark arts of *never*!" Lord Elal practically roared. "I know your designs on my daughter, how you attempted to seduce her. You've displayed a surprising amount of ambition for a Harahel bookworm, but it will do you no good. Alise will be taking a familiar and training to become Lady Elal after me. She doesn't wish to see you, ever again, and I support her in that decision."

"I'd prefer to hear that from her own lips."

"I don't care what you prefer, boy. Perhaps you should have thought of that before you had your grandmother send my daughter packing rather than offer her the simplest hospitality at House Harahel. Turning her out without even a meal or a night's sleep, simply because she doesn't trust an Elal." He barked out a bitter laugh. "Well, if Órlaith thinks I'll treat her scion better than she did mine, then she's gone batty over the years. An Elal isn't welcome at House Harahel? Fine then. No Harahel is welcome here. Begone."

Feeling sick, the truth of what had happened while he was unconscious hit him, along with pure fury at his conniving grandmother. The pieces of the puzzle fell perfectly into place, fitting into a seamless whole. Alise hadn't left him, not of her own will. That's why it had never made any sense. His grandmother, Lady Harahel, had given Alise the imperious boot and Cillian hadn't been awake to interfere. No wonder Alise hadn't written him. No wonder she didn't want to see him.

No wonder she'd agreed so readily to save her niece by returning to House Elal with her father. He knew Alise and it would have wounded her to be expelled from Harahel, and then to hear no word from him. Or perhaps he didn't know Alise as well as he thought, as he hadn't figured this out until now.

Piers Elal, following at least some level of Cillian's sequence of realizations, nodded. "So, you see. You will leave and—"

"I'm afraid I can't do that," Cillian interrupted with quiet dignity. It wasn't really in him to stand up to others, especially someone who outstripped him in rank, wealth, and power as Lord Elal did. But this was important. Maybe the most important thing he'd ever do. No matter how it worked out between Alise and him, he had to clear up this terrible misunderstanding. He withdrew the paper from his pocket. Because he'd sealed it with his archivist's magic, the simple note was as fresh and crisp as on the day Alise had grudgingly penned it, her contained fury showing in the bold strokes and slashes of her handwriting. She hadn't meant to grant him the favor, a slip of the tongue in her determination to protect him and get rid of him.

Finally approaching Elal, presiding behind his desk like a king, Cillian came around the side, forcing Lord Elal to turn to face him. He would be no supplicant. Holding the note between his first and middle fingers, Cillian offered it. "Wizard Alise owes me a favor to be determined later. I'm calling in that favor by requesting a private audience with her."

Piers Elal snatched up the note in clear outrage, his face crimson, his magic intensifying as if he'd love nothing more than to reduce Cillian to a steaming pile of goo on the spot. He glared at the note, fuming. "That fucking idiot," he snarled. "Wait until I give her a piece of my mind about this."

"Not until the favor is granted," Cillian reminded him lightly. "I know you wouldn't want your house to be foresworn."

Elal's one good eye glared daggers at him, the metal patch nearly glowing with a swirl of maddened spirits. Then his expression shifted craftily and he made to tear up the note. Nothing doing. In growing rage he summoned a fire elemental to burn the thing, with no greater effect. Cillian watched politely, in mild amusement.

"Archival quality preservation," he finally said, all friendly helpfulness. "Librarians aren't good for much, but we do know how to preserve documents from, ah, tampering."

Elal tossed the note on his desk, lip in that contemptuous curl. "Only you and I know about this. I can have you eliminated."

"And Alise," Cillian corrected, gesturing to her handwriting. "She knows."

"My daughter also knows when to keep her mouth shut."

"Oh," Cillian inserted as if he'd just remembered, "and my grandmother knows, as does all of House Harahel. Why do you think she granted me the introduction to come here? She wasn't any more eager to send me than you are to have me."

Piers Elal gripped the edge of his desk. "You think you've outmaneuvered me, but you are gravely mistaken, book boy. Alise doesn't want you. She'll simply tell you to leave and you will have wasted—wasted!—a favor from House Elal. And you're supposed to be so smart."

A fool for love, Cillian supposed, so he only smiled. "Nevertheless, this is the favor I ask of her."

Lord Elal fumed, but finally threw up his hands. "Fine. You can stay for dinner and see her then."

"I did specify a private audience."

"Which you will have, *after* dinner." Lord Elal smiled in malicious satisfaction. "If you still want to at that point. I advise you to consider otherwise. You might wish to cash in that favor for something better than a conversation that will only disappoint you. Wealth, a sinecure. I understand you were fired from Convocation Academy. Incompetence, was it?"

"I look forward to seeing Alise at dinner," Cillian said, not allowing his resolve to waver. "Shall I remain here until then or…?" He allowed the question to trail off, highlighting Elal's lack of hospitality, for all his blustering about it.

"I should make you wait in the carriage," Lord Elal snarled. "But no, I shall offer what Órlaith couldn't be bothered to do. Likely House Harahel had no spare rooms nor enough food to go around to offer my daughter. I'll do better. You can stay the night. Have dinner. Plead your pitiful case to Alise, then be sent packing in the morning. I'll enjoy seeing you creep off after my daughter shows you the road."

Cillian figured that was as likely an outcome of any.

~ 19 ~

I T HAD BEEN a long day, but a rewarding one. Alise had mastered a new skill and felt terribly pleased with herself. It had helped that her father had left her alone in the arcanium for a time, giving her the opportunity to experiment with trial and error without his forbidding presence.

Yes, he'd become far more free with praise, but he was also quick to point out her mistakes. Professor Cixin, in particular, had extolled the virtues of making mistakes, saying one learned more from failures than from successes. And learned she had from those many failures, then found the way through. Feeling accomplished, Alise sipped her wine, enjoying the company of her boys, the musician among them playing a new tune, the others keeping up quiet conversation in a demure, undemanding way that allowed her to listen or not. She could live this way. It wasn't a bad life. She nearly laughed at herself for the thought as she allowed her gaze to travel over the luxurious, even ornate smaller dining room for intimate family. "Intimate" meaning the table sat twelve easily. Though only the six of them currently nibbled at the hors d'oeuvres course, two more place settings awaited more company. One for Lord Elal, assuredly. Alise idly wondered if the other was for Brinda or some guest of her father's.

For all but a few of the people in the Convocation, her current opulent lifestyle exceeded anything they could imagine, let alone hope for. She was privileged, lucky to have all of this, and she needed to appreciate that. Never mind that she hadn't chosen it. Strike that. She had made a choice. She'd known the stakes and consequences when she agreed to accompany her father back to House Elal. In truth, she'd fully expected to be miserable, a tormented prisoner as she'd been initially. But, once her father saw the error of his ways and began treating her like a real member of the family, like his heir and colleague… Well, everything had obviously gotten much better and she should be happy.

She *was* happy.

Or, at least, content.

Satisfied.

She didn't really understand why, under it all, the restless misery persisted.

You miss Cillian, a tiny voice inside whispered, quietly, but so insistently that she couldn't ignore it. All right, fine. She drew out the feeling and let it sit, probing the pain of missing him like checking a bad tooth, the responding twinges shockingly sharp. Deliberately, she studied each of her boys, all so reminiscent of Cillian yet none able to hold a candle to him. Noticing her attention, they each smiled warmly in return, sitting up straighter and preening for her. Of course, they were all familiars and so they couldn't compete with a full wizard. That wasn't their fault; they were all perfectly fine people.

Still, they weren't him, and Alise fought a sense of drowning despair that she'd forever feel the lack of Cillian in her life. Maybe if she could see him one more time, she could get over him. Surely he hadn't been all that sweet. He'd flown into a rage once and he could be cranky. He'd been an absolute pill in the carriage on the flight to House Harahel, not to mention that he'd never bothered to write to her. Yes, if she could see him again, she'd recognize he'd been a passing crush during a difficult phase of her life, she decided, sipping her delicious wine. She wouldn't feel this—

Crushing shock scattered every thought as the door opened and Cillian walked into the room.

Alise actually choked on her wine, bobbling the glass and spilling the crimson down the front of her pale gown. The nearest of her boys leapt to her in concern, patting her back and taking the glass from her hand. Another scurried to a side cart to get a towel to clean up the spill. Two others exclaimed in dismay and the musician stopped playing in a horrified, discordant strum.

The happy smile Cillian had worn walking into the room fell away. He stopped there, at the far end of the long dining table and stared, his gentle black eyes going cool as he took in his five near-doppelgangers. Alise flushed with shamed embarrassment. Feebly—because she was still choking on the wine and had yet to draw in a full breath—she batted at the boy trying to help her. The familiar who'd fetched the towel returned with that and a bowl of iced water, dabbing solicitously at the broad stain on her bosom, clucking in distress, even though she tried to get him to stop also. Cillian observed both her half-baked efforts and those of the two familiars with chilly cynicism.

Yeah, all right. It looked bad.

Her father stepped into the dining room behind Cillian, looming over the shorter and slighter wizard, his smirk at Alise's discomfort clear on his face. Several realizations slammed home in that moment and she struggled to assimilate them all at once, not easy while trying to suck in a breath and squirm away from the two attentive familiars.

Cillian had come for her.

Her father delighted in her misery.

She'd been a fool.

If withering away to slide under the table in a puddle of ectoplasmic goo was an option, she would have seized it without hesitation. Feeling the contempt in Cillian's unrelenting gaze, seeing the expression of jaded betrayal on his face that a heart as pure and noble as his should never experience, Alise wanted nothing more than to disappear.

Cillian's frozen hesitation evaporated and he made to turn, as if to immediately leave, but Piers clapped a meaty hand to the librarian wizard's shoulder, stopping him. "Don't run, boy. We set a place for you to have dinner, so you don't want to waste that. And here is Alise, as you demanded. Plead your case."

He steered a now unresisting Cillian to a chair before one of the empty place settings, the lookalike familiars giving him a friendly smile that Cillian couldn't seem to muster to return. Alise's father raised his brows at her, fulminating anger boiling through his magic and looking to her like crimson bubbles forming around him and popping to shower lava-like drops.

"This nobody of a wizard has something of yours," he informed her in silky tones. A small gremlin appeared, snatched a card of some sort from Cillian's fingers and ran it down the table to her.

Oblivious to the fraught undercurrents, several of the familiars laughed. Alise had finally managed to clear her windpipe. "I'm fine," she told the ones hovering so embarrassingly. "Leave me be."

They looked like wounded puppies at her sharp tone, but obeyed immediately, settling back into their chairs. Cillian observed that, too, looking from one to the other, then returning his acid-drenched gaze to hers in patent disgust. She tried not to wither beneath that unflinching inspection, keeping her spine straight and chin high, taking the card from the gremlin with as much dignity as she could muster.

She read it, not quite able to comprehend its meaning at first, blinking as though focusing her vision was the problem though she could see just fine. Her handwriting. Promising Cillian a favor to be named later. With a spiraling sensation, she remembered that night, her desperation to protect him, to push him away, how she'd recklessly offered a favor and how he'd asked her to write it down. Always the record-keeper. And he'd sealed it with his archivist magic, the paper encased in a perfect magic shield. She'd forgotten about it entirely, never once dreaming he'd use it against her.

Lifting her gaze from the note, she found Cillian's eyes boring into her. "I decided to call in the favor, Wizard Alise," he said with distant formality. "As you can see."

Dumbly, she nodded, still holding the note with numb

fingers. "To have… dinner with me?" she squeaked. It didn't seem likely. Armed with the power of a favor like that, Cillian could have requested House Elal provide him with an army and a fortune. No wonder her father was so enraged.

Piers had seated himself at the other end of the table, at the head, eating from a plate he'd already filled. Or that someone had filled for him. She couldn't quite look directly at her father. With Cillian three people down and to the side of her, she could keep her line of sight angled away. Dealing with her father's repercussions would come soon enough.

"No, not to have dinner with you," Cillian answered slowly, as if she were dense. "Lord Elal was gracious enough to invite me to stay for dinner and to rest the night here."

Her father grunted, making his level of graciousness abundantly clear. "The boy wants a private audience with you, Daughter," he said, every word ripe with disappointment. "I calculated that it's a small enough price to pay for something that could have cost us a great deal more."

She knew it. But what was Cillian's game, coming here now, calling in that favor? It wasn't like him to use something like that—something they both knew had been part of a much more intimate exchange than a negotiating token between high-house scions—as political leverage. Unless Lady Harahel was behind this. Briefly closing her eyes to clear her mind, she opened them again and made herself face Cillian squarely.

"Of course I'm happy to grant you a private audience, Wizard Harahel. Since you're only staying the one night," she added, figuring it couldn't hurt to repeat that stricture, lest he get ideas about remaining underfoot, "shall we discuss after we eat? Unless you'd prefer morning, before you leave."

She maybe didn't need to say that last bit, as Cillian gave her another of those long, cool looks, clearly communicating that he saw right through her. Well, she didn't care if he did. He'd been the one to lie about his grandmother's rank—even if only by omission—and he'd never tried to reach out to her before this oh-so-convenient calling in of the favor he'd manipulated her into writing down. Really, this current ploy called into question their entire relationship. Maybe Cillian *had* been using her. His unswerving attraction to and pursuit of her had never made much sense. Alise knew full well she was no raving beauty, with her odd face and boyish figure. Cillian certainly possessed the brains for this kind of long-term strategy, and the fact that he'd concealed his lineage went a long way toward calling his motives into question. Maybe he'd been more conniving in that relationship with Szarina than he'd made out.

Maybe Szarina had been the smart one, to use him first, before Cillian could use her in whatever scheme he and his house had planned. Well, as her father had been reminding her, House Elal had thrived all these centuries through cleverness and healthy suspicion. The Convocation was a competitive and often cutthroat society. Wizards didn't share power if they could help it, and apparently even benign houses like Harahel carried on with deep agendas, their own interests always in mind.

"No time like the present," Cillian remarked. "After supper would be ideal."

"Fine," she replied. To show it didn't matter at all to her, she reached for her wine glass, then paused, having forgotten she'd spilled it all down the front of her gown. So much for regal dignity. One of her boys hastened to fill the glass, murmuring an apology. Cillian tracked the interplay, raising a brow and smirking at her. She didn't care what he thought.

In the morning he would be gone and she wouldn't have to bear witness to the condemnation in his eyes. She'd told him from the beginning that she had no good in her. What she did have was a healthy portion of Elal wiles. If Cillian thought to shame her into playing along with whatever House Harahel wanted, well he'd discover just how hard she could be.

Better for him to learn that as soon as possible and depart, leaving her to her fate. Her glass filled, she toasted him with it, then looked away, not quite able to bear the brutal knowing in his face. Yes, better for him to know the worst of her and go away. Forever.

~ 20 ~

CILLIAN DIDN'T KNOW exactly what he'd expected to find when he finally laid eyes on Alise again. Being who he was, he'd naturally spun a few fantasies of their reunion. He was no raging Silas and Alise was definitely no fragile, helpless Lyndella, but he'd still leaned heavily in the direction of storming in to find Alise weepingly grateful to see him, perhaps rushing into his embrace. He'd imagined holding her tightly, murmuring to her that she was safe now, that everything would be all right.

Alise seated at the opulent dining table, radiant with magic and elegantly gowned and jeweled, being fawned over by a group of male familiars, had never entered his imagination.

He made himself eat, mostly because it gave himself something to do to pass the time, which moved with excruciating slowness. Alise had been rattled by his sudden appearance, and not at all pleased by it. He'd anticipated surprise on her part, figuring her father wouldn't have prepared her, but not the look of sheer horror on her face. She was drinking more wine than she was eating food, the idiot beside her refilling her glass far too often and liberally.

Lord Elal ate in glowering silence, the five familiars at the table carrying on pleasant conversation for all of them, determinedly filling the fraught silence like it was their job. Probably it was.

Surreptitiously, Cillian studied the five young men. Was it just him or did they all look rather unsettlingly like… well, himself? That could be vanity on his part, or maybe Alise had settled on a type, but all five were slender with dark hair and gentle demeanors. As familiars, their eye color varied, but otherwise they could be his brothers. None of them were bonded to her, his wizard senses told him that much. So why were they there?

He suspected he wouldn't like the answer, but asked the question anyway, posing it as a general inquiry to the table, whether they were general familiars for House Elal or…?

"Oh no, Wizard Harahel," one answered with shy enthusiasm.

No one had offered their names, which seemed perfectly in line with Lord Elal's fulminating disdain for all of them, but was out of character for Alise. She, however, seemed to have retreated to some internal landscape, her face nearly blank, gaze turned inward as she mechanically ate and drank—still mostly drank. Cillian decided to mentally call them by the names of the five identical brothers in the children's tale: Wim, Bim, Tim, Gim, and Zim. The one who'd answered him became Wim.

"None of us belong to House Elal," another of the familiars chimed in—Bim—then slid his gaze slyly to Alise, "… yet."

The one who'd been attentively refilling Alise's glass, Tim, gave Cillian a sweet smile. "We're all hoping that someday

Wizard Alise will choose one of us to be her bonded familiar."

"Ah, congratulations in advance then," Cillian replied. "May I?" He held out a hand for the wine carafe, adding a small amount to his own glass and deliberately setting the carafe down again on his other side, well out of reach. Sipping, he hoped to swallow the bitterness of knowing Alise was auditioning familiars. That had been the logical explanation for the little scene, and Cillian had obviously known that Alise would eventually bond a familiar. She possessed far too much potential as a wizard to hamper herself by not having one.

Still, he hadn't expected her to move that direction so soon. And not in this distasteful fashion. With what he had to acknowledge as jealousy, he contemplated that she might have been testing them out in bed, too.

The familiar holding an instrument, Gim, strummed a thoughtful chord, glancing at Alise for a reaction, though she noticed that no more than anything else since she'd retreated inside her head, then turned his attention to Cillian with speculation in his thoughtful gaze. "Do you have a bonded familiar, Wizard Harahel?"

Before he could answer, Alise made a snorting sound, proving she was paying attention after all. "Sainted High House Harahel doesn't employ familiars, do they, Wizard Cillian?"

"No such thing as a library emergency," he replied, enjoying that she at least flushed slightly at the reminder of their running joke. "Speaking of which," he said, pushing his empty plate aside, "are you finished eating, Wizard Alise? If so, we can proceed to wherever you'd like to have this conversation."

She met his gaze, the burn of betrayal in hers. Oh, she was not at all happy to see him. Fine then. No matter how this went, they'd at least have it out, once and for all. She stood, carrying her wine glass. "Yes, let's get this over with."

"Would you like one or more of us to attend you, Wizard Alise?" Zim, who'd been quiet so far, asked deferentially.

Cillian cocked his head at the promise she'd discarded by her plate.

"No, thank you. A private audience was requested and I shall abide by my written word." She said the words with plenty of bite, speaking them entirely to Cillian. "Good night, Father."

He took his attention from his plate long enough to give her a speaking glare, which he transferred to Cillian. "Be smart about this, Daughter," he advised. "Remember what's at stake."

"As if I could forget," she replied crisply, then led the way out of the dining salon. Cillian followed behind, eyes on her rigid spine and the soft hollow at the nape of her neck that her short haircut revealed. Despite everything, he wanted to kiss her there. Truthfully, he wanted to bend her over and kiss her there, while pulling up that sheer gown to reveal her perfect ass. He wanted to kiss her all over until her scent covered him, until he smelled her at odd moments on his body, unexpectedly, and in many different places.

He hadn't expected this deep, sexual ache in her presence, this edged craving to have her against him, skin to skin, to slide into her warm and willing sheath, to lose himself in her. He'd always been more a person of the mind than the body, easily forgoing sex for periods of times so long as he had a project to focus on, and particularly after Szarina and that terrible legacy of the passion he'd once felt for her. But around Alise, with her magic twining all around him like sun-warmed roses blooming in hot sunshine, their vines entangling him and thorns piercing him to the quick... He could only think of having her naked and in his arms again, of being inside her and hearing her whimpers in his ear.

Not the most productive frame of mind for what promised to be a logistically difficult conversation.

Alise led them to a smallish salon, not her father's office, but some room in what felt like a different wing. One of the fifteen discrete wings of House Elal, his memory—made eidetic by his library wizardry—informed him relentlessly. One of one-hundred and ninety-three separate rooms in the sprawling complex, at least according to the most recent history, and not including bathing rooms and outbuildings, or hidden spaces.

Alise prowled directly into the room and stopped pointedly in the center, holding her wine glass with false insouciance, tapping one toe in clear impatience and obviously disinclined to sit. So, Cillian took care of the niceties, closing the door, triggering the Iblis lock with a flick of magic, then imposing a privacy shield around the room.

She raised a sardonic brow. "I thought 'private' was a euphemism. Is this a conversation or...?"

"A private conversation," he replied, going closer to her, but not so close as to drive her away. Still, he had no intention of standing across the room from her and shouting. "Do we have eavesdroppers?"

"You *are* in House Elal," she answered, unrelentingly unhelpful.

He took that to be a confirmation of what he suspected, that spirit spies watched them regardless. "Then I formally request you ensure the privacy of the audience that your favor grants me."

Her delicately winged brows forked down in irritation. "Must you?"

"Yes." He kept it simple. He also knew banishing any spies lay well within her capabilities. Holding her gaze, he waited for her to comply. If her father listened in even now, he would know Alise had abided by the agreement his house was bound to honor. That wouldn't make Lord Elal any less angry, but Cillian had come all this way, had put both of them in danger for this conversation. He wouldn't pull any punches now.

Still glaring at him, Alise unfurled her magic, the pure tendrils of it snaking through the enclosed space as she calmly sipped her wine. No dramatic gestures for her or giving any appearance of effort. As Cillian had no spirit magic to speak of, he couldn't sense exactly what she did, but he knew she'd cleared the room because she raised her brows expectantly. She had grown in skill and power, exponentially.

"Well?" she prompted with considerable impatience. "You wanted this conversation so badly you cashed in an invaluable favor for it—though why now after all this time, I have no idea—so you might as well start talking."

"Can we sit?" he asked gesturing to the nearby chairs and settee.

"I'd rather stand, thank you," she bit out.

"I'd rather sit." He picked a spot on the settee where he could see her. Thought about where to start. As many times as he'd imagined this moment, none had included this formal awkwardness, his mind going completely blank.

"I suppose there's no time limit on this audience," Alise commented drily, "but if we're to spend it in silence, I'll want more wine."

"You never used to drink so heavily," he commented.

"I didn't used to need to," she retorted, then flushed, clearly annoyed with herself for admitting that much. "Elal is famed for our wines," she added defensively. "It's a perk of being in the house of my birth."

"Has it been very bad, Alise?" he asked softly, his heart aching for her. She was doing her best to drive him away again. She might succeed this time, but he wouldn't go easily.

"What do you care?" she snapped, draining the last of her wine and casting about for more. When she saw there wasn't any, she gripped the stem, ticking the glass back and forth like a pendulum.

"I care," he told her. "I've always cared. You know that."

"Do I? You have a funny way of showing it. Not one word in all this time."

"My grandmother prevented me from communicating. She wouldn't allow me to contact you, or anyone outside House Harahel. When she finally relented, I sent a message to you here at House Elal to tell you I wanted to visit. And then that I planned to. I imagine you didn't receive it."

She didn't acknowledge that with even a blink, instead

pouncing on something else. "About that, your *grandmother*. How is it that you somehow neglected to mention that she's the head of House Harahel?"

"It was wrong of me not to tell you that, it's true. I thought I had time to explain. I apologize."

"Apology *not* accepted." But some of the fire went out of her at his admission anyway.

"It never mattered to me, my grandmother's rank." he explained slowly, searching for the right words. "Harahel isn't like other high houses. To my mind, she has always been simply my grandmother and I'm just another moderately talented librarian wizard. Her heading the house had no relevance most of the time."

"Until an Elal scion has the temerity to arrive on her doorstep unannounced and uninvited, at which point she breathes fire as well as any high house head."

"I apologize for that, too, Alise," he said, pouring his earnest regret into the words. "I didn't know she'd done that until just recently. It never occurred to me that she'd treat you so badly, that she'd force you to leave. I was as shocked to discover the truth as anyone."

Alise gave him an exaggerated look of disbelief. "Then, what? You thought I just dropped you off and left? That you were on the brink of death from carrying that archive and that I'd nearly killed myself getting you to Harahel, in the midst of nowhere, and then went tra la, tra lay, I guess I'll just go." She widened her eyes as she took in his expression, then threw back her head in a bitter laugh. "Oh, you did think that. How galling."

"I didn't know—" he began, but she cut off his words.

"No, you didn't know, but you assumed. I see now. You leapt to the conclusion that I'd just leave you, even after all we'd been through. That my word meant nothing to me, that our relationship meant nothing. You thought I was just another Szarina, that I'd gallivanted off without a note or a backward look now that you'd served your purpose." She swigged from the empty wine glass, clearly forgetting she'd emptied it. Glared at the dregs. "Well, fuck you, Cillian. Fuck you for that!" She nearly screamed it, then hurled the glass at the stone fireplace.

She'd surprised them both and they stared together at the point of impact, as if expecting something more. Cillian slid her a careful glance. "I suppose it was your turn," he commented, remembering how he'd thrown a plate at the wall in a similar fit of rage.

A high flush gracing her cheekbones, she folded her arms, wizard-black eyes snapping, the scent of her wine-red magic deepening to a scorching redolence. "It was more surprising coming from you," she said like an accusation, "Lord Mild-Mannered Librarian."

"We seem to bring out intense passions in one another," he admitted. "I'd never done anything like that before."

"This is a first for me," she admitted on a sigh, her gaze resting on the fireplace in a bleak stare. "Cillian..." She let out another long breath. "*Why* are you here?"

"May I approach the bench?" he asked carefully, and she rolled her eyes at him.

"Fine, I'll sit." But she chose the other end of the settee, curling up like a cat with her back against the arm rest, drawing her knees up and resting her chin on them, eyes large and black in her drawn face. With the gorgeously embroidered and sparkling gown pooled around her and that wistful expression, she looked like a little girl playing dress-up—an impression only enhanced by the red stain on the bodice from her spill—and an analogy he'd never speak aloud as she'd no doubt hate it. But he wanted to pull her onto his lap and comfort her, knowing he couldn't yet, not with that anger burning in her still. Instead he pulled up a knee and turned sideways to face her.

"I am here to rescue you," he told her, well aware of how absurd and grandiose that sounded. But it was true and he felt saying anything else would be a prevarication.

Her lips parted and she shook her head slightly, breathing a laugh. "Always the white knight."

"Guilty." He searched for something more to say, to mitigate that. "But in complete sincerity. I know you're not here of your own free will, Alise."

"But I am."

"I heard what happened at Bria's naming, and I'm more sorry than I can say that I wasn't there with you. I know you agreed to come here to protect her."

"Of my own free will," she insisted. "No, Cillian. You can't argue that with me. I made an agreement with my father with my eyes wide open and dozens of witnesses. I'm not a prisoner here." She hesitated over that, for some reason, making him wonder, but she plowed on. "I'm learning from him. I'm his heir as you always said I should be."

"I said you should be Lady Elal if you wanted to be," he felt compelled to clarify, "not that you should become your father's creature."

Her mouth fell open and she straightened. "My father's creature—is that what you think I am?"

"Are you saying you're not?" he fired back, the decadent scene in the dining salon roaring back into his mind with full force. Never mind that Lord Elal had clearly engineered that little scenario, wanting Cillian to see Alise in that setting. She'd still been fully immersed in it.

"You have no idea what I'm trying to do here," she gritted out. "No idea what this is like for me."

"That's why I asked," he pointed out, as reasonably as he could manage, which admittedly wasn't very. "Almost the first thing I asked you was how you're handling this."

"No, you *assumed*," she emphasized the word, sneering, "that it's been bad."

"A reasonable assumption, you have to admit," he retorted.

"Why, because Harahel hates Elal?"

"Alise."

She shoved her fingers into her blue-black hair, clenching and pulling, baring her teeth in a grimace. "Oh, *why* did you come here?"

"I—"

"How did you even know where I was if you've been so isolated and incommunicado?" She demanded, interrupting him again and springing up to pace. Spinning, she pointed an accusatory finger at him. "Nic told you, didn't she?"

"No," he answered. "Actually—"

"Because she has no business interfering in my life! You can tell her to stop sending me couriers. Live her life. Raise Bria. Be happy. That's what she needs to do. That's the whole point of this…This…" She cast about the room as if the word would offer itself.

"Sacrifice?" he suggested. "Martyrdom?"

"You're not funny," she replied sourly.

"I was dead serious. How *would* you describe this?"

"A savvy career move," she shot back, looking triumphant.

He couldn't help it. He burst out laughing.

~ 21 ~

Alise's face heated at Cillian's laughter. Maybe she'd overstated the case, but he didn't need to be so morally superior. So patient and understanding. So fucking sweet. Of course almost the first thing he asked when they could speak privately was about her wellbeing.

Has it been very bad, Alise? The bald question had nearly made her break into tears. Only reminding herself of her father's fury—and righteous retribution in the very near future—had allowed her to regain some control. He'd never forgive her for banishing his spies, whether or not she'd been honoring house integrity by agreeing to the strict terms of Cillian's favor redemption. The price for her giving Cillian that favor to begin with would be high indeed, and anticipating her father's punishment made the sweat drip chill down her back.

A tremulous part of her kept expecting her father to knock down the door at any moment, but if he hadn't by now, he wasn't going to. No, he'd save her punishment for later, until after Cillian had gone and she was alone again. She didn't seem to have much spine on her own. Worse, her father seemed to know that, easily bending her to his will. She'd been molded into the kind of daughter he wanted now. Sensitive to his desires and priorities, attuned to even his unspoken wishes, always just a little bit afraid. Not exactly broken, but too far distorted to be returned to her previous shape.

"I'm sorry, Alise," Cillian gasped, recovering. "I didn't mean to laugh. Please come and sit."

She hadn't been aware of standing, but she stayed on her feet, the nervous energy propelling her into agitated circles around the salon. She needed to complete and end this conversation.

"If Nic didn't tell you, how did you know where I was?" Part of her, some romantic remnant she once would have scoffed at, imagined Cillian searching for her. Going to Convocation Academy or House Phel, hoping to find her. *Well, he's found you now,* a jaded voice said in the back of her mind. *And you sure aren't rewarding him for the trouble.*

Well, no, but then she was a terrible person, so no one should be surprised.

"It's a long story," Cillian answered, patting the settee invitingly. "And telling you about it is part of why I'm here."

"I'd rather stand." She moved restlessly to the window.

"And pace."

"Yes."

He sighed. Cillian had a range of expressive sighs, all evocative of various shades of disappointment in her. "Han and Iliana told me."

She paused mid-step. Not at all what she expected. "I don't understand. You went to House Phel?"

"No," he replied gravely, holding her gaze. "They came to House Harahel."

She was sorry she wasn't sitting, feeling suddenly wobbly, the sense of the world having rushed onward while she was sequestered here making her dizzy. Probably she shouldn't have drunk so much wine. "I don't understand."

As the words came out, she realized she'd repeated herself. Dark arts she was a mess. She both fervently wished Cillian would leave already—or, ideally, that he'd never come—and wanted to throw herself into his embrace and beg him to make everything better. Except there was no better. This was as good as she could have, which was why she'd been making the best of it.

"Then let me explain," Cillian said gently, as if intuiting her inner turmoil. Probably he did. He told her about the bargain he'd made with his grandmother once he recovered from the impact of the magic debt—which made her realize she'd been so busy being angry and ashamed that she hadn't asked about his health or anything about what he'd been doing. Which had been single-mindedly working on unlocking the folded archive. For her.

By the time Cillian finished telling her about the code embedded in the archived texts, the earth-shattering implications of the research of the ancient Phel scientist, Alise had relented, returning to curl up on the settee—though still a cautious distance from Cillian. She had no idea where they could go from here, except that it seemed blatantly clear that they couldn't go back to how things had been. It might be best to allow the break between them to stand, perhaps bridged with a distantly formal acquaintanceship. Nothing more.

"I brought this to show you," he said, the light of enthusiasm shining from him as he dug in his satchel. At times like this, when he talked books and libraries and linguistics, his magic looked to her like sunlight dappling through shadows, illuminating odd nooks, glancing over dust motes so it seemed to make them dance. It hit her hard and painfully how very much she loved him. Numb from the realization, she reviewed the ancient committee meeting minutes and listened with dawning understanding to the shocking information contained within. Of course, only a secret as Convocation-shattering would embolden so many houses to conspire, to move against House Phel in such a thorough, dedicated, and far reaching plan.

Her mind racing, her stomach tight, she accepted the various booklets from Cillian's hands, pretending to look at them while he excitedly explained how the code probably worked and how they'd determined there was one and what Han and Iliana were doing next to decipher it.

After a while, she found herself simply studying his face as he bent over the materials he'd brought, his long, sensitive fingers pointing out particular elements, watching his lips move and hearing nothing. She'd been such a blithering idiot. Somehow, in Cillian's grounding, rational presence, her world shifted and resettled into new patterns. The picture that emerged as if seen from his perspective only shamed her further.

She'd been pretending to herself that she was going along with her father, lulling him into complacency, and planning some vague vengeance when all the while he'd been playing her, softening her with praise and gifts and luring her into being exactly what she'd always feared most, what she'd promised herself she would never become: just like him.

"Alise?" Cillian set a hand on her cheek, a fleeting touch that only made her crave more. And more is what she couldn't have.

"This is an amazing discovery," she said, trying to sound excited. And it was amazing and she was excited. So why did she feel like her heart was breaking? "Have you told Gabriel and Nic yet?"

"No." Cillian frowned a little, seeming puzzled. "I wanted to tell you first. This was your project. I knew you'd want to be in on next steps."

And there was the rub. She couldn't be "in" on anything but her commitment to House Elal. She wasn't a prisoner, exactly, that much of what she'd told Cillian had been true, but neither was she free. And they both knew where Elal stood in this conspiracy to suppress such dangerous information. She was suddenly, fiercely glad Cillian had asked her to banish the spirit spies. The moment her father knew about what they'd found, he'd explode. He'd kill Cillian—a small transgression compared to the violence to come—and possibly her as well. She should be so lucky.

"What are the next steps, do you think?" she asked, rather hoping he wouldn't notice that she'd sidestepped his assumption on her involvement.

"We need to take this evidence to the Convocation. We have proof here of grounds for the original conspiracy against House Phel and the ongoing targeting of the house and you."

Alise didn't think they did, but she nodded with enthusiasm. "I think you should take this to House Phel and find out how Nic and Gabriel want to proceed."

"I know that's your first impulse and not a wrong-headed one, but I think it's time to escalate. Provost Uriel told me to bring her evidence and I've got it. House Uriel is our best bet for—" He paused, his ears catching up to his thoughts. "*I* should take it? You mean *we*."

And there they were. "No, I mean you. I can't leave here."

His frown crystallized. "You said you're not a prisoner."

"Maybe I should say I won't leave. I am the House Elal heir now. My father is teaching me everything. I have access to the House Elal arcanium. Working in it is… extraordinary."

"And you're auditioning familiars," he noted darkly. "Are you seriously considering Wim, Bim, Tim, Gim, and Zim?"

The names rang a bell. It came to her. "From the Five Idiot Brothers of Nod?" she asked incredulously.

Looking vaguely embarrassed, he waved that off.

"It's unlike you to be cruel, Cillian," she said softly, "especially to those less fortunate than you."

He met her gaze steadily, not denying it. "At the moment, they don't seem less fortunate, at all."

Ah. That paused her breath a moment. "My father has persuaded me of the potential usefulness of a familiar, yes." She watched his face, the shifting emotions, her heart aching. "Cillian, if House Elal is one of the conspirators against House Phel, as we both know is almost certainly true, we are now on opposite sides. I can't assist with this."

"What about being on the side of truth," he demanded. "Don't you want to be on the right side of history?"

"Those are relative concepts," she replied, aware that she used her father's reasoning. "Think about it, Cillian: if this information about familiars having the potential to become wizards comes out, it will upend the Convocation. It could cause all out war. Is that being on the 'right' side?"

"You'd rather we allow a deeply unjust, predatory social system to continue in the name of a surface peace?" he demanded in turn.

"I think it's more than surface," she countered. "We don't have the raging and devastating wizard wars of long ago. Most of our citizens are prosperous and enjoy decent lives. The current balance has existed for a long time for a reason."

"Because it's built on the backs of familiars," Cillian retorted. "People like your own sister who could be wizards if they hadn't been stunted."

"It introduces bias to use words like stunted. We don't know that it's not a natural process and that Anciela Phel's discovery wasn't flawed in some way. That's why the committee wanted more research. What if this reversal or unblocking or whatever causes even more damage, like my dissolving of the bond did?"

"It would be worth it to find out," Cillian insisted. "If there's a way to liberate familiars from the restraints that make them second-class citizens, we owe it to them to make that possible."

"Do we? I don't see that we owe anyone anything. I certainly don't. What you do is up to you."

He gazed at her for a long, throbbing moment. "I feel like I don't know you anymore."

There was her opening. "You don't," she said baldly, steeling herself against his flinch, the hurt in his eyes. "Arguably you never did."

"That's a lie."

"Cillian," she said in a tone of infinite patience, not caring if it grated. All the better if it did. "We barely had a few days together. It was nice, but—"

"Nice?" he interrupted in a harsh voice. "I'm in love with you and I know you love me too."

She forced herself to plow on. "I'm sorry to hurt you this way, but that's not true. I don't love you. I never did."

"Another lie."

"I'm sure it's painful to have feelings for someone who doesn't return them. That's not something I can help though." She gave him a regretful smile. "You don't have the best record of judging women, after all." A ruthlessly aimed thrust.

"You're trying to drive me away again," he said, the words certain, but worry threading through his voice. "I apologize that my grandmother sent you away and that I didn't follow up. That's on me. You're absolutely right: I assumed that you left me, that you didn't care and…"

He trailed off and she raised her brows to highlight the point, smiling in sympathy. "You knew, deep down that what we had was a… a fling of the moment. Transitory at heart."

She reached out to pat his hand, to underscore her regret. He turned his at the last moment, surprisingly quick, and held hers in a fierce grip. "Tell me, Alise. Why do all your potential familiars look like me?"

"I don't think they do." She tugged at her trapped hand.

"Let me go."

"You know they do. Do me the bare courtesy of admitting that they look like me because of me."

"If there's a resemblance, then it's my father's doing. He thought that might help."

"Help," he echoed in a dark and musing tone. "Help with what—getting over me?"

She forced a laugh. He still didn't let her go, staring into her eyes with more intensity than she could bear. "Cillian, let me go."

"No, I don't think I will."

"I could make you." Her wizardry could outpower his and they both knew it.

"You could," he agreed. "I don't think you will."

"Cillian…" She made his name into a plea, her will eroding at the seductiveness of his touch. It had always been like this with him—the barest touch of hands, the lightest kiss, and the passion flared to life between them.

"Alise." He said her name like he'd answered a question. With his free hand, he touched her cheek, tracing the skin along her jaw up to her temple, the caress reverent. She felt as if her skin drank it in, that touch, as if she'd been starving without realizing it. His fingers threaded into her hair and he drew closer, gaze on her lips.

She wanted, oh, she wanted, needed, craved, longed for that kiss. She couldn't give into it. This would only lead to more pain. And yet the lure of the momentary pleasure proved more than she could resist. "We can't," she whispered, unable to pull away. "*I* can't."

"You can," he insisted. "Let me remind you of what we have between us."

As if she needed reminding. Her heart already jolted in her chest like a wounded thing, a fish out of water, flapping on the shore and gasping for breath. *Her father's creature.* She'd gone too far to come back.

And there was Bria to protect.

And… Cillian's lips brushed over hers.

And she was lost. The will-sapping sweetness of his taste, his touch, the abundant affection radiating from him like sunshine on frozen ground—it all poured into her and she clung to him, unable and unwilling to break away. She made a sound of helpless despair and he pulled her in closer, laying back against the couch and draping her over him, holding her close and kissing her with ravenous need. Feeling that from him and from herself, Alise found she couldn't withhold herself, couldn't recall all the very good reasons that this had to be in her past.

Instead she surrendered utterly, giving over to the all-consuming need to be held and cherished and loved. To be touched in earnest joy and feel herself blossom in return. Vaguely, in the back of her mind, she recognized that she'd been pretending to herself that the affection and praise her father had generated had been enough to sustain her.

But it had never been enough. No, it had never been real, no more than drinking wine could nourish her instead of real food.

Cillian's hands roved over her, sparking new flames and fanning old ones, his breath coming harder and his magic more urgent. "Alise…" he groaned. "This isn't why I came here, why I asked to see you—or not entirely why—but can I, can we…"

"Yes," she answered recklessly. "Yes. Please now."

They were alone and as private as could be in House Elal, she reasoned. Or whatever facsimile of reason she currently employed, as she had no doubt her more rational self— temporarily drowned out by lust and the sheer need to be touched—would judge this little episode harshly. Indulging herself in Cillian's ardent sweetness would solve nothing. In truth, this would only complicate her feelings and his.

But she couldn't refuse. Instead she told herself this would be the last time, that she should savor for the last time what she'd never have again. Not with him. Not like this.

So she allowed him to trigger the fastening of her Ophiel gown and draw it off of her. She worked away the buttons of his shirt, no wizardry to his clothing, always the slow and rustic way for the Harahels. Once they'd wrestled the extraneous aside, they sighed in unison at the full body, skin to skin reunion. Alise melted into him, surrounded by the scent of cinnamon and sugar her mind evoked, a full metaphor of the rich and delicious things he meant to her.

His hand closed over her breast, teasing her taut nipple, knowing exactly how she liked it, his mouth drawing on hers, their tongues twining in a near silent language of a breath and a slide and tremor of exchange. Her heart swelled, feeling as if she bled inside, with joy and grief entangled inextricably. If only she could have this always. Hold this moment forever suspended with no thoughts, no past, no future.

Cillian rolled her under him, breathing the question she

didn't need him to ask, poised there at her weeping entrance, her hips lifting to ease his way, to welcome him home.

"Alise," Cillian said roughly in her ear, his breathing harsh, his hands vising on her eagerly pumping hips. "Did you hear my question?"

"Yes," she panted. "Yes, I want you."

"Not that. Did you have your fertility unlocked? I don't want to…"

He didn't finish. He didn't have to. He thought she might be testing her fertility with the boys, her potential familiars, trying to get with child. It would be funny if it weren't so tragic. If only, if only. She wound her arms around his neck, her legs around his narrow hips. Never let him go. Her fingers wound into his silky dark curls, she met his warm gaze. "No. I didn't want them. I only ever wanted you."

Making an animal sound, so unlike her quiet, reserved bookworm, Cillian surged into her, piercing her with pleasure so exquisite, she could only cry out in return, throwing her head back to release the intense wave of ecstasy. Moving in her, knowing her body and her needs, he thrust her higher, soon hurtling her over the edge. She shuddered in wave after wave of climax, gripping his shoulders as if she might fall. He rode her orgasm through with her, then resumed the dance, taking them both up.

She squirmed beneath him, deliciously pinned, needing more and more. He gave her more and all, rocking her into new heights, his lips along her throat, teeth nipping her collarbones, words in her ear that chanted his love his need his longing their forever.

Blurring and blending, she lost time to the endless love-making, climaxing over and over as he held off, watching her face and kissing her in long, lingering swallows. As if he'd thirsted for her, too. At last, his face a rictus of erotic pain, he gritted out that he couldn't hold off any longer.

"Then don't," she purred, clasping him to her, holding on as if she inevitably wouldn't have to let go. Receiving him, gripping him with everything in her, she opened as he flooded her, crying her name and his love and the sweet ecstasy of it all.

He collapsed on her, face in the crook of her neck, lips pressed to the hollow of her throat, their bodies slick with sweat and clinging at every possible nook and curve. She buried her nose in his silky curls, knowing she only imagined he smelled of cinnamon sugar and glorying in it anyway.

"I love you, Alise," he said against her skin, pressing a kiss to seal the words there, like a promise, like a vow, like a gift she couldn't keep.

"I know," she breathed, uncertain if he even heard her, saying it more to herself. She did know that. Nothing with Cillian was ever a mystery that way. He felt what he felt, with his whole heart, earnestly and without reservation. She was the problem, riddled with holes and rotting inside. Seeing how she'd spent these last weeks and months, seeing herself clearly, she had to confront all the lies she'd swallowed. She'd taken them in and built herself out of them.

Too late to change now.

Cillian must have felt the shift in her because he levered up, gazing down at her in the dimness. She'd never lit the fire for them, or even very many lamps, so intent on ending the interview and getting rid of him as fast as possible. Where Cillian was kindness, she was unkind. Stingy to his generosity, sour to his sweet, empty to his wholeness. Reaching out with her magic, she brought the fire elementals to life, encouraging them to warm and light the dark salon.

Cillian smiled at her, close-lipped and wistful. "You don't have to say it back to me. I won't bother you about how you feel and if you don't want to be with me, I promise I won't trail after you like a puppy."

Her own lips curved at the image, the tenderness she felt for him almost overwhelming. She could nearly weep for losing this, for not having him. But she'd gone too far down a dark path. Even Cillian couldn't forgive her the things she'd done, the way she'd used Brinda, how she'd treated the boys. How quickly she'd fallen into treating those familiars like her private feast. She couldn't bear for Cillian to see how truly awful she was.

She shifted restlessly and he slid out of her, that primal, intimate connection disrupted. Cillian didn't move, his weight on her, his gaze expectant as he waited for her to look at him. Finally, knowing he'd outwait her, she met his eyes, expecting gentleness and affection, not the expression of steely determination he focused on her.

"I won't pressure you about any of that," he told her, "but when I leave in the morning, you're coming with me."

~ 22 ~

Hᴇʀ ɴᴀᴋᴇᴅ ʙᴏᴅʏ beneath him, Alise's tension, which had been gradually increasing since that final, delicious climax, suddenly leapt to high intensity, as if she were a bird that might take flight. Also like a bird, however, her delicately boned body easily yielded to even his meager strength. "I'm not taking no for an answer," he warned her and her lushly fringed, wizard-black eyes sparked fury at him.

"How can I say no when you didn't even ask the question," she spat.

"Alise, will you come away from House Elal with me?"

"No!"

He sighed, dropping his forehead to her bosom. "I'm not taking that answer."

"What happened to not pushing?" she demanded. Her magic heated with the room, the wine scent intoxicating, the feel of roses so palpable he almost expected the prick of thorns. But she didn't use her wizardry against him, which he counted on. Alise might not want to admit she loved him, just as she had pretended to be entertaining the courtship of those fawning familiars, but he knew her through and through. He saw the goodness, the kindness, the generous heart in her,

242

even if she didn't. The way she'd responded to him, first the touch of hands, then the kiss, then the ardency of her lovemaking—it all erased any doubt he'd harbored.

And there was no way he would leave her here. Her father had tried to warp her into his mold. Given more time, he might even succeed. Cillian didn't know what methods Piers Elal had used to change his daughter's thinking, but he doubted Alise had been aware of them.

"I said I wouldn't push about our relationship. Even though you were the one to propose that we have a love affair," he reminded her, not above needling her, rather enjoying her embarrassed and annoyed flush.

"That was a long time ago."

"A few months isn't a long time."

"Time and place," she snapped, making a sudden furious attempt to wriggle out from under him. He was very glad that he'd been the one to set the privacy shield. She'd done it to demonstrate her unwillingness to talk privately, but had ended up handing him leverage. If she got mad enough, she might've tried to dispel the shield to end this interlude. "That was then; this is now and I'm not going anywhere with you, Cillian Harahel."

"You could always come back," he said reasonably, calmly, willing her to listen. "What are you afraid of?"

"Not you," she countered, glaring, her struggles subsiding.

"Well then. Come with me."

"I can't."

"You can," he insisted. "Remember? Not a prisoner."

"Cillian, you don't understand." Tears welled in her eyes,

though she tried to sniffle them back, and he suspected he understood far too well.

"Maybe not," he told her gently, kissing the tears from the corners of her eyes where they leaked out. "Maybe you can never tell me all that happened to you here, but I do understand that I can't leave you here, all alone, with that monster."

"He's not so bad," she protested, though weakly.

"Yes, he is. And the fact that you even say that makes me more determined to get you away."

"Cillian…" She'd begun crying in earnest, so he shifted to the side, cuddling her close, no longer needing to keep her from flying away. "I'm not a good person."

Though he wanted to deny it immediately, he knew it would make more impact if he took her seriously, gave her a thoughtful answer. "I think that maybe none of us are good or bad people," he said slowly, "only the actions we take and how that affects us, others, and the world."

She'd buried her face against his chest, so he stroked the short, silky feathers of her black hair. So infinitely precious to him. "That sounds like an excuse," she said, muffled. "And, besides, I've done bad things. You don't know what I—"

"Shh." He kissed the top of her head. "You can tell me another time, if you still want to. But you should know I don't care. I love you no matter what."

She gave a watery laugh and pulled back to look at him. "Yes, well, you loved Szarina and look what a shit she turned out to be."

"I never loved Szarina," he told her gravely, then kissed her, tasting salt and regret and fear on her lips. "I only knew real love when I met you."

She gazed at him, a myriad of emotions passing over her face. "You're absurd."

"Very likely, but that doesn't change how madly, deeply I love you."

Shaking her head, she pursed her lips. "I thought you were all determined to let me go, to bond a familiar, live my life and become Lady Elal."

"I can and will do all of that and still love you."

"But you won't just go and let me stay here."

He studied her face, so lovely in the flickering light, the despair in her so clear. "No. I can't in good conscience abandon you to him."

"Cillian, he'll take Bria in my place. I can't—"

"I have news on that front, also. Grandmother, once we settled our differences, allowed me to present the problem to House Harahel's finest legal librarians. They believe we have plenty to keep this issue tangled up in the courts for years. By then we'll have dealt with him—along with all the conspirators against House Phel."

She cocked her head, clearly surprised. "House Harahel would help with that?"

"We already are. No one is touching Bria. She's safe from your father."

"You're that confident."

He considered, going through all the logical points he'd assimilated. "Yes."

She smiled, started to laugh, then sobered. "You're serious."

"I've never been more serious in my life. Come away with me in the morning and I'll show you."

"He might not let me go easily."

"I have a solution to that," he told her.

Her winged brows climbed. "Even this newly confident and daring Cillian Harahel can't be planning to engage in a duel with my father."

He liked that, that she found him newly confident and daring—and that she even considered the possibility that he might duel her father for her. Not Sylus devastating his enemies, but a wizard worthy of the name. Someone to be reckoned with. Except that he wasn't that sort of wizard. He planned to win by guile. And the old-fashioned Harahel way.

"You'll see," he promised.

"What will you do?"

"It's better if you don't know. You'll see in the morning."

"I think it almost is morning.

She was probably right. He slid his thigh between hers, kissing her deeply, loving how she went hot and supple against him. "I know just how to spend the time," he said against her lips.

To his everlasting delight, she agreed.

THEY ASSEMBLED FOR breakfast in a different salon, this one filled with morning light. Alise had harnessed a grooming imp for him, so he was at least clean, though he wore the same clothes, considerably more rumpled from a night on the floor. She had slipped out in the early morning hours, returning to her chambers, and had donned a fresh outfit. Fancier than she'd been in the habit of wearing as a student, with pants of Ophiel-fitted black leather and a deep green blouse with flowing sleeves caught up in embroidered cuffs at the wrist and a black vest over it embossed with the Elal crest. Her skin glowed with satiated happiness and her dark eyes sparkled like the green jewels she'd fastened to her ear lobes.

The five familiars joined them, exclaiming over her loveliness, fussing with each other to be the first to provide her with her favorite pastries and beverages. Cillian found he didn't mind. Alise was incredibly lovely this morning—and he took full credit for the bloom in her cheeks. Even the advent of Piers Elal didn't dim her radiance much.

Elal scowled at them all, levelling an extra hard glare at Cillian. "Still here?" he grunted.

"Leaving directly after breakfast, Lord Elal," Cillian answered cheerfully.

"Good." He sat, a servant placing a generous platter of eggs, beef, beans, and bread before him. Then he took note of the glass bottle of red oil beside his place. "What's this?"

"Regards from Lady Harahel," Cillian answered, placing a hand over his heart in a polite gesture, bowing slightly from the waist.

"Órlaith means to poison me, does she?" Piers barked out a laugh and held up the bottle. "It won't work. I can detect poison."

"Of course, Lord Elal," Cillian replied smoothly, "so you'll have reassured yourself that there's no poison here. My grandmother sent this with her apologies for her inhospitality to Wizard Alise. She mentioned that you'd been fond of her ERS oil back at Convocation Academy, and had particularly enjoyed it to spice up your eggs at breakfast."

Lord Elal considered Cillian and the flask. "That was a long time ago. I'm surprised Órlaith remembers that."

"She said you would." Which was absolutely true. Cillian skipped pointing out that his grandmother, as a librarian wizard powerful enough to head her house possessed a meticulously trained and magically fueled memory. Careless of Elal to ignore that. "She also mentioned that you were one of the few she'd ever known who could withstand the heat level."

"True, true." Piers Elal considered the sauce, the spirits trapped in the metal-bound globe of the mechanical eye whirling idly. He dabbed a bit on his finger and tasted it, then blew out a sharp breath, shaking his head. "Ah, that's the stuff. Volcanic. Would you like some?" He extended the vial toward Cillian's plate.

Cillian made a pained face and pressed a hand to his stomach. "It's far too spicy for me. I'm afraid I have a rather, ah, delicate constitution."

As he'd calculated, Lord Elal sneered at that, casting a speaking look at Alise, who'd been watching the exchange in silence, quietly eating the pastry Wim had plated for her. "This fragile pretty boy is who you picked?" he asked, disgusted, pouring a great deal of the ERS oil over his eggs, making a show of it. "I don't understand your taste, Daughter."

Alise gazed over at him, black eyes wide and thoughtful. "I like pretty boys." The other five, admittedly very pretty young men around the table all looked at Cillian, too.

Cillian simply watched Lord Elal as he shoveled the spicy eggs into his mouth, pretending to be admiring. "I've never seen anyone capable of eating so much of my grandmother's oil before."

Lord Elal waved that off, though his face had gone bright red, beads of sweat forming on his temples and forehead. "The burn is the best part," he declared, then thumped his chest with the meat of his fist, punching out a juicy belch that had one of the familiars flinching in disgust and Alise rolling her eyes.

"Excellent," Piers proclaimed, then pointed his fork at Cillian. A smear of red oil stained his beard. "You tell Órlaith she hasn't lost her touch. Exquisitely brewed, as always. Perhaps even hotter now."

"She's been tweaking the recipe over the years," Cillian replied.

"Eh, well, good that she has something to do with her time. Never did understand the charm of living out at House Harahel in the back of beyond. 'What do you do all day?' I asked her once and she said 'read.' Ha!" He bellowed a laugh that smelled unpleasantly of ERS oil combined with digestive fluids.

Alise caught Cillian's eye and raised her brows slightly. He gave a reassuring smile. Any moment now. "Speaking of House Harahel," he said, "I should be heading home soon. If I could trouble you, Lord Elal, to ask that my carriage be readied?"

"Already is." Piers shifted in his chair, gaze turned inward, an odd expression on his face. Then he pinned Cillian with a glare with his one remaining black eye. "I didn't want any delay in seeing the back of you."

"A perfectly understandable sentiment," Cillian noted mildly, rewarded by Lord Elal's frown as he sorted through the remark for insult.

"Once you—" Lord Elal broke off, a loud gurgle coming from his gut. "Something seems to not be sitting well with me."

"It *has* been a long time since you had my grandmother's ERS oil," Cillian replied with sympathy, "and you mentioned she's brewed it hotter than it used to be. Perhaps you've lost your tolerance?"

"I've only grown stronger over the years," Elal insisted. He got a very odd look on his face, then actually squirmed in his chair. "You'll have to excuse me, young Harahel," he said, stating it like an order. "I must, ah, take care of something, so I won't be able to see you off personally. But don't get ideas, you—" He paled and stood abruptly. "I want you gone. No lingering."

"Oh, believe me, Lord Elal, I intend to go immediately," Cillian promised with absolute sincerity.

The wizard practically fled the room and Cillian found himself hard-pressed not to show his amusement and satisfaction. That had worked even better and faster than his grandmother had promised, no doubt due to the excessive amount of ERS oil Elal had slathered on his meal.

"What happened to Lord Elal?" Zim wondered. Gim and

Tim snickered.

Cillian turned to Alise. "Would you see me out Wizard Elal, in lieu of your father?"

"I'd be delighted Wizard Harahel," she replied demurely.

The five familiars watched Cillian escort her out of the room, looking rather forlorn. He felt sorry for them, but not so much that he didn't indulge himself by setting a hand on the small of Alise's back as they passed through the doorway. *Mine.*

She slid him the side-eye. "Did you just pull a possessive move?"

"I'm a librarian and an intellectual," he answered in a lofty tone, "which does not make me a more evolved human being. Fuck those guys."

A sound suspiciously like a giggle suppressed into a snort came out of her. "We should hurry."

"Yes, but not so fast as to look suspicious. He'll be out of commission for a while."

"What did you do to my father, anyway?"

"You were right there. You saw exactly what happened. I did nothing." Since his hand was still on the sweet curve of her back, he stroked her there, savoring that he could.

"It wasn't poison."

"It wasn't poison," he agreed. "Just my sweet little old grandmother's ERS oil. Do you know how it got its name? When we were kids," he continued without pausing, "my grandmother made a batch of her usual spicy red sauce. Partway through the simmering process, she became distract-ed." Looking back, it occurred to him that likely Lady Harahel had been distracted by house business. "She served it at dinner that night to add some fire to a fairly bland meal of potatoes and white fish. And every one of us spent the night in the loo."

He laughed at her horrified expression. "Oh, we were fine. Eventually, but those hours of extremity." He mock shuddered. "Well, I only wish them on my worst enemy."

"My father is—"

"Is your father," he interrupted firmly. "I won't tell you how to feel about him, but neither can you direct how I think and feel." She was quiet a moment, the great doors to the outer courtyard looming. Cillian began to worry that he should've kept his big mouth shut until he had her in the carriage. Though what would he do if she'd changed her mind even then—restrain her?

She paused, and he braced himself, ready for the argument where she'd changed her mind and would refuse to go with him. But she reached behind a podium holding a suit of armor and pulled out her bag, which she'd clearly hidden with excellent forethought. She resumed their purposeful stroll into the courtyard and his carriage waiting there.

"Cillian?" She said his name as a question, and he kicked himself. You only had to wait a few more minutes. "You didn't say why you called it ERS."

He nearly laughed in relief, taking her bag, and holding the carriage door open for her. "E.R.S," he spelled out, "for evil red sauce."

$$\sim 23 \sim$$

ALISE LAUGHED AT the joke, maintaining a poised exterior, but inside she was a churning mess. When she'd been in Cillian's arms, safe inside that bubble of intimacy that he somehow created so effortlessly, as if by magic, she'd been able to see her way clear to this crazy plan of his, that she could just walk away from House Elal and her father. That somehow everything would be all right.

But it wouldn't be all right. Nothing could be, and her jangling heart knew the truth. Even as they passed under the portcullis and crossed the drawbridge, she knew the illusion of escape was exactly that. She might be out of House Elal proper, but it was a long way out of Elal and the umbrella of her father's power. Bria might be safe, but she was not.

"He'll come after us," she said into the silence of the carriage, realizing only then that Cillian had been waiting for her to speak.

"He'll be occupied for a while yet," Cillian said calmly. "Hours."

"Long enough for us to get out of Elal?"

He didn't reply, only cocked his head slightly, as if expecting her to say more.

Yeah, that's what she'd thought. "What will we do?" she fretted.

"If he comes after you," Cillian said, moving to sit beside her on the carriage bench, "he'll use his wizardry against you. He'll send spirits."

"Exactly!" she agreed, imagining the power of what he could send, what she'd seen him do in the arcanium, powered by Brinda's white hot magic.

"And you'll use your wizardry to combat him," Cillian continued evenly, as if discussing what route they'd take.

Alise goggled at him. "You're not serious."

"Of course I am."

"*This* is your plan?" her voice rose to a squeak and she began sweating in anxiety. Oh, she should not have left her father.

"It's a working plan," he admitted. "Mostly I wanted to get you out of House Elal—which you have to admit has worked admirably—and I had and have confidence that you will be able to fend off anything your father throws at us."

"Over-confidence has killed many a wizard," she noted darkly. "And you have no idea what my father has been up to."

"Besides summoning demons? Has he gone beyond that in his hubris, attempting to harness djinn?"

Alise gave him a long, considering look. "What do you know?"

He took her hand, holding it in both of his, enfolded like something precious he needed to protect. "I'm well-read enough to recognize from the descriptions what your father intended to attach to Bria."

"Nobody else but me knew that was a demon."

Cillian shrugged a little. "I asked Han and Iliana to describe what they noticed and that was the obvious conclusion."

"You're amazing."

"I'm glad you think so." He smiled warmly and leaned in to kiss her.

She pulled back just enough that he missed, scowling at him. "That wasn't a compliment, Cillian. You have no idea how far in over your head you are!"

"I believe in you."

"Well, you shouldn't," she snapped, feeling the weight of his belief.

The carriage wove around a curve, climbing the first rise out of the river valley, and the massive structure of House Elal filled the view. Spring had rushed headlong into full bloom during her time inside, coming late to these mountainous climes, but fully in place now and edging into summer.

"You're not going back," Cillian informed her with quiet resolve, "so don't even think about it."

"Or what," she fired back, turning her fear and anger on him. "You can't stop me."

He cupped her cheek with one hand, sliding it around to the back of her neck when she tried to pull away again. This firmer, more assertive Cillian had her a bit off-balance, but… that probably wasn't fair or true. He'd always been determined in his interest in her, just more polite about it before. Her father had totally bitten on the bait Cillian had dangled about being delicate and unable to withstand much adversity, but the person who underestimated Cillian—and she had to include herself in that group—found out to their sorrow that beneath his sweet and mild personality lay a will of iron.

"Alise," he said, gaze holding hers, "please don't leave me again. I'm begging you."

"I didn't mean to leave you to begin with," she pointed out crisply. "And besides—"

He stopped her with a kiss, a long, lingering, dreamy kiss that sapped all thoughts from her mind. Oh, how she'd missed him. His taste, his feel, his wry humor, his generous affection, the way he looked at her like the rest of the world had fallen away and he didn't care if it ever returned.

Pulling back just enough to lean his forehead against hers, he whispered. "Just don't leave me again, for whatever reason. I don't think I can withstand it. Bond a familiar, bond all five of the Nod brothers if it will make you happy. Just let me be with you, too."

"I don't want any of them," she confessed, also whispering, for no good reason. "I didn't bed any of them, either."

"It wouldn't matter if you had."

"Thank you. I didn't mean to hurt you."

His fingers flexed on the back of her neck. "I didn't mean to hurt you. Maybe we'll get better at not doing that over time."

"Over time?"

"Yes. Our lifetimes. I want to go where you go. I don't care where that is, so long as it's with you."

Shaken, she set that aside, not ready to deal with the implications. "Where *are* we going?" it occurred to her to ask. There was only one way out of the river valley, by design, but soon they'd have to choose a direction and that would determine how soon she'd have to fight off her father. He might be indisposed for a few hours, but when he recovered, he'd be looking for her and his anger would be something she did not care to behold.

"It's up to you."

"Why?" she demanded. "Is this also part of the 'I didn't have a plan past getting Alise out of House Elal?'"

"I don't know how I missed that sharp tongue of yours." He kissed her, flicking his own tongue against hers in a sensual and loving caress, then sat back, still holding her one hand. "This is still your project. We have the code to break, which could take a very long time, but the fact that we've come this far is entirely because of you. So what we do next is your call. I have three options in mind, but you might think of something else. First, we can go to House Harahel and—"

"No, thank you."

"I promise to be conscious this time and, no matter what, my grandmother will never turn you away again. You have my word on that."

She withheld comment, but she'd believe it when Lady Harahel laid down the attitude along with a welcome carpet.

"If we go there, you can examine the texts we extracted and see what you think. Then we can take Han and Iliana back to House Phel and you can tell your family about your discovery."

Her family. The pang of longing to see Nic, and everyone else, to be at House Phel once more hit her like a punch of magic breaking through her shields.

"We can also go directly to House Phel," Cillian said softly, watching her.

Was she that transparent? Probably. "What's the third option?"

"Convocation Academy," he answered promptly.

"To take this discovery to Provost Uriel," she mused.

"And Professor Seraphiel. I think they'd both be very interested."

She considered it. "Much as I would love to go to House Phel, I think there's merit to going to Convocation Academy. If we take this discovery to Meresin, we run the risk of the information dying there with us all over again. I take it no one outside of you, me, Han, and Iliana know everything?"

"Correct. My grandmother most decidedly did *not* want to know."

"Plausible deniability?" she asked, amused by Lady Harahel's game-playing. Alise doubted she'd ever come to like the woman, not after the way she'd come between Cillian and her.

Cillian shook his head in dry amusement. "She is far more canny than I ever imagined. Now, this is in our laps. And I defer to your wishes."

"You trust me to make that decision?" she asked. "I could be an Elal shill now."

He met her gaze, taking her hand and twining their fingers. "You are Alise, who possesses such a huge heart you liberated familiars, and couldn't bear to be unkind to a puppyish librarian in love with her, and who gave up everything to protect her infant niece."

Tears pricked her eyes. "I aspire to be the person you believe me to be."

"Easily accomplished then." With a smile, he leaned in to kiss her, lingeringly. "Where to, my lady?"

The archaic gallantry made her smile. "Let's show Tandiya Uriel what we've got."

He grinned. "That's my girl."

Coming July 8, 2025 from Jeffe's new pen name:
Jennifer K. Lambert
Never the Roses

TITLES BY JEFFE KENNEDY

FANTASY ROMANCES

BONDS OF MAGIC
Dark Wizard
Bright Familiar
Grey Magic
Familiar Winter Magic
(Also available in Fire of the Frost)

RENEGADES OF MAGIC
Shadow Wizard
Rogue Familiar
Twisted Magic

HEIRS OF MAGIC
The Long Night of the Crystalline Moon

(also available in *Under a Winter Sky*)
The Golden Gryphon and the Bear Prince
The Sorceress Queen and the Pirate Rogue
The Dragon's Daughter and the Winter Mage
The Storm Princess and the Raven King
The Long Night of the Radiant Star

THE FORGOTTEN EMPIRES

The Orchid Throne
The Fiery Crown
The Promised Queen

THE TWELVE KINGDOMS

Negotiation
The Mark of the Tala
The Tears of the Rose
The Talon of the Hawk
Heart's Blood
The Crown of the Queen

THE UNCHARTED REALMS

The Pages of the Mind
The Edge of the Blade
The Snows of Windroven
The Shift of the Tide
The Arrows of the Heart
The Dragons of Summer
The Fate of the Tala
The Lost Princess Returns

THE CHRONICLES OF DASNARIA
Prisoner of the Crown
Exile of the Seas
Warrior of the World

SORCEROUS MOONS
Lonen's War
Oria's Gambit
The Tides of Bára
The Forests of Dru
Oria's Enchantment
Lonen's Reign

A COVENANT OF THORNS
Rogue's Pawn
Rogue's Possession
Rogue's Paradise

CONTEMPORARY ROMANCES

Shooting Star

MISSED CONNECTIONS
Last Dance
With a Prince
Since Last Christmas

CONTEMPORARY EROTIC ROMANCES

Exact Warm Unholy
The Devil's Doorbell

FACETS OF PASSION
Sapphire
Platinum
Ruby
Five Golden Rings

FALLING UNDER
Going Under
Under His Touch
Under Contract

EROTIC PARANORMAL

MASTER OF THE OPERA E-SERIAL
Master of the Opera, Act 1: Passionate Overture
Master of the Opera, Act 2: Ghost Aria
Master of the Opera, Act 3: Phantom Serenade
Master of the Opera, Act 4: Dark Interlude
Master of the Opera, Act 5: A Haunting Duet
Master of the Opera, Act 6: Crescendo
Master of the Opera

BLOOD CURRENCY
Blood Currency

BDSM FAIRYTALE ROMANCE
Petals and Thorns

Thank you for reading!

About Jeffe Kennedy

Jeffe Kennedy™ is a multi-award-winning, bestselling author of 66 published titles, primarily in epic fantasy romance. She is a Past-President of the Science Fiction and Fantasy Writers Association (SFWA). She is best known for the RITA® Award-winning *The Pages of the Mind*, the recent trilogy, *The Forgotten Empires*, and the wildly popular *Dark Wizard*. She recently signed a six-figure deal with Tor for a new romantasy series writing as Jennifer K. Lambert™, with book one, *Never the Roses*, forthcoming in hardback July 8, 2025. Jeffe lives in Santa Fe, New Mexico. She is represented by Sarah Younger of Nancy Yost Literary Agency.

Jeffe can be found online at her website: JeffeKennedy.com, on Facebook, Goodreads, BookBub, Twitter, YouTube, Instagram, and—just like all the kids these days—TikTok.

jeffekennedy.com

facebook.com/Author.Jeffe.Kennedy

twitter.com/jeffekennedy

goodreads.com/author/show/1014374.Jeffe_Kennedy

bookbub.com/profile/jeffe-kennedy

Sign up for her newsletter here.

jeffekennedy.com/sign-up-for-my-newsletter